Wildflower

Dorelyn Kunkel

Wildflower

Copyright © 2018 by Dorelyn Kunkel

ISBN: 978-1-7327237-3-3

Library of Congress Control Number: 2018960360

To my mother, Gertie, who raised me to be independent and think for myself.

You have been gone for many years, but your love and support live inside me every moment.

You truly believed and taught me that I could achieve anything I wanted, and you knew I always wanted to write. It took a while. But here we go.

I only wish you could be here to share it.

Acknowledgments

This has been a long process, and this story might have fallen by the wayside except for the support and encouragement—and maybe prodding—from a number of people.

The first of these is my partner, Lynn Blackburn. Lynn was the first to listen as I read new chapters. He offered editing advice, some of which I followed and some I didn't. He expected that; and never let it phase him. But I prized his honest reactions, because they gave me clues regarding how readers might react to my story.

I would also like to thank my four children; Josh Levine, Seth Levine, Dustin Cooper, and Ashley Cooper for broadening my life experience and providing me with insights that added credibility to my writing. Also, thank you for sharing my joy upon its completion.

I especially want to thank my daughter-in-law, Melanie Cooper, for her work on the Wildflower book cover. And I appreciate her sharing her positive emotional reaction and enthusiasm for the story after being the first in the family to read the final draft.

My longtime closest friend, Pam Cullen, and I share a love of reading and writing. She has supported my efforts since they began, through plot discussions and long-distance editing via Internet. Her encouragement has always meant a lot. Thank you, Pam.

Throughout the writing process, I was fortunate to participate in Central Phoenix Writer Meetup groups with fellow aspiring authors who offered valuable critique and encouragement. Two of these, Kathleen Martin and Nim Stevens met with me regularly to focus on the novels we were all working on at the time.

Kenneth Weene, a fellow author whom I frequently encountered at Phoenix Meetups, encouraged my early efforts and after Wildflower was complete, put me in contact with his publisher, All Things That Matter Press. ATTMP became **MY** Publisher. Thank you so much, Ken!

And, finally, I want to thank ATTMP. Thank you especially, Deb, my editor, for your efforts and patience in removing hundreds of unneeded commas and noting repetitive word use. It is good to have a clear, experienced, and unbiased eye to review one's work.

Prologue

Will the Circle Be Unbroken?

Trudy stared down the hospital hallway at Mama and took a moment to reflect on what she saw before her mother looked up to see them coming.

So old! I should've expected that, I guess. But so little. You always seemed so big.

But that had been nearly twenty years ago. Mama might have shrunk with age, but Trudy knew that couldn't entirely account for how tiny she was. The handmade blue and gray flour-sack dress that brushed the tops of her shoes looked exactly like the one she wore in Trudy's memories, but the figure inside was rounder, bosom blending into stomach. Mama looked up, and the hint of a weary smile crossed her face then fled like the shadow of a bird in flight.

Millie, tall and raw-boned as she'd always been, stood beside their mother. Now, though, she wore glasses, and her long, wavy brown hair was streaked with gray. She approached Trudy and took both of her sister's hands in her own.

"How's Papa?" Trudy sought the answer in her sister's eyes. What she saw added to her grief.

"'Bout the same, I guess. They're cleaning him up and refilling that bag of morphine or whatever it is. For the pain." They stepped back to allow a bed on wheels holding an unconscious patient to pass. The nurse steering it smiled and mouthed a silent "Thank you."

Trudy caught her mother looking at her from the corner of her eye. "Hello, Mama." She leaned forward and kissed her mother's cheek, then stepped back.

"Hello, Trudy. Been a long time." Mama's hand touched Trudy's forearm then withdrew. "Are these your childern? They look like you, 'cept this one." She pointed at Molly.

"Yes. She's more like her father." Molly hid behind Trudy, holding her mother's dress and peering up at her grandmother.

"This is Will. And Bob. And Molly." Each boy said "Hello, Grandma," and bent over in turn to kiss her cheek. Trudy's younger sister, Mary, broke the awkward silence by stepping around her to hug their mother.

A nurse came out through the doorway to Papa's room. "You can go inside now. He's awake. But don't expect him to be that way long. I'm afraid I tired him out some." She smiled and walked away down the corridor. Bob and Will stayed in the hall with their grandmother and little sister. They'd meet their grandfather after this first visit.

Papa's head swiveled on the pillow to face Trudy and Mary as they entered. His hair was snow white and his face was gaunt, but his blue eyes twinkled like they always had. When he saw Trudy, they lit up even more, and he smiled a slow, peaceful smile.

Oh, Papa, I'm so sorry. I never meant to be gone so long.

She fought back tears, but felt her eyes fill despite her efforts. "My baby girl," he said in a voice that was barely audible. There was no doubt he was talking to Trudy, although Mary was younger.

She stepped up to him and gently kissed his forehead and both cheeks. "Papa, I'm so sorry I didn't come sooner. I wanted to." She could no longer control her sobs.

The arm without the IV lifted slowly and pulled her to him. "I know you did, small fry." He patted her back, then stroked it as he spoke. "Sometimes the Lord has other plans for us."

Chapter One

Can She Bake a Cherry Pie, Billy Boy?

It was already dark when Trudy and Betty got to church for the Saturday night pie supper, but the church ladies had set up lanterns and there was a full moon. They handed their pies off, threw an old quilt on the ground, and plopped down to watch the bidding.

Papa and Mama and a few church elders occupied folding wooden chairs a few yards away. The rest of Trudy's family, except John, sat nearby on quilts and blankets. John was off on his own. At twenty-three, he had not yet married, but spent little time with the family. Still, he remained Trudy's silent ally. He'd been regularly sneaking her off to the Tahlequah library for the four years since her twelfth birthday. A Brontë novel currently hid under her mattress.

Trudy's eyes sought her mother, who turned to gaze back at her briefly with her usual dour expression, then turned away. As the murmur of quiet conversations flowed around her, Trudy remembered the first time she'd heard her brother say the word bitch. He'd said it a few times since.

You should taste my pie, Mama. It's better than yours ever was.

She noticed her sister Millie leaning against her husband on a quilt next to Mama's chair and watching her with a puzzled frown. Trudy grinned and waved. Millie waved back with the hand that wasn't holding Sam's.

Papa paused in his conversation, and Trudy caught his eye. His familiar soft smile bloomed. Trudy remembered when he'd helped build the old church. Now it had a weathered look, but, in a clearing, on a hill, with the bell tower stretching up, it was still the tallest thing around. It strained upward towards heaven like everything Papa did.

The bidding started. Betty leaned over and whispered. "I bet Joe's gonna get your pie again." Joe Dobson had been bidding on her pies at the church's auctions for charity most Saturday evenings for a few months now. He won almost every time. Trudy's pies were good, but she knew he bought them to win her company, not for the flavor. As children, she, Mary, and Joe had played tag in the woods. Trudy remembered one time he'd almost caught her, but she'd grabbed a possum grapevine, swung up into a tall oak tree, and grinned down at him. Trudy smiled at the memory as the bidding closed.

Betty poked her in the side. "Told you so."

***

After the bidding ended and everyone dispersed, Trudy and Joe sat apart from the others. Joe dipped his fork and took a large bite of her blackberry pie straight out of the pan. Then he rested the hand holding the fork on his denim covered knee and stared into her eyes.

"I've decided to get outta this place, Trudy. Ain't no future here. Paw'll leave the farm to Elton, anyway, but that's beside the point. I don't want it. Who wants to scratch out a living from the dirt? I'm heading for California in a day or two." Trudy's eyes widened with surprise.

"What? Why, Joe? What are you gonna do there?" She felt a trace of sadness. She'd known Joe most of her life, and now he was leaving.

Joe took a second bite, chewed, and swallowed. "They got truck driving jobs there, and a man can save some money and buy his own truck. I can get good wages. Someday be my own boss. Maybe even start my own business." He took another bite. Purple juice dribbled down from the corner of his mouth.

"You're leaking, Joe." Trudy pointed her finger at his chin. He wiped his face with his hand and then rubbed the residue on the leg of his overalls.

"It's beautiful there, Trudy. The weather's better'n here. The air's mostly dry, so they don't have all these darned bugs." He dropped his fork into the pie pan to swat at a mosquito then continued. "It never snows. You can drive right up to the ocean. "Look." He reached into his overall pocket and pulled out a picture postcard that showed a sandy, shell-covered beach with people in bathing suits and caps lying under umbrellas.

"It's beautiful, Joe. Do you have family there?"

"That's the point, Trudy. I don't. I wanna be on my own; make my own decisions." A frown darkened his brow, and his lower lip jutted out. Trudy struggled to keep a straight face.

You look just like Davy when he don't get his way; a spoiled, pouty little boy.

"I'm sick and tired of Paw and Elton telling me how to live my life. I've broke my back for as long as I can 'member, and what good's it done? We're still dirt poor, and *they* always will be. But I'm gonna make a better life, and I want you to be with me, Trudy. Will you come? I know you're only sixteen, but we could get married in Texas. They couldn't stop us."

"You're asking me to marry you, Joe? I don't know what to say. I never saw this coming. You know I like you, but I've never even thought about getting married yet. We're still so young." She'd gone walking with him a few times, not counting the pie suppers, and even kissed him once or twice. She hoped she hadn't led him on. Millie accused her of being a bit of a flirt.

Oh, no! I don't want to hurt your feelings, but you're just not my Heathcliff, Joe.

"It sounds exciting. But this is a big surprise. I need time to think about it. Can you be a little patient?"

I can say I'm not ready to be that far from home. That's completely true.

"'Course I can, honey. But think about it and let me know soon as you can. I want you to come, but I need to get outta here. I'm all ready to go. And please don't talk about my plans to nobody. I don't want Paw to try and stop me."

"I won't. I swear. And I promise I'll give you my answer in a day or two at most."

They finished the pie and rose to stroll through the nearby woods. Joe kept his arm around her shoulders as they walked. Trudy looked over her shoulder and saw the family rise and begin to drift away with the rest of the crowd. Mama caught her eye.

Are you scowling? What's wrong now?

Trudy gazed up at the stars. She couldn't see many. The moon was too bright. A bat flew overhead and landed somewhere in the trees. Trudy hoped it would catch some of the mosquitoes. One landed on the hand Joe rested on her shoulder. She swatted it, and he jumped and looked at her. She laughed and showed him the mosquito on her palm. He brushed it off then raised her hand to his lips. Joe first kissed her hand, then bent to kiss her mouth.

It can't hurt. He'll be gone in a few days.

She leaned into him and relaxed her lips against his. Joe ran his tongue across them and pulled her against him. Her physical response surprised her a little. Then he thrust his tongue down her throat. Her warm, tingling stopped. She didn't know if she was going to laugh or choke. She pulled away.

"It's late, Joe. I have to get home. Papa might be worried."

***

Joe escorted her home, and they exchanged a chaste goodnight kiss. Trudy looked forward to a moment alone with Papa. He often stayed up later than the others. He read his Bible, and sometimes, overcome with private joy, exclaimed "Praise Jesus." But when Trudy came inside, it was not her father, but her mother, who was awake. Mama glared at her.

"So, you finally decided to come home, did you? I won't bother to ask what you were up to this late. I don't need to." She looked Trudy up and down. "I do hope you know he ain't gonna marry you. Why buy a cow when you can get the milk for free?"

Trudy's cheeks burned and her temper flared like a snake striking. "Who'd you think I am? Just 'cause you're a miserable, suspicious old hag who thinks the worst of everybody, don't give you the right to say such a thing to your own daughter. I'd never hurt Papa like that!"

Mama slapped her. Trudy clenched her fists. Davy stirred on his pallet near the stove. "Mama, what's going on?" Trudy heard him yawn over her pounding heart.

"Nothing, David. Go back to sleep," Mama said.

Tears stung Trudy's eyes as she rushed into the bedroom she still shared with Mary and Evelyn. They were both asleep. Evelyn was snoring. Trudy slipped the pillowcase off her pillow, careful not to disturb Mary, and stuffed all her clothes she could find inside. She added her hairbrush and a few other belongings, including a notebook and pencil, from the top of their chest of drawers.

She hesitated a moment then stuck the extra quilt from the bottom of the bed under her arm. She looked at Mary, sound asleep in their bed, then brushed her lips across the side of her sister's brow. Mary murmured in her sleep and rolled onto her side.

Trudy hurried out of the bedroom. On his pallet in the front room, Davy snored like a purring kitten. She looked around for Mama. Her mother had disappeared.

I'm never gonna let you judge me again. I stood it all these years, but I can't anymore.

Out back in the barn, she scrambled onto the back of the family plow horse and fled her home. As she rode, she relived the pain she'd felt as long as she could remember; the longing for Mama's approval and love, the failure to ever see anything but contempt or indifference reflected in her mother's eyes.

It was too late to wake up Betty's family, and she hadn't the heart for any more commotion, so Trudy rode to the closest neighbor's farm. The farm dogs knew her. They gathered around without raising a fuss when she entered the barn. They wagged their tails and licked her hands.

She spent the few hours until morning there, lying on her quilt in an empty stall, with the murmurs of the livestock for company. She lit a barn lantern with a match from a box left there by the farmer, and used its dim light to write two letters.

The first was to Papa. She couldn't bring herself to tell him what had transpired between her and Mama, so she lied to him for the first time in her life. She told him she loved Joe, and they were eloping. She would write to him after they were settled.

The second was to Joe.

"I made my decision," she wrote. "I'll go with you to California if we leave right away. But as soon as we get to Texas we have to get married. And you must promise not to touch me until after I am your wife. If you try, I'll make you take me back home." She knew it was an empty threat, but he didn't. Only she knew she would never go home.

The next morning before dawn, Trudy rode the horse home and left it and the quilt in the family barn. Then she crept up to the front door and slid her letter to Papa underneath. As she rose, an owl swept by headed for the barn loft where it had spent the days sleeping for as long as Trudy could remember, and the realization of what she was doing made her weak.

She walked to Betty's house and relief flowed through her when Betty answered the door herself. Her friend looked at her with raised eyebrows. "What are you doing out so early?" She glanced toward the pillowcase hanging from Trudy's hand and frowned. "What's wrong, honey?"

"Nothing's wrong. I need your help with something, that's all." Trudy forced a smile. "Can we go to your bedroom and talk?"

"Sure." Betty opened the door wider and stepped back.

Trudy entered and led the way to Betty's room at the back of the house. No one else was in sight. "Where're your folks?"

"They're over to Grandma's. She's feeling poorly. They might be taking her to the doctor." The girls sat side by side on the bed, and Betty reached for Trudy's hand. "Lord, your fingers are cold. So tell me. What do you need my help for?"

"Me and Joe are gonna elope."

Trudy's friend's eyes flew open. She lifted her free hand to cover her gaping mouth.

"He asked me last night. We're going to California, but we'll get married in Texas first. I need you to give him this note." Trudy slipped her hand out of Betty's, replacing it with the letter to Joe. "It's my answer to his proposal. Please don't talk to anybody but him. Our families can't find out 'til we're gone. They might try to stop us."

Betty recovered her power of speech. "Trudy, I'm so thrilled for you! 'Member when you lent me *Wuthering Heights* from the library? We talked about true love? This is so exciting and so romantic; I can't believe it's happening to you! I'm so jealous. 'Course I'll help!" Betty threw her arms around Trudy and hugged her tight.

"One more thing. Can I hide here 'til Joe comes?"

"Sure you can. I'll make sure nobody finds out."

***

He came for her that very night. As they drove away in Joe's old Ford, Trudy remembered her friend's reaction to their elopement.

Let her keep her dreams. It's better for everybody this way.

Joe hadn't put up the top of the Tin Lizzie, and Trudy gazed up at the Milky Way as tears filled her eyes. Then Mama's sour face displaced the stars, and Trudy felt herself soar away from that face into the darkness ahead as the lights of Tahlequah and all she had ever known faded away behind.

Chapter Two

California Blues

Tahlequah, Oklahoma, forty miles west of Arkansas, rested at the end of the Trail of Tears, or Nu na da ul tsun yi, the Place Where They Cried, as the Cherokees called it. At three years old, Trudy Kelly hadn't known the name. Home and family had comprised her universe, apart from Heaven. She didn't comprehend a whole lot about Heaven yet, either, but she trusted Papa. He'd told her that someday, Heaven would be her home as well.

Not long ago Trudy had sat on Papa's lap looking at pictures in the front of his Bible. Eve held an apple out to Adam. Satan was there, too, his horns curled like a ram's. She'd touched the page, thin and delicate, edged in purple, as she'd listened to her father's comforting voice. "Don't let him scare you, small fry. He's sneaky, and he's always looking for a way to tempt us into sin. But as long as we keep Jesus in our hearts, the devil can't get in. There's just no room for him."

The image of Satan flitted into Trudy's mind now as she watched her mother. Mama had been in the garden, pulling up the dead tomato plants, but she must have heard the crash. She stood at the edge of the front room and glared at her mute children. The lantern's broken pieces lay scattered on the front room floor. Kerosene seeped into the faded rag rug and old floorboards. The smell pricked Trudy's nostrils, and her eyes watered.

"Look at this mess! You're driving me crazy." Mama dug her fingers into her hair and yanked. Trudy watched the ends of her mother's eyebrows and the corners of her eyes rise up with her hair. Mama's fists knotted against her head.

Mama looks scary. Is Jesus in her heart?

"Who's gonna clean it up? Me, of course."

Trudy looked around at her brother and sisters. They were all watching Mama. Trudy's oldest sister, Mildred, lowered her gaze and spoke. "We'll clean it up, Mama."

"No, you won't. You'd just make it worse." The corners of Mama's mouth dropped down as she released her hair. Her eyes looked as full of poison as the cottonmouth Trudy'd seen down by the creek that morning. Mama glared at each of them, one after another, then bent over to pick up a piece of glass. She cut her finger. Blood ran down her palm. It dripped into the kerosene puddle.

"I can't take no more of this. I'm gonna end it once and for all!" She dropped the piece of glass and marched to the door. The children trailed behind her. Millie, John, and Evelyn looked at each other. They all frowned.

"She sounds like she means it this time," John said. They started after Mama.

"Wait. I have to see 'bout Mary." Millie ran back inside. "She's sound asleep. Hurry," she said when she came back.

Trudy hustled after the others, trotting to keep up. Mildred reached back, clasped her hand, and dragged her along. They rushed across the front yard and past the garden. The dry tomato plants lay in a pile near the gate. Even the okra was turning brown. Soon it would be winter.

Why are we running? I want Papa.

"Millie, where's Papa?"

"He's gone to church, Sis. You know that. It's Wednesday."

They passed through a stand of oak and blackjack trees, bare limbs clawing the sky, and headed across the field toward the train tracks. Trudy saw Mama a few feet away. She stood like a statue on a railroad tie, right in the middle of the train tracks. Her arms hung straight down, and her hands were still.

Trudy stared, but Mama never looked back at her.

Mildred stopped on the weedy railroad right-of-way and jerked Trudy back when she tried to go closer to Mama. The tall yellow grass and brambles scraped Trudy's legs. She reached down with her free hand to scratch them.

A loud whistle moaned in the background. Trudy looked at the pink, purple, and orange clouds on the horizon; just like the box of crayons Evelyn had brought home from school, but softer, prettier. Evelyn had taught her the names of all the colors.

The train whistled again, louder now. The sound filled the air the way color filled the sky. She looked up the track at the giant steam engine. A man in a blue cap leaned out the side window. Black smoke puffed out of the stack, and Trudy could feel the ground tremble under her bare feet. John, Mildred, and Evelyn were crying.

"What's the matter, Millie?" Trudy felt tears rise in her own eyes, although she didn't know why. Her sister didn't reply. She, John, and Evelyn leaned across the track and touched Mama. They grabbed at her arms and tried to catch her hands. Mama jerked her arms away. She swatted their fingers like she was slapping away flies. The wind whipped Mama's hair around her face and her house dress clung to her legs.

The train had started whistling again and the man in the blue hat was leaning out the window, waving his arms. His mouth was open.

Is he saying something?

"Please, Mama, don't. We don't want you to die! We'll be good!" John's voice cracked. Tears ran down his face. "We'll mind you, Mama!"

I want Mama!

Trudy tried to pull her hand from Mildred's grasp, but her sister tugged her back. She snatched Mildred's hand to her mouth and bit her, but Mildred was too strong.

The ground shook harder. Mildred stepped back from the tracks and yanked Trudy with her. She spun Trudy around, pressed Trudy's face against her stomach, then curved her body around her little sister, enveloping her, blinding her.

Trudy's hands were free now. She hammered her fists against the sides of Mildred's legs then tried to push herself loose from her big sister's grasp. All at once Mildred released her. Trudy stumbled backwards then turned around to search for Mama. She was walking right towards them.

The whistling freight train thundered past. It spewed black smoke, and the wind from its passing rocked Trudy's body. She almost fell. Mildred grasped her hand again, but Trudy reached out to her mother.

"Mama, Mama!"

Mama walked right past without even looking at her. Trudy tried again to pull away, to run after her mother. Mildred held onto her. Gradually Trudy quieted herself.

Evelyn bent over and hugged her. "It's okay, Little Sis. Everything's okay now."

John stepped closer to the rails. He reached down, picked up a big rock, and slammed it down on the train track. It made a loud clang. "Bitch," he said, and rubbed his eyes with the backs of his hands.

Mildred and Evelyn looked at John, then at each other.

"John, don't say that," Evelyn said. "It's our fault. We was too loud and rowdy, and we did break that lantern. You know we ain't supposed to play like that in the house."

"She's just mean. Next time I'm gonna let her go. She can do whatever she wants."

"You don't mean that," Mildred put her hand on his shoulder. He was nearly eleven and taller than she was even though she was almost two years older.

Trudy saw her mother in the distance, near the house. She'd never looked back at them. A sadness spread through Trudy as evening spread across the sky. The lonely sound of the train whistle drifted back to her through the gathering dark.

I want Papa. I want Papa.

Joe and Trudy crossed the Texas border after driving all night. Trudy gazed into the brightening sky, exhausted, but too tense to sleep. She pushed Papa's face from her mind. She knew he'd be all right. He would see whatever happened as God's will and make his peace with it. Besides, she'd told him she loved Joe in the letter. He always believed her and trusted her decisions.

Mama's cold, blank stare filled her memory, and a wide grin spread over her face.

I'm free of you, Mama. You can judge me however much you like, but I'm free.

Three hours later, Joe tracked down a Justice of the Peace in Amarillo. The old coot spoke only to Joe, but Trudy felt his eyes crawl all over her as he discussed the procedure to obtain a license and his fee for performing the ceremony. When they left the Potter County Courthouse, Joe took Trudy's hand and led her back to the decrepit brick building that housed the JP's office. Trudy resolutely distanced herself from the forlorn setting as the man officiated at their sad parody of a wedding.

Wearily, Trudy vowed to love, honor, and obey. Squeezing her hand, Joe promised the same, except for the obey part. As he looked down into her eyes, she struggled to meet his gaze and felt a fresh wave of guilt. At least Mama wasn't there to mock her. "Act in haste, repent at leisure," she'd have said.

They checked into a scruffy motel on U.S. Route 60 just beyond the city limits. It was still daylight outside, but as soon as he closed the door behind him, Joe stripped down to his underwear and turned down the well-worn bedclothes. Her eyes on the floor, Trudy took her nightgown and hairbrush out of the pillowcase she carried, stepped into the bathroom, and stared at herself in the cloudy mirror.

Her large gray eyes stared back at her as she brushed her auburn hair until it gleamed. She chewed the inside of her lip until she tasted blood, then slipped into her nightgown and returned to the bed where Joe waited for her.

She'd seen farm animals woo more than Joe did, maybe because the male knew the female had the option of refusing. Trudy didn't. She was Joe's property now, according to everything she'd learned from her parents and God's Holy Book. She was a wife.

Joe peeled off her nightgown and became so intent on her breasts and other private parts that he barely paused to kiss her. When they had kissed in the woods two nights before, his tongue brushing her lips had made her shiver. She'd felt a warm, tingling desire for more—at least until he'd stuck his tongue down her throat.

But in the dim motel room, a strange detachment crept over her as Joe took her virginity. All she found herself able to do was to close her eyes and wait for it to be over. When his hands pried apart her thighs, she felt blood rise to her cheeks and had to restrain herself from pushing him away. She was surprised by how fast it ended, but at least it hadn't hurt much.

She was grateful for that, but her expectations, nourished by romance novels, in contrast with the stark reality struck her as black humor. She pressed her face into the pillow, smothering a hysterical urge to giggle, and listened to Joe snore, determined to ignore the part of her that wanted to cry.

It'll get better. When I love you.

She fell asleep, grateful to be in a bed at least. Joe woke soon after and didn't let her exhaustion curb his desire. Trudy tried to distance herself from her body. She was so tired it was almost easy to do, especially by his third advance, but she roused enough to worry about his stamina.

How's he gonna stay awake to drive tomorrow?

***

They continued across the Panhandle and into New Mexico the next day. Trudy had never been anywhere but Oklahoma. She leaned out the window, feeling the wind in her face, and watched the landscape change as they headed west. Long, flat fields of wheat faded away to high plains desert where little except dry grass grew.

By late morning they dropped down off the high caprock and into an alien landscape that took her breath away. An endless vista of dry earth, dotted with strange, stunted plants and occasional stone buildings stretched toward all horizons. She tried to recall pictures of the desert she'd seen in a book she'd glanced through at the Tahlequah library.

Joe pulled the car to the side of the road, got out, and walked over to a plant with shaggy stalk-like branches and pale green leaves arranged in circles. With his back to Trudy, he began to relieve himself.

Trudy jumped off the running board and raced to examine a cactus with fat circular leaves. It and others of its ilk shared the dry land with those of the sort Joe was watering. Some were covered with waxy yellow flowers. She made the mistake of touching a leaf, and jerked her hand back. Her fingertip sprouted a batch of fine brown needles.

"Ouch!"

"C'mon, Trudy. Let's go." She ran back to the car, and, as Joe pulled back onto the highway, carefully extracted the needles with her teeth.

Late that evening, the landscape changed again. They stopped for groceries at one of the small truck stops and motels made almost entirely of earth that they saw occasionally, along with trading posts advertising Indian curios. Joe told her the building material was called adobe. Mud bricks were used to compensate for the lack of nearby lumber. They were finished with a thin layer of mud.

Then a river appeared and grew. It was lined with tall cottonwoods in some places and reeds in others, its current deep and powerful compared to the shallow gurgling creeks Trudy had grown up with.

"Do you know the name of that river, Joe?"

"I think it's called the Rio Grande. That means Big River in Mexican. Mexico used to own this part of the U.S. The people that live 'round here kept the name."

"I'm glad. It's a pretty name, and this is a pretty place."

Joe smiled. "Just wait 'til you see California, Trudy."

But they didn't get any closer that day.

Chapter Three

Have a Little Faith in Me

The next morning, Trudy and Joe followed the road along immense red rock cliffs dotted in places with small, six-sided buildings with dirt roofs. According to Joe, they were inhabited by Navajo Indians. Trudy observed it all with wide eyes, too astounded by the view to be frightened that the narrow road bordered a sheer cliff just beyond the Model T's wheels.

Later, Joe explained the term Continental Divide to her as well. As they entered Arizona, Trudy looked at him with growing respect tempered by doubt. Outside Phoenix, she watched as the Model T sucked gasoline out of the hose like a starving nestling latched onto its mother's beak.

Joe left his wallet behind to make a trip to the men's room. Trudy peeked inside and wished she hadn't. The sun had almost set and it was growing dark, but she could still see well enough to count the money, and, as Mama knew, she was good at arithmetic. She saw Joe approaching and put the wallet back where it had been.

"Joe, honey, are you sure we got enough money to make it to California and get a place to live while you find work?

He hesitated. "No, I can't say I am. I been thinking 'bout that. Jesus, Trudy, I guess I didn't figure how much gas costs some places and how far California is from Oklahoma. I'm kinda worried 'bout the tires, too. We got a spare, but it ain't in very good shape.

"Driving through the desert could be bad if we get a flat, or, God help us, something else goes wrong with the car. I'd like to trade those old wood spoke wheels for some of the new all steel ones, too. A broke wheel could strand us, for sure. I gotta decide what's best to do."

"How much money've we got left?"

He looked surprised that she had asked. He exaggerated a little, watching her out of the corners of his eyes rather than meeting her gaze. She kept a straight face as if taking what he said as gospel. She waited for him to say more, but he started the car and pulled back onto the road. He drove a quarter mile before he turned onto a dirt side road and parked.

Joe stared out his window in silence at the streaks of fading purple clouds west of them; the direction of California. Then he turned back to face Trudy. "I'm thinking it might be a good idea to find a temporary job 'round here someplace. We could stay long enough to save up some money, buy some new tires, maybe at least one spare wheel." Joe glanced at her then looked down at his hands. "I'd rather hold onto as much of the money we got now as we can. We could sleep in the car for free."

Trudy touched his shoulder. "Sure we can, Joe. It's definitely not cold. It might be fun, sleeping under the stars."

So they stayed on the dirt road with the roof back for air. The temperature dropped somewhat with the sun, and a sliver of moon rose to hover above a distant mountain peak. There were no houses in sight. By the moon's faint light, Trudy could see the vague shapes of unfamiliar vegetation on her right. To her left, beyond Joe, the far edge of the irrigation ditch was lined with tall trees that looked like cottonwoods. Beyond the trees lay acres of bare fields.

Must be a farm over there someplace. They haven't planted yet.

An eerie quavering cry pierced the silence. Startled, Trudy grabbed Joe's arm. "That's just a coyote, Trudy. Don't worry." He squeezed her hand. Another cry followed the first. "They're probably howling at that moon."

"It startled me, Joe. It's kinda spooky out here." Trudy released Joe's arm and climbed into the rear of the Ford. She stretched out as much as she could on the cramped, hard bench seat.

Joe followed her. Even within those cramped confines, he managed to satisfy his passion, but after he did, he returned to the front. The front seat was wider, although he still had to curl up his long legs and tuck his feet under the steering wheel.

Trudy lay on her side, knees bent. Her head rested on one hand as she looked up at the stars. The sky was the same as the Tahlequah sky, although the stars glinted more in the dry air. The Hunter strode through the heavens above the southwest horizon, his faithful hound at his heels. She could have been lying on a quilt in a field back home watching this same journey. After all the excitement and strangeness of the previous days, it was comforting. She fell into a deep, dreamless sleep.

The next morning, using supplies they'd picked up on the way, Trudy fixed herself and Joe peanut butter sandwiches on Wonder Bread for breakfast. She made extra ones for herself and for Joe to take with him in case he was gone past noon. She handed Joe his breakfast sandwich, and they leaned against the car, chewing and sharing their last warm Coca Cola. She looked around for a shady spot where she could wait while he was gone, but saw none.

"Trudy." Joe swallowed his last bite and licked his fingers. "I decided not to take the car. I don't know my way 'round this town at all." He rubbed his nose with the back of his hand. "The main thing is gas. Anyway, I think it's better for you to have the car to stay in. I don't wanna leave you wandering around when I don't know when I'll be back."

Trudy felt relieved, but didn't understand. "But how'll you get to the places that are hiring? Are you sure you won't need the car?" She wiped the sweat off her upper lip. The sun was barely up, and it was already getting hot. She took another small bite and relished the softness of the store-bought bread.

"I'll hitch rides. I done that lotsa times back home, before I had a car." Joe finished his sandwich and drained the last of the Coke. He stood and stared into space. Trudy looked around for a good-sized bush. It had been too dark to wander around the night before, so she'd relieved herself behind the car.

Now she looked at the empty land on the side of the dirt road nearest the Ford. It was mostly barren. Tall, yellowish Bermuda grass covered the sides of the irrigation ditch lining the road. Roundish weeds with small leaves, or thorns, and some yellow-green bushes with tiny stick-like branches and miniature leaves dotted the dry, cracked earth beyond.

Across the road, cottonwoods that looked about as old as Papa lined the far side of that irrigation ditch. Now Trudy could see that the fields beyond had been planted after all. Tiny green sprigs divided the neat rows. Further north up the road she saw a field of small green trees with spots of orange nestled among the branches.

"Oh, my goodness, Joe. Are those oranges?" She pointed. Oranges had been a rare treat back home, usually reserved for Christmas.

"Yeah, they probably are. I don't know too much 'bout Arizona, Trudy. But I think they do grow a lot of oranges and lemons. They even had some for sale at that service station."

Trudy gazed in awe for a moment, then turned back to the uncultivated land on their side of the road. One of the bushes was big enough to hide behind. She lifted her dress above her knees, jumped the irrigation ditch, walked back from the road, and squatted behind the bush. She brushed against it as she rose, and a clean, sharp scent permeated the air. She pulled a branch toward her, sniffed, then pulled some twigs and leaves off and crushed them. She sniffed her fingers and smiled then jumped back across the ditch and held her fingers out to Joe.

"Smell this, Joe."

He regarded her a moment through narrowed eyes then grasped her wrist and pulled her fingers close to his nose. "Yeah, so what? What is it?" He stared at her.

She shrugged. "That bush over there. Don't it smell clean and fresh? Do you know what it is?"

"No. Don't think it grows in Oklahoma. We need to plan, Trudy. Pay attention. I'm gonna drive back to that grocery store we passed before we turned off. I'll buy a newspaper and look through the want ads. I can ask 'bout trucking and construction businesses 'round here, too. The main thing is to talk to people. I'll find something." Trudy handed him his extra sandwich and he tucked it inside the bib of his overalls.

***

Joe parked in the grocery store lot, raised the Ford's canvas top against the sun, then left Trudy waiting while he went into the store. He returned a few minutes later with a newspaper under his arm. He extracted a few pages and dropped the rest on the car seat. After giving her a distracted kiss, he climbed into a car that was waiting for him with the engine running.

Already got a ride! You're good with people, ain't you, Joe?

Trudy waited inside the Ford until the heat drove her out. She loitered inside the A.J. Bayliss. Enjoying the coolness and trying to be inconspicuous, she strolled the store aisles, noting the price of cans of vegetables and the even higher cost of fresh vegetables in the produce section. She remembered Mama's dedication to her garden and the time she spent canning.

How much money did you save us, Mama?

Leaving the store, she strolled across the street to eat her sandwich in the shade of a huge cottonwood. More of the bushes she'd seen earlier grew in the vacant lot next to the store. After she swallowed the last bite, she walked over to examine them again.

A man in a business suit passing by on the sidewalk tilted his head and stared at her. "Is everything all right? Do you need help?"

"No." She laughed. "I was wondering what these bushes are. They're just 'bout everywhere. They smell so clean and fresh."

"Those are greasewood. You should smell them after a rain. And, yes, they are just about everywhere. They're tough, don't take much water, and don't mind the heat. Like some people, they're hard to get rid of." He grinned at her.

Is he flirting with me?

"So you must not be from around here," he said. "Where are you from?"

"Oklahoma. We only been here a couple of days."

A shadow crossed his face, and his eyes shifted away from hers. "Well, I'd better get back to work. Good luck to you." He walked away and never looked back.

The exchange puzzled Trudy. She sniffed her underarms and detected a faint odor of sweat.

Did he notice I ain't had a bath lately? Could he smell me from that far away?

***

Late that afternoon, when Joe returned, she was sitting on the ground under the cottonwood leafing through the newspaper he'd left in the car. As they drove back to their parking place along the dirt road, Trudy pointed to the bushes. "They're called greasewood, honey. A fella told me that today."

"Greasewood, huh." He began to tell her about his day.

He didn't ask for details about hers. She was glad. She hadn't understood that man's attitude, and it had left her with an uneasy feeling. She tried to push it away.

Maybe people 'round here ain't as friendly as they are back home, or maybe I just imagined it.

Loneliness suddenly swept through her. In that instant, she felt ready to trade all the greasewood bushes and Rio Grande rivers in the universe to go back to slip barefoot over moss-covered rocks in a murmuring creek, gathering watercress with Mary.

***

When Sunday came, Joe was still unemployed. He couldn't look for work on the Lord's Day. Nothing was open. Instead, he and Trudy walked downtown along Washington Street then meandered around Phoenix.

Trudy gazed with longing at the S. H. Kress sign. It advertised a soda fountain, but Joe said, and she agreed, even a shared soda would be too extravagant. Besides, even if they had wanted to yield to temptation, the store, like all the other businesses, was closed.

"We'll come back after I get a job, honey. Buy a iced vanilla Coke. Maybe even a chocolate milkshake. You'd like that. We can share the straw, if you promise not to chew on it." Joe grinned at her, wrapped his arm around her shoulder, and pulled her close.

Monday, he began his search again.

Thursday, he returned to the parking lot earlier than usual. He broke into a run as he approached the car where Trudy waited. "They hired me, Trudy! I got a job! Johansen's Sand and Rock. I have to get a Arizona Commercial driver's license. That won't be any problem. Lord knows I can drive a truck.

"You can help me study for the written part. They give me all the materials. I can start loading and working 'round the yard right away, but I can't drive 'til I show them the license."

That evening they celebrated with dinner at a small roadside cafe. Joe explained how he had stumbled upon the job as they gobbled hamburgers and French fries. "It was pure, dumb luck, honey. I catch a ride out Van Buren to the Tovrea stockyards. I think maybe they could use a hand with something, but they don't have nothing. So I'm 'bout ready to eat my sandwich 'fore I head back towards town, but I want a cup of coffee to go with it. There's this little cafe, 'bout like this one, on the corner 'cross from the stockyards. I go in and get my coffee and decide to sit outside on their porch in the shade to eat my sandwich. I get to talking to a guy eating his lunch, too. I tell him I'm looking for work, and getting pretty desperate."

He paused a second to put a catsup-soaked French fry into his mouth, then, still chewing, continued. "He says the place he works, this Johansen's Sand and Rock, is just getting ready to put out a sign for truck drivers. He takes me back with him after he finishes eating, and I talk to his boss, and guess what, honey?"

He didn't wait for her to guess. "The fella's from Oklahoma. He's born somewhere right 'round Muskogee. Ain't that something? He likes me right away. I tell him 'bout the hauling I done back home, and next thing I know, he offers me the job. No application form, no nothing." His pride shone in his deep brown eyes.

Smiling, she reached across to feed him a French fry. "That's great, honey. I knew I could count on you."

Chapter Four

What is This Thing Called Love?

That Friday, Joe hitched a ride with the coworker he'd met at the sandwich shop for his first day of work, parking the Model T in the A.J. Bayliss lot as was becoming a routine. Trudy loitered up and down the store aisles, then returned to the Ford at lunch time to eat her peanut butter sandwich. She avoided the vacant lot with the greasewood bushes, afraid she might encounter the man who had spoken to her then left so abruptly that first day.

She was grateful that Joe had found a job but tired of examining cans of green beans and comparing bread prices. She gazed with longing at a magazine rack, but she knew Joe would consider such a purchase an extravagance they couldn't afford. Waiting for a time when the store had few customers, she used the public restroom to scrub her face and arms. That helped somewhat, but did nothing for the grime accumulating on the rest of her body or the smell of sweat that permeated her dress. It was getting hard to ignore.

After Joe returned that evening, as she watched her husband steer the Model T toward the side of the dirt road where they camped, she decided to test the waters. "When will you get your first paycheck, honey?"

"Why, Trudy? I still got money left. When I do get paid, we need to save most of it for California, anyhow. What are you thinking?" He frowned and glanced at her sideways.

"We need to start looking for a place to live. We can't stay here forever."

"We could stay 'til I get my first paycheck, anyhow. That'll be next Friday. They pay ever two weeks. I get 'bout half pay the first time. A little more 'cause I worked today."

"Joe, if we stay in this car 'til next Friday, it'll be over two weeks since we even had a sponge bath. I know some of the guys you work with might not be too clean, either, but you don't want your boss to see you with your hair all greasy and your clothes all filthy, do you? You already smell a little strong."

He glowered. "So do you."

"I know. That's my point. And all our clothes are dirty. In another week, they'll be even worse. We need a place where we can clean up, Joe. Besides, we can eat cheaper if we have a stove. I can buy flour and lard and make some biscuits and beans. I don't know 'bout you, but I'm tired of peanut butter sandwiches. And store-bought bread is lots more expensive, too. Besides, it sure would be nice to sleep in a bed."

Joe sat in silence for a few minutes, then sighed and conceded.

***

That Saturday they rented a tiny furnished house, using most of the remainder of Joe's California savings, in a neighborhood northeast of the city, among other frame, brick, and plaster stucco houses. A fireplace with a brick facade graced the cramped living room. As they carried in their scarce belongings, Trudy stood for a moment, staring at it in disbelief.

Does it ever get cold enough here to use this thing?

The tiny walk-through bathroom had a shower, toilet, and sink. Neither of them had taken baths in anything other than galvanized tubs before. Joe tried to squeeze in with her, but Trudy held her ground.

"Not this time, Joe. I need to concentrate on getting clean. Maybe next time."

As night fell, Trudy unfolded the sofa on the screened-in porch where they would sleep to try to escape the heat inside. She hung wet sheets in front of the screens for privacy and to cool the circulating air, thankful that Joe had managed to pack a few practical things besides clothes.

The early nighttime heat did nothing to stifle Joe's passion. He still barely kissed her and never seemed to notice Trudy's lack of response. She'd become accustomed to it. Rolling onto her side, she used her toes to push the sheet further down the sofa and let the faint, warm breeze evaporate Joe's perspiration from her body. As she stared into the darkness, listening to his faint snores, she recalled scenes from *Wuthering Heights* and *Jane Eyre*.

Maybe all those romance novels are fairy tales, anyway. A man has to have passion, or he can't make children. All us women really need to do is lie there.

By their two month anniversary, she was pregnant with their first child. The night she was absolutely sure, she told Joe, hoping he would be excited. He wasn't.

"Lord, Trudy! 'Course I want us to have a family, but this just ain't the right time. Couldn't this've waited 'til we get to California?" He regarded her, jaw clenched.

"Well, I'm not sure you have that much will power, Joe. Maybe if I slept somewhere else." She glared at him, trying to ignore the pain under her anger.

"I just thought there was something women could do so this didn't happen."

"Well, if there is, I don't know what it is. I never learned. Why don't you just ask around and find somebody who can get rid of it? I'm sure some of your new friends must've got girls in trouble before." Her eyes dared him. She wondered what she'd do if he rose to the bait, but she was angry and hurt.

"God, no, Trudy! I'd never do that! It's just, " his voice trailed off. "We'll just have to make the best of it."

"In my family babies were blessings." Trudy curbed her tongue. She wanted to apologize for inconveniencing him, but even Joe, dense as he could be, would have caught the undertone of sarcasm. She couldn't change him, and fighting wouldn't have helped matters.

Trudy's mother had had seven pregnancies and six babies that Trudy knew about. She might have even had other miscarriages. It was almost certain that Mama didn't know any means to stop having babies except menopause. That hadn't occurred to Trudy before.

Did you ever regret that, Mama?

***

Grown-ups from Thomas Kelly's church had come to the cabin one night in October the year Trudy had turned four. The old folks had come to ask Papa to entreat the Lord's help to protect their two sons who were fighting in the Great War. They'd been praying out loud with Papa and quoting Scripture since they'd arrived after supper. Trudy didn't remember their names.

The parishioners sat on the couch, and Mama and Papa sat on the soft chairs on either side of the coal stove. Little sister Mary, two years old, slept on Mama's lap. John, Mildred, and Evelyn had dragged wooden chairs away from the dinner table to sit close to the stove. Trudy sat cross-legged on the new rag rug in the front room with Mama's old shawl wrapped around her. A small island of lantern light enveloped the family and guests, leaving the house outside the circle in cold darkness.

Trudy liked the rug. Mama had made it to replace the one her children had ruined the year before. She'd made it out of scraps left over from Trudy and her sisters' dresses. When the grown-up talk bored Trudy, which it did a lot of the time, she searched the braids for scraps that matched her dresses.

Trudy watched Evelyn's head drop down onto her chest. Mama glanced at the visitors, who were looking at Papa, and reached across to poke Evelyn in the side. Evelyn jumped and her eyes flew open. Mama frowned and thrust her chin toward the bedroom.

Evelyn got up and touched Mildred's arm. Millie rose, and they headed for bed. Trudy yawned. She was sleepy, but she wanted to wait until Mama put Mary to bed so she wouldn't have to crawl under those cold covers alone. She was about to lie down on the rug when she heard Papa say her name.

"Yes, wherever they are, no matter what the danger may be, always remember, the Lord's there, too. His eye is on the sparrow. Hallelujah, I should know! When I dropped Trudy she couldn't of been more than two or three weeks old. She could of died, or been hurt real bad, but I know the Lord caught her in His loving hands!"

"You dropped Trudy? How'd that happen, Reverend? That must be quite a story!" The soldiers' father caught Trudy's eye and grinned.

"Well, it never should of happened. Lord forgive me! But such a tiny mite, she was. I didn't feel like I needed to hold onto her. She was sort of resting on top of my arm. Then Melissa come up behind me and touched my shoulder." Papa glanced over at Mama, who was frowning.

"No, dearest, I don't mean it was your fault." He looked into her eyes as if no one else were there. "I should of been holding her tighter." He turned back to the visitors. "It startled me, and I jumped. Well, Trudy slipped right out of my arms. I tried to catch her."

He shook his head. "There was this loose board in the floor." He looked down at the wide wooden planks that formed the floor of their tiny share cropper's shack as if he were reliving the memory. "That one over there." He pointed.

You dropped me, Papa?

He glanced at Mama again. "I'd been meaning to fix it, but I hadn't gotten 'round to it yet. Wouldn't you know she'd hit it? It tipped sideways, and she went right through to the earth underneath the house." He slapped his knee hard.

"But the dear Lord caught her. He must of, 'cause she landed so gentle, she barely cried at first. Praise Jesus!" He laughed and shook his head. Black hair fell down over his forehead. He brushed it back, looked at Trudy, and smiled. His blue Irish eyes crinkled.

"I don't think it hurt her very much at all. She was mostly mad at me. I could tell by how she squeezed her little fists tight and yelled after we got her out. I tried to tell her how sorry I was. I don't know if she believed me or not."

Trudy got up off the rug, walked over to Papa, and stood by his side. He gripped her waist with his large hands and lifted her onto his lap. She laid her head against his shoulder and felt the steady thumping of his heart.

"If Jesus hadn't caught her, and she'd been injured, I don't know what I'd of done." He laid his hand on top of her head and took a deep breath. "Thank the Lord! I fixed that board that very day. She's too precious to risk losing." He put his arms around Trudy and hugged her tight. The visitors smiled. Trudy smiled, too.

Suddenly, Mama stood. She looked at Trudy. Mary perched on Mama's hip, rubbing her eyes. "'Scuse me, I'll just put these childern to bed. C'mon, Trudy."

Trudy kissed Papa goodnight, climbed off his lap, and followed her mother into the bedroom where Evelyn snored and Mildred muttered in her sleep. Mama turned down the handmade quilt on the bed the younger sisters shared and tucked Mary inside while Trudy changed into her nightgown. Her little sister was almost back to sleep when Trudy scooted in beside her and snuggled up to her warmth. Mama pulled the covers up over them, turned, and left the room.

Mama, you didn't say goodnight. You forgot to kiss me.

The covers on Mildred and Evelyn's bed rustled.

"Millie, are you awake?"

"Yeah, what is it, Little Sis?" Trudy heard her sister yawn.

"Did you know Papa dropped me when I was a baby? I fell through the floor."

"Yeah, of course I knew 'bout that. I can still remember. It was a real hullabaloo. You'd a thought he killed you."

"I didn't know."

"Why'd you think he always treats you like you're so special? Kinda makes the rest of us mad sometimes. Now go to sleep."

Is Mama mad?

Trudy slipped out of bed and walked back into the front room. The visitors had left, and Papa was reading his Bible. Mama was adding coal to the stove for the night and banking up the ashes with a little shovel. Papa looked up from his reading. "Why ain't you asleep, small fry?"

"I forgot to kiss Mama goodnight." She walked over to her mother. Mama bent down to kiss her, and Trudy wrapped her arms around her neck. "I love you, Mama."

Do you love me?

***

After her anger died down, in the spirit of making the best of it, clash as it did with her idealistic nature, Trudy tried to reassure Joe about the baby. She waited a couple of weeks to give him time to recover from the shock of her announcement then brought the subject into their conversation over dinner. They'd opened all of the kitchen windows and the living room door in hope of catching a breeze. It was still June and early evening, but the temperature must have been in the low hundreds at least.

"You know, Joe, babies don't add that much expense, and they really aren't any trouble, at least 'til they start walking." She put a fork full of fried potatoes and beans in her mouth and chewed, watching him.

He looked back at her in silence. His skepticism hung in the air.

She swallowed. "I'm serious, Joe. I know some women go to the doctor, but I won't. Mama never did. It's not like I'm sick or anything. It's a natural condition."

"What if I save enough for us to get to California? What happens then? You can't travel like that." He stared at her, reminding her of an old rooster working himself up for a fight.

"Sure I can. Why not? I'm healthy as a horse, and in the old days pregnant pioneer women traveled in wagon trains." He'd gone to school longer than she had. He must know that was true.

"Well, that's probably not gonna happen anyway, saving enough. What with paying rent on this place and all. It's gonna take a while longer."

Chapter Five

Life is Just a Bowl of Cherries

After her experience with the stranger in the lot next to A.J. Bayliss, Trudy was hesitant about reaching out to her nearest neighbors, although she did wave and say hello when she saw them outside. They all seemed a lot older than she, and appeared to be absorbed in their own lives. Trudy occasionally saw what were probably their grandchildren playing in their yards.

Instead of socializing while Joe was at work, she resolved to scrub the tiny house from top to bottom. She waxed the ugly, worn linoleum in the kitchen, and got on hands and knees to wash baseboards, too intent to be bothered by the sweat-damp strands of hair falling into her face. As she scrubbed, when she felt her baby flutter inside her, she thought about Mama.

Do you ever miss me, Mama? Sure, like a dog would miss its fleas.

***

It had been the first day of third grade, and Trudy sat in a big desk that year. The top was marred with carved initials. Only the tips of her shoes had touched the floor. She could swing her legs back and forth if she lifted her toes. She loved school. Sometimes she got so excited she had to move. She swung her legs that afternoon as Mrs. Bromley poured ancient Egypt and mummies into her imagination.

Mrs. Bromley finished the lesson and rang the bell. Trudy darted through the door after the others. She wanted to run straight home but had to wait for Mary. Her little sister stood in the doorway of the first grade classroom waving at a little girl in pigtails and a flowered dress who was skipping away. Trudy hurried over to her.

The girls walked the half mile home holding hands. Mary chattered about her first day. Trudy listened and resisted the urge to tell her sister about mummies. She was saving that for Papa. Mary trotted over to the garden to look for Mama when they got home.

Trudy burst through the door into the front room where Papa sat in the rocking chair reading his Bible and making notes for sermons. Dragging a stool out of the kitchen, she perched in front of him.

"Papa, Miss Bromley read us a book today. Did you know when

people died the Egyptians turned them into mummies?"

"Really? How'd they do that?" He set his open Bible on his knee and smiled at her.

"It's very complicated. They only did it for important men, like kings. They just buried other people sort of like we do. But for kings, they cut them open and took out their insides first, so they wouldn't rot so fast." Trudy paused. "They left the heart 'cause their gods would use it to find out if the man was good enough to go to their heaven."

"You know there's only one Heaven, don't you Trudy?"

"Yes, Papa, but the Egyptians didn't know about Jesus. He hadn't been born yet." She looked into space, relishing her new knowledge. "This was thirty-two hundred B.C. That means Before Christ. Anyway, the worst thing they did, they stuck a thin stick with a hook on it up his nose and swished it around 'til his brain was like mush. Then they sucked it out. Euuugh! Pretty disgusting, huh?" She giggled. "I guess his heart was more important than his brain."

Papa nodded. "That's very interesting, Trudy. I guess even the Egyptians knew a man's heart is what guides his actions. It don't matter how smart you are if your heart ain't in the right place."

Mama and Mary came in the front door. Mama carried a basket of turnip greens.

"Trudy was just telling me about a story her teacher read today." Papa looked up at Mama. Mama stepped into the kitchen and set the basket on the table, then turned to inspect Trudy.

"Oh, ain't that interesting?" Mama's mouth twisted into a false smile. "So tell me, Miss Priss, did they teach you how to bake a pie yet? How to sew a dress?"

Trudy looked down. She knew by the smirk on Mama's face that she didn't expect an answer.

"Them are the things you need to learn." Mama turned back to the kitchen.

Trudy looked at Papa. He was staring out the window, his hand resting on his Bible.

***

Trudy had been exchanging letters with Papa and Mary since she and Joe had arrived in Arizona. In her first letter to Mary, she'd asked her sister to have John return the Bronte novel under their mattress to the Tahlequah library, but she never explained the circumstances behind her abrupt departure. In her letters to Papa, she always wrote "Dear Papa and Mama" as a salutation for Papa's benefit, but only heard about Mama indirectly when Papa used the word "we" or used her name.

'Course Mama can't write, not that she ever would.

When the serious heat of early July moved in, Trudy persuaded Joe to buy a small electric fan they could switch from room to room for some relief. They had no garden, so she had to buy their vegetables at a nearby Piggly-Wiggly, mostly in cans, which were less expensive than fresh produce. As she shopped, she heard people in the grocery store talk about the weather, and invariably they finished with the comment, "At least it's a dry heat."

Hell probably is, too.

July and August crawled by with temperatures up to a hundred and ten degrees and higher. The summer rains came. They broke the heat briefly, but it returned a few hours after each storm, and no one could call it a dry heat any longer. It reminded Trudy of muggy, itchy Oklahoma heat, filled with mosquitoes.

Her only brief respite came when Joe surprised her with a Saturday trip to the air conditioned downtown Rialto movie theater to celebrate a small raise in wages after six months with Johansen's Sand and Rock. She relished the cool almost as much as her first motion picture.

Then in September the clouds disappeared, and the dry heat was back. Now she could appreciate the difference. Finally, in late October, the heat broke for good, and Phoenix slid into its glory season.

That winter, with increased energy despite her expanded abdomen, Trudy longed for something to read. She could only cook and clean so much, and magazines were too expensive. Besides, she wanted more than fashion articles. She wanted books. Memories of the Bronte sagas and other novels she'd hidden from Mama under her mattress filled her with longing. As she wended her unwieldy way to the Piggly-Wiggly one morning, she pondered the possibility of locating a public library.

But Phoenix is so big! Even if I found a library, how would I get there? Joe's too depressed to take me. All he thinks about is getting to California; anything else is just a distraction or a bother.

She decided to at least find out about public libraries in Phoenix. She asked the grocery cashier. He knew her by now and was happy to chat. "Sure, honey, we have a library," the cashier said. "Where do you think you are, in Timbuktu?" He rolled his eyes and raised his shoulder in mock offense, then grinned at her.

The woman in line behind her smiled, too. She wore a white nurse's uniform and was unusually pretty with dark wavy hair and perfectly arched brows. The Good Samaritan Hospital was a few blocks away. She touched Trudy's arm. "It's called the Carnegie Library, and it's downtown. Not far from here at all."

The Carnegie Library was west of downtown, near the state capital. If Trudy walked a few blocks west, she could take a public streetcar south to the station on Washington near the S. H. Kress Five and Dime and about nine blocks from the library. In Phoenix, streetcars only ran north and south, but she wouldn't have to walk very far. It would cost a total of ten cents for two tokens; one there, and one back. She considered as she trekked home.

Surely, with a decent job, you can give me that much, Joe. Maybe you can even give me a nickel for that vanilla Coke. You did promise me.

When she got there with the groceries it was just past noon, but Joe was already sitting, scowling, on the living room couch. She stopped in surprise, still holding the bag supported by the side of her protuberant belly.

"What happened?" Her heart drummed in her ears.

"They cut my damned hours." Joe didn't look at her.

"How much?"

"From forty to thirty a week." His mouth turned down, and a sullen scowl covered his face.

Trudy did a quick calculation. *That's twenty-five percent less!*

"Can we make it?"

"Maybe. I guess we'll have to." He laughed, but there was no humor in the sound. "I don't have enough money saved to buy tires and get a place to stay in California. Anyway, if we went there, I might not get a job at all what with this goddamned Depression. We're stuck." His voice sounded bitter and angry.

"Things will get better, Joe."

At last he glared up at her. "Is that right? Is that right? Well I guess you would know, you being so damn smart and all."

She stared at him, speechless, turned, and walked into the kitchen. She set the bag down on the counter and started to put the groceries away along with her hopes for the library. John wasn't here to help her this time.

***

Mama had decided that Trudy would not return to school that year, despite her pleas to continue. When Mary came home after the first day of classes, she handed Trudy a small, sealed envelope. Trudy glanced at the name printed at the top. It was from Mrs. Bromley. She pushed the screen door open to step outside, and her sister followed. Mary grabbed Trudy's arm. "I told her you wouldn't be back this year, and she told me to give you that note."

They hurried past the garden, and only the crunch of dry leaves broke the silence until they stood under a blackjack in the small stand of trees beyond. Mary rocked back and forth on the soles of her feet as her sister read Mrs. Bromley's note.

"Well, what does she say?

"She says she's sorry I won't be coming back. She says if Mama will give her permission she will lend me books I can read at home, but she can't unless Mama says so. It would be against the rules. So that's never gonna happen."

Mary walked up to her sister and laid her hand on Trudy's arm. Then Trudy brightened. "She says when I turn twelve I can get a library card from the Tahlequah library. I won't even need Mama's permission for that."

"That's nearly two years, Trudy. Besides, how're you gonna get to town without Mama knowing?"

"I'll find a way. Meantime, maybe I can borrow books from some of my friends like Betty. She's still going to school. When I turn twelve I'll get to the library. Don't you worry about that."

And she had, thanks to her trusted and beloved older brother.

***

Nothing had prepared Trudy for labor, and after sixteen hours she'd sworn she'd never have another baby. She would find out about birth control, or Joe would never touch her again. A local midwife attended her while Joe waited in the living room, pacing and staring out the window. She shared her resolve with the midwife, who was noncommittal. Then, after a final tremendous push, the pain stopped, and she heard Johnny's first cry.

"It's a boy." The midwife cut and tied the umbilical cord. Then, wiping the baby off with a towel, she placed him in his mother's arms. By this time, alerted by the birth cry, Joe stood in the doorway of the tiny bedroom.

"Come on in," the midwife said. "Come and meet your son."

He entered. Trudy shifted her attention from her infant to her husband's face. He was grinning like a Jack-o-lantern. She searched his eyes.

What's behind that grin, Joe? Your manly pride or a father's love? I guess time will tell.

She brushed her lips across her infant's forehead and examined his tiny fingers and toes. Her newborn nuzzled her breast, and the midwife guided him to his mother's nipple. He began to nurse for the first time. The instinctive strength and ferocity of motherhood flooded through Trudy. She looked up at Joe.

This is what matters, Joe. Not romance. Family. We're a family now.

The next day, Joe presented her with a rocking chair he'd built himself at a co-worker's house. Trudy kissed him with a surge of genuine affection, and her spirits soared.

Chapter Six

Wrap Your Troubles In Dreams

Willie was just over a year old, and the Great Depression had wrapped its dark wings even more tightly around the nation when Trudy could no longer deny that she was pregnant again. She dreaded telling Joe. Despite her efforts, their relationship had worsened over the previous year, at least for her. As far as she could tell, Joe was oblivious to her growing resentment. She felt invisible to him except when he used her for a whipping boy or an outlet for his primal urges.

Trudy knew Joe's frustration was in large part due to the indefinite postponement of his California dream. She tried to make allowances for that, even though any conversation with him could turn into a stroll through a minefield. One misstep from her and he exploded. Nasty, cutting words sliced through Trudy like metal shards. Sometimes he reminded her so much of Mama she wanted to scream. Papa had lightened his family's struggles with his sense of humor, but Trudy had seen no evidence that Joe had one.

Nearly a month after she was sure, in February of '32, she decided she couldn't put off telling Joe any longer, or he might figure it out for himself. He came home in the early afternoon since his hours had been cut, and moped around the house. He was sitting at the kitchen table that day, leafing through the meager want ads.

"Joe, I haven't had my monthly visitor for two months now, and I been throwing up most mornings. I'm pregnant." She steeled herself, waiting for his reaction.

Shoulders slumped, he glared at her.

She felt her chin rise in defiance, despite her effort to remain calm. "You know we can't afford for me to go to a doctor. How'm I supposed to learn how to keep this from happening? Who am I supposed to ask? If you hate me having babies so much, why don't *you* do something?" She was too embarrassed to say it directly, but after Willie's birth, the midwife had told her that men could get something called rubbers to put on their Johnsons to prevent pregnancy.

It's so easy for a man. You must know that. Surely guys talk.

"How in hell am I ever supposed to save enough money for us to get to California, if you just keep having babies, Trudy?" He didn't wait for an answer, just got up and stalked out the front door.

So, Joe, is this another Messiah I'm having, then? Or did you maybe have something to do with it?

Even if he hadn't been gone, Trudy would have bitten her tongue rather than express the thought. Fighting with him wouldn't help. It would only make matters worse, especially for their son. Willie toddled over to her and held up his chubby arms. Trudy scooped him up. "Hey, big boy, want to hear a story?"

"Story," he said.

She planted a kiss on his cheek with an exaggerated smack and walked to the dresser where she'd hidden a copy of A. A. Milne's *Winnie-the-Pooh* beneath her underthings. She didn't want Joe to know she'd squandered money on such a frivolity. Right now, though, she didn't care if Joe caught her. She could only bite her tongue for so long, and it was starting to feel bloody.

He didn't catch her. He didn't return until suppertime, and they ate in silence. But later in bed, he curled himself against her back, putting his arm around her as he fell asleep. Trudy allowed herself to be mollified by the rare gesture of affection.

***

In May, when Trudy was five months pregnant, Joe came home earlier than usual one Friday afternoon. He sank down onto the living room couch, his face stone still. Trudy watched him, afraid to say anything, but panicking inside.

Finally she had to ask. "Joe, what is it? What's the matter?"

He handed her his paycheck with a note on company letterhead attached. Trudy read it. Johansen's Sand and Rock was closing its doors that very day. They apologized for the short notice.

"Short notice, my ass. No notice more like it." Joe jerked the note out of Trudy's hand.

"What are we going to do?" Trudy glanced over at her son sitting in the corner.

"How the hell am I supposed to know?" His voice was loud and filled with anger. Trudy jumped. Willie looked up from his building blocks. His face crumpled, and he started to cry. Trudy rushed over to soothe him.

"I'm sorry," Joe said, staring at nothing. "I'll find something. Don't worry."

Don't worry?

***

That night, Trudy lay sleepless. She'd heard about the Wall Street crash before they left Oklahoma, but it was far from the reality of a tenant farmer's family. The only 'stock' that held meaning for her was livestock. Now everywhere she looked she saw boarded up businesses and men wandering the streets. Sometimes they knocked on her door, offering to do some odd job for a sandwich. Trudy never asked them to do anything, but she always gave them sandwiches.

These drifters told her stories. Most were working their way toward the West Coast by riding the rails, sleeping in Hobo Jungles, and working for food — or money, if they could get it. One of them had traveled all the way from Chicago. He told her there were no jobs anywhere. She stared into the darkness, her mind racing.

Now Johansen's Sand and Rock's dried up, too. How can Joe ever hope to find a job?

She could tell by his demeanor the next morning that Joe didn't have much hope, either. He went through the motions for the next few days, but, finally, he spoke bluntly over his bowl of oatmeal one morning. His voice held an unusual note of resignation.

"It's a waste a time, Trudy. I'm not gonna find a regular job with a regular paycheck. Not now. The best thing for me is catch as catch can. I'm gonna go over to that old Texaco where the day laborers wait. I'll do whatever I have to 'til the farmers get to know me. If I show 'em I work hard enough, and do a good job, maybe someone'll hire me regular."

"Whatever you think best, Joe." She searched for something else to say. "You're one hell of a hard worker. I know that, and they'll see it, too."

He looked at her in silence, and she saw a flash of anger cross his face. Trudy stepped over to Willie, lifted him onto her hip, and walked out onto the porch.

***

Even after his hours were cut, Joe had brought in enough money for them to live frugally and pay their bills. Now he picked up farm work in the fields just outside the city limits wherever he could find it. He tended livestock, mucked out barns, and weeded and irrigated the endless acres of cotton fields.

At first, Joe waited with other day laborers, but soon some farmers began to schedule him in advance to come directly to their farms to help out. He helped one elderly local farmer tear down a barn and build a new one.

Oddly enough, his treatment of Trudy improved. He still mostly ignored her, but he rarely lashed out. That almost frightened her more.

When he told her his plans for the fall, he couldn't seem to look her in the eye.

"Picking cotton don't pay much, but at least it's regular. After the season starts, I can make enough to buy us food, anyways. If them little Mexicans can do it, a Okie should be able to. I picked enough as a kid. Never thought I'd have to pick it again." He sat, shoulders slumped, and stared at his hands curled in front of him.

"Joe, we'll get by. These are hard times. Everybody's in the same boat." He glanced up, and she caught a brief glimpse of the old resentment before he looked away.

Now I see. You think you're better than the rest. It's not just that you feel responsible, you feel ashamed.

Trudy was too worried about how they would survive to focus much attention on her husband's feelings. She wanted to help, but with a baby on the way and a toddler to care for, it was hard to think of ways she might.

The next day she waited until she saw the elderly woman who lived to the right of them outside watering flowers. Trudy overcame her reluctance and approached the picket fence. When she brought up the possibility of doing their laundry, the white-haired woman gave Trudy a sad smile.

"My daughter and son-in law are gonna be moving in with us for a while. The way things are, they're having a hard time. It just makes sense. This place is paid for," she thrust her head toward the house, "and we have an extra bedroom. I'll ask people I know, but with my daughter to help, I, personally, don't need laundry service. But good luck to you."

At least you'll have family to share these hard times.

"Thank you," Trudy said. "I bet you'll enjoy having your grandchildren here all the time." The woman returned Trudy's smile without meeting her eyes.

While Trudy was thinking about knocking on the door of the neighbors to the left, a moving van pulled up in front of the house and began to load furniture. The old couple stood outside and watched. As the van pulled away, an old Plymouth arrived. The neighbors climbed in and the car drove off. The next morning a For Rent sign was on the lawn.

The old man across the street had either moved, too, without Trudy noticing, or died, judging from the For Sale sign out front. Trudy didn't know which. That made her sad. Back home she would've known.

Neighbors farther away in a nicer part of the neighborhood could afford to have their laundry done. But Trudy discovered that most preferred to drop it off at the public laundry down on West Madison. There, customers could rent the latest ringer washers: Maytag Model 60s, which were electric, and 62s which ran on gasoline. For a small extra charge, the owners did drop-off laundry. They did ironing as well.

Trudy couldn't compete. The only additional service she could provide was home pick-up and delivery. That won her a few customers, but not enough to add to their income substantially. Even so, she spent hours bent over her tub and scrub board, hanging wet clothes, then ironing them as sweat dripped down her face. But at least she felt she was doing something.

More than ever, Joe assumed total control over their money, even the few dollars Trudy brought in. He paid the bills, and refused to discuss their financial situation. Then one day he disappeared on foot, carrying his tool chest. When he returned, he had no tools, but carried a huge, rolled-up tent. He stared at Trudy in silence. The muscles in his jaws clenched, released, and then clenched again. She stood on the porch, wiping a dish with an old towel.

"Trudy, if we don't leave on our own, the landlord's gonna call the sheriff to throw us out. I ain't been able to pay the rent for almost two months now."

"We're gonna have to go to that camp out by the farms. I took my tools to the pawnshop. I was able to get us this tent. It's a pretty nice one, and bigger than most. You can stand up and walk around in it." His eyes pleaded for understanding. "It's only for a little while." He looked at the ground.

"It's okay, Joe. We'll just have to make the best of it."

Will we ever do better than make the best of it?

Mama's careworn face shimmered in her memory, and she felt a flash of understanding.

You've been making the best of it your whole life, ain't you, Mama? And look what it's made of you. God take me before I let it do that to me.

Chapter Seven

Brother Can You Spare a Dime?

Trudy kept an eye out for the sheriff. She found herself walking over to the front window every five minutes over the next few days. While she waited, Joe established a residence for his family among dozens of other tents, cardboard shacks, and shelters patched together from scavenged scrap wood or tin. By lantern light, using weathered lumber given to him by the farmer whose barn he'd helped tear down, Joe built a floor between them and the bare earth.

Trudy hadn't actually seen the tent city yet, but she'd known of its existence for at least a year. She'd heard about these dilapidated "Hoovervilles" from the hobos who'd eaten her sandwiches back when she was able to feed them. She knew that these makeshift camps were named after President Hoover. Democrats, and even many Republicans, and especially those displaced drifters, blamed the president for the country's economic distress. Trudy'd never paid much attention to politics, but lately it had begun to seem more relevant.

During the time Joe was working on the platform for the tent, he managed to acquire a Coleman camp stove fueled by white gas, a mattress, a barrel for hauling water, and a few other basic necessities besides food. He even bought one luxury: a used, battery-powered Zenith Companion radio. He surprised Trudy with it the day before they were to move into the tent. She suspected his underlying motive was to be able to listen to the news.

The economic news was dire, so Joe could be assured that their situation wasn't his fault. Trudy knew he was also more interested in politics than she was. Still, she could listen to music now. She smiled, remembering dancing to Papa's fiddle strains. Music always cheered her up. She kissed Joe as he handed her the radio, and she felt his lips curve into a smile against hers.

"Thank you, Joe."

Whatever happens, however mad you make me, I swear I'll never tell you that you only caught me because of Mama.

***

Trudy avoided looking at the camp as they turned off the road. She kept her eyes on Willie, pretending she'd just discovered him sitting there in her lap. He giggled and buried his face against her as she poked and kissed him. The car bumped to a stop, and she heard Joe set the parking brake.

With her son perched on her hip, Trudy stepped out of the car onto the running board and fastened her attention on their new home. The rest of the camp hovered in the background like an unacknowledged stranger.

The tent was large, as Joe had said, ten by sixteen feet and over six feet tall at the ridge pole. It rested on the platform Joe had built from wooden planks nailed up on two by fours. The platform extended about four feet beyond the edge of the canvas in the front and ropes holding the tent upright were attached to stakes driven into the earth beyond.

Joe came around the Ford and stood beside her. She laid her hand on his shoulder and forced a smile when his eyes met hers. "The floor is perfect."

He's doing his best. Things could be a lot worse.

Joe shifted his gaze to Willie. He lifted the toddler out of her arms and, taking Trudy's hand, helped her off the running board and onto the tent platform. She took a deep breath, exhaled, then at last confronted the surrounding camp.

Acres of ragged tents of all sizes mingled with shacks thrown together out of scrap wood, tin, and cardboard. Tin cans, newspapers, and other trash lodged in greasewood bushes. Here and there, flies buzzed above dark mounds. Trudy shifted her eyes, cringing inside.

Lord, I hope that's from dogs, not people!

Her gaze was drawn to a pair of tumbleweeds, clutching each other and rolling in the grip of an errant dust devil. Then she glimpsed other movement at the corner of her eye and turned to see a fat, gray rat skitter under a newspaper. Its beady eyes gleamed out at her. About a hundred yards away, a man stood in front of a bush with his back toward her. His legs were spread slightly, and his trousers drooped a little in the back.

She turned back to the tent, pulled the flap aside, and entered, followed by Joe. A sharp chemical scent assailed her nostrils.

"What's that smell, Joe?"

"It's some spray they use to waterproof the canvas and keep it from growing mold. Don't worry. It'll air out after a while. It's good 'cause it's a sign this tent ain't been used much. The guy in the pawn shop told me it was nearly new, but I wasn't sure whether I could trust him or not."

An old dining table and two chairs sat to one side near the front of the tent. Across from the table, the Coleman stove rested on an orange crate. Two more crates rested side by side holding a white enameled dishpan and a pitcher. Further back, at the far side of the tent, a blanket hung a couple of feet to the side of the ridge pole, concealing most of a thin mattress.

Joe set Willie down next to a box containing his scant assortment of toys. The toddler busied himself with a pair of toy trucks.

"I'll get the rocker." They'd tied it to the back of the Model T.

Trudy pulled a rickety chair out from the table and braced herself with her legs until she was sure it would bear her weight. As her eyes traveled around the tent, a vision of the fly-covered mounds she'd seen outside intruded, and she shuddered.

Surely that was dogs. What kind of person wouldn't even throw dirt over their poop?

She remembered playing in the woods as a child. Rather than walk back to the outhouse, she and Mary had dug holes behind bushes, then scratched dirt over their leavings like cats. She'd done that when she and Joe were traveling. But there was no real privacy here, surrounded by strangers, so that couldn't be a solution.

Joe returned with the rocking chair and set it down across from the mattress. She decided to bring the matter up. They had to resolve it.

"We can get a big pot for a slop jar, I guess, honey, but where do we dispose of it? What do the other people here do, or should I ask?"

"Don't worry," Joe said, "I'm gonna handle it. I should a done it already, but I was worried 'bout the sheriff coming before we got out of the house. You stay inside the tent. I gotta talk to some people."

He clenched his jaw and stepped outside. Trudy scooted her chair closer to the tent flap, pulled it aside, and peered through. She watched Joe weave his way among the neighboring tents and shacks until he disappeared.

She rose, dropped the tent flap, and began to rummage through the meager supplies Joe had stacked in additional orange crates in the middle of the tent. Minutes later she heard his voice and peered through the opening again.

Joe stood on the edge of their tent platform. A group of ten or more men had gathered in front of him. They greeted each other with nods and a few handshakes.

Who are these people? Do they all live here?

"So what did you want us all to come over here for, Joe? Is this a welcome party? Where's the moonshine?" A bald man in an undershirt and dirty tattered Levis spoke in a loud, raucous voice.

A short, stocky man standing near the speaker laughed and shoved him sideways. The bald man staggered as if off balance. He mugged at the crowd like Charlie Chan. It reminded Trudy of the motion picture they'd seen before Joe's hours were cut. Most of the crowd looked mildly annoyed.

"No, 'fraid not, Lou. I want to talk 'bout something serious." He paused and looked around the group. Trudy watched him.

What is he up to?

"It's not right we have to live like this, working hard like we do. But that's the way it is. At least for now. But we're good men, ain't we?" There were nods of agreement. "So we got to have some pride. I know there are some fellas 'round here who just answer nature's call wherever they happen to be."

The bald man broke in. "Well, who gives a shit?" A few responded with chuckles, others with looks of contempt and head shakes.

Joe held up his hand and waited again. "I do. I'm serious. I brought my wife and son here. I don't want them living like this. Do any of the rest of you fellas have women living with you?" A few raised their hands, some nodded.

"Well, don't they need somewhere private to do their business? For that matter, wouldn't some of you fellas like that, too? I know I would. I got more pride than a damn dog."

There were murmurs of assent, and most of the men nodded. The bald man and his sidekick scowled and walked away.

"Good riddance," someone said.

"If I get the wood, how many of you'll help me build outhouses; one for us men, and one for the women? If we work together, we can do it in a few hours. I know a farmer who'll give us the wood. He's a decent guy."

Hands went up. Several men came over, slapped him on the back, and agreed to help. Trudy gazed in amazement.

I guess I should have had more faith in you, Joe.

***

The next few days, after the men returned from the fields in the evenings, Trudy followed the progress on the construction of outhouses for each gender. The men laughed, cursed and yelled instructions at one another as they worked. Their disembodied voices filtered through the canvas walls of the tent where Trudy eavesdropped.

"Hey, what'd you do with my hammer, asshole?"

"It's right there by your hand, jackass!"

"Charlie, hand me that board, will ya?"

"Ouch! Hey, somebody gimme a piece a sandpaper, or some lady's gonna get splinters in her ass."

The sense of camaraderie and common purpose reminded Trudy of a barn raising back home, although maybe a little more vulgar. She heard Joe's voice as he moved among them, joking and directing. It was a side of him Trudy hadn't seen before.

***

After the brisk activity of organizing the move and resolving the toilet situation was over, Joe's customary moodiness returned. It was a mixed blessing for Trudy when he left at sunrise every morning and didn't return until near sunset. Even his sullen presence did provide some distraction and company. When he was gone, she sometimes felt like a rat in a trap.

If she could have gone for walks, it would have helped. But although she knew most of their neighbors in the tent city were decent folks who had fallen on hard times as she and Joe had, she'd noted a few men openly leering at her even when Joe was with her. She suspected there were some even shadier characters than the bald man and his sidekick that she'd seen that first day. Joe had warned her. She didn't want to expose her son, or herself, to the risk of unpleasant encounters, so except for necessary trips to the outhouse, she stayed near or in their tent.

The heat was stifling. Even with the flaps over the windows rolled up, there was little breeze, and she knew it would only get worse as they slipped into summer. She wrote weekly letters to Papa and Mary. Joe mailed them and collected their replies from the post office for her. She tried to organize the tent, but quickly ran out of things to do.

Willie provided her only relief. She played with him for hours on end, sometimes enjoying their interactions so much she forgot her surroundings as they created their own world. When he grew tired, she sat rereading chapters of *Winnie-the-Pooh* while her son fell asleep in her arms.

When Joe came home from the fields he ate dinner—pinto beans and fried potatoes or rice with biscuits or cornbread—in silence. Afterward, he listened to news on the Zenith for a while then rolled a cigarette and sat outside, staring up at the stars and smoking until bedtime.

If Willie were asleep, sometimes Trudy sat and smoked, too. Joe didn't speak much, but he was always willing to roll her a cigarette, and Trudy sensed he enjoyed her silent companionship. It helped her, as well, and she liked the taste of the tobacco and the satisfaction she got from smoking. But she needed more. At last, an idea began to grow.

Chapter Eight

Oklahoma Hills

"Honey, after Willie was born I laid in bed for a while, 'member? It took me over a week to get back on my feet, and even then I had to sit around nursing him a good part of the day. You helped me fix supper after work for a week or two. You even helped me with the laundry."

The sweltering heat of the end of August engulfed the tent. Joe sat next to the old dinner table that held the Zenith radio. He was listening to the news and replied without looking at Trudy. "Yeah, I had to wear unironed shirts to work for a couple a weeks. Why?" A bitter grin spread over his face.

Been a long time since you wore an ironed shirt. Is that what you're thinking, Joe?

"Well, this one's gonna be harder 'cause I'll need help with Willie, too. You can't stay home. We need all the money you can earn." Joe started to interrupt, but Trudy pretended not to notice. "You know I been writing Mary. She could come out here for a few weeks to help me. It wouldn't cost us a nickel. She can take the train, or a Greyhound, and she'll buy her own ticket."

"Trudy, for God's sake, we live in a tent! I can't afford to feed your sister. It's all I can do to feed us."

Trudy lowered her voice as if she were calming a fretful baby. "We thought of that, honey. We don't want to put more of a burden on you. I can get along without help for part of the day. I'll manage 'til lunchtime so Mary can pick cotton with you in the mornings.

"The season will start soon, and you know she's a good cotton picker. She got enough practice back home, like we all did. Why, if you bring in enough money to feed you, me, and Willie, she can at least bring in enough to feed herself. She can probably even help us out a little."

After a moment's silence, Joe responded. "But where would she sleep?"

"We can hang up a blanket at the back of the tent, like we did around our mattress. She can sleep on a pallet like Willie does. She could probably even buy herself a cot, or a mattress, if she picks enough cotton. Wouldn't it be fun to have some company, Joe? We sure could use the help." She waited for him to speak.

"I'll think about it."

I bet you will. You know she's a hard worker, and she's cute as a button, too. You might like a little distraction. God, am I getting as cynical as Mama?

***

Although Mama had never picked on Mary as much as she had Trudy, Trudy knew from her younger sister's letters that Mary was anxious to fly the coop. Mama had voiced no opinion or emotion regarding Mary's proposed trip to visit Trudy. But both sisters knew their mother seldom expressed herself openly in Papa's presence. As usual, her eyes had said it all: good riddance to bad rubbish. Or at least that was how Mary interpreted Mama's expression in her letter to Trudy. After what Mama had said outright to her, Trudy supposed her sister was right.

"I got the bus fare," Mary wrote. "John gave it to me. Sam is gonna give me a ride to Muskogee. I can catch the Greyhound there." Trudy had told Papa in her letters that she needed Mary's help, so when Mary told him her plans, he hadn't protested. Trudy figured that by now Papa was resigned to all his daughters leaving the nest. Besides, his children were in God's hands, not his. Trudy envied his faith but sometimes wondered where personal responsibility fit in.

How strange to let life flow over you like a river, accepting everything that happens as God's will. I guess we're not as much alike as I once thought, Papa. I wonder if you ever had any idea of how we all protected you?

***

It had been the morning after Trudy had first seen Mama stand on the train tracks. Papa sat at the kitchen table watching as Mama measured coffee into their old percolator, cracked eggs into a bowl, and heated a frying pan on the wood stove. He'd glanced up as Millie walked by leading Trudy by the hand toward the front door. He grinned, but Mama spoke before he could.

"Where're you off to?" She frowned, regarding Millie with suspicion.

"Trudy ain't seen the new chicks yet, Mama. She wants to see them. We'll be right back, I promise. We won't be late for breakfast." Mama turned back to the frying pan without a word. Millie pulled her little sister through the front door.

"I seen them yesterday, Millie," Trudy said as they stepped off the porch, and Millie tugged her toward the chicken coop.

"Hush, Little Sis. We need to talk 'bout yesterday."

Trudy's chin began to tremble. "I want Papa." Millie lifted Trudy inside the coop and squatted down in front of her to look her in the eye.

"You can't talk 'bout what happened yesterday to Papa. You don't want to worry him and make him sad. It's done. She just wanted to scare us and make us mind her. Besides, if you tell Papa and she finds out, which she would for sure, she's really gonna be mad. We'll all be in trouble. Do you understand?" Trudy nodded, but her eyes filled with tears.

Millie took her into her arms. "You have to be strong for Papa. Can you do that?" Trudy nodded again, blinking away her tears. "She's done it before, but nothing's ever happened. We never told him. That would just make everything worse."

***

Trudy hovered outside the Phoenix Greyhound Terminal at nine on a Tuesday morning in late September. The temperature was a hundred and five degrees. She lifted her bangs and wiped the sweat off her forehead as she watched Mary get off the bus. Her sister's eyes swept the gathering group of travelers and those waiting to either pick them up or send them off.

"Sis! Over here!"

Mary saw her. They weaved toward each other through the milling crowd, laughing and crying at the same time. When they touched, Trudy bent awkwardly over her belly to hug Mary and kiss her on the lips. They broke apart and clasped hands. As she stared into her sister's eyes, Trudy felt the time and distance between them sweep away.

Time changes nothing that's important.

Mary jabbered about her first bus ride as they headed back inside the terminal. "Goodness gracious, it took forever! But the seats were soft, and they leaned back, so I managed to sleep some. We stopped a few times to use the toilet and eat. I got coffee and sandwiches. None of it was very good, though."

Trudy left her for a few minutes to make an emergency stop at the terminal ladies' room.

Lately seems like I'm running to pee every fifteen minutes. I'll be so glad when this is over!

She rejoined Mary, and they walked past the old wooden benches and through the front doors to where the Model T waited out front. "So, how are Millie and Sam doing? How's the baby?"

As Trudy drove back to camp, Mary filled her sister in on all the details about the current state of family members that she hadn't been patient enough to include in her letters. Both their brothers were still at home. Millie's son, Sam Jr. was beginning to walk. Evelyn was pregnant. Trudy knew she'd married, but had never met her husband Jim.

"He's not the sharpest knife in the drawer, or the best looking. But he's got a good heart, and Evelyn adores him."

Trudy thought about her horse-faced older sister, the plainest of the four. "I'm glad she found someone to love. She'll make a sweet mother."

After Trudy finished her questions, it was Mary's turn. "So how are you, Sister? Are you happy? Besides living in a tent, that is."

Trudy could feel her sister's stare, but she kept her eyes on the road. "Well, times are hard, as you know, but Willie makes it all worthwhile. Wait 'til you see him. He's cute's a button."

"How 'bout you and Joe? Are you happy?"

Trudy continued to focus on the road ahead of her. "I imagine we're happy as most." She glanced sideways at her sister. "You know, life ain't always as romantic as we'd like it to be, Sis. But Joe's a good husband. He works hard. It ain't his fault he can't find a job. It's this goddamned Depression."

Trudy instantly realized Mary had never heard her swear before and slammed a hand over her mouth. Mary giggled and laid her hand on her sister's shoulder.

"Yeah, this Depression is really a sonofabitch," she said.

The Tin Lizzie bumped over a rut in the dirt road as Trudy turned left and guided the car toward the space beside the tent. She glanced over at Mary, who was staring saucer-eyed at the sprawl surrounding them.

Trudy grinned, remembering the first time her sister had worn that look of incredulity.

Not quite as pretty as those jars of candy back at McAlester's, though, is it, Sis?

***

"Your Papa and me are going to McAlester's, childern," Mama had said.

They'd all been in the front room, except Papa. Trudy had started second grade a month before, and Evelyn had started fourth. But it was Saturday morning, so they both sat cross-legged on the bare wood floor with Mary and played jacks. Millie stood by the sink, drying the breakfast dishes and putting them away. John, fourteen that fall, sat in Papa's chair by the coal stove. He'd picked up Papa's old *Farmer's Almanac* and was thumbing through it. He didn't look up when Mama spoke.

"Ya'll can come along, if you're ready by the time we leave. But we ain't gonna wait for you. Papa's hitching up the wagon right now."

Trudy looked at Mary. They sprang up, grabbed each other's hands, and began to jump up and down until they saw Mama's frown. Still holding hands, they ran to their bedroom to find their shoes. Evelyn and Millie hustled after their little sisters. John took a well-worn baseball and glove and stepped out into the bright fall morning, letting the weathered screen door slam shut behind him. Pausing on the porch only a moment, he took off across the field toward a neighbor's house without looking back.

Trudy and Mary stood near the rear of the wagon. They were about to scramble in when Millie tapped Trudy's shoulder. Trudy glanced up and saw her big sister looking at Mama, who sat swiveled around on the driver's bench next to Papa. She was staring at them. She raised her hand in a silent summons. Trudy and Mary followed the older girls over to her.

Did we do something wrong? Are you gonna change your mind?

"Here. This is for candy, but if you lose it, you won't get another." Mama handed each of them a nickel.

"Thank you, Mama," Millie said. Each girl echoed the phrase as nickels plopped into their outstretched palms. They circled back to the rear of the wagon. Trudy gripped her coin as she and Mary clambered into the back in front of Mildred and Evelyn. She dropped down to the hard, wooden bed behind Papa.

As the girls settled, and the wagon began to move forward, Trudy stared at the nickel in her hand. Since she'd been a baby, she'd watched Mama place every cent Papa got from his collection plate into the pocket of her apron. It was always mostly pennies and nickels, and Mama's face, when she looked at Papa, said it wasn't enough. Yet, somehow, she managed to buy everything they couldn't grow with those pennies and nickels. Trudy struggled to understand why Mama had decided to spare four nickels just for candy.

She caught Mary's eye, opened her mouth, stuck her coin under her tongue, and grinned at her sister. Their dresses didn't have pockets, and she would have been afraid the nickel might fall out anyway. It felt very secure under her tongue, safer than in her fist. She glanced up front to make sure Mama hadn't seen her then held her empty hand out toward her sister and wiggled her fingers. Mary grinned back and put her nickel under her tongue, too. They joined hands.

Trudy liked the strange, metallic taste of her coin. She played with it then held it firmly with her tongue. The sisters swayed as the creaky wagon bumped along the dirt trail leaving a cloud of dust behind them.

"Trudy, what're you gonna buy?" Trudy could see her sister's tongue gripping her coin as she spoke. She sounded so funny both girls began to giggle and couldn't stop. They turned loose of each other's hands and took the nickels out of their mouths to keep from choking.

Trudy tried to remember the last time she'd been there as they entered the edge of town. She was seven years old now, and could only remember one other time in her whole life. They passed a filling station on Main Street with a shiny black Model T parked alongside, and the whole family swiveled to stare at the automobile.

"Would you look at that," Evelyn said. "I wonder who that belongs to?"

"Nobody we know," Millie said and cackled. Their mother glanced back and frowned. Evelyn turned to look behind her, hiding her grin.

Papa parked the wagon and tied their horse to a post out front. They all followed Mama through the door of McAlester's General Store, the biggest building on the street. Trudy looked at Mary then popped the nickel back into her mouth, savoring the taste. Mary put her coin in her mouth, too, and they clasped hands again.

Inside, Trudy looked at her little sister. She'd heard grown-ups say 'eyes big as saucers." Now she understood what that meant. Mary stared with round, bright blue eyes at the rolls of cloth, work boots, shovels and other farm tools, sacks of flour and sugar—and candy!

Near the back of the store, a whole row of giant jars filled with mints, gumdrops, bubble gum, taffy, butterscotch, chocolate peanuts, every kind of candy they had ever tasted, and some that Trudy had never seen before, sat on a shelf. A man wearing spectacles and a blue-and-white-striped apron stood at the counter in front. He glanced up at them and smiled.

Trudy remembered when Papa had preached about Moses, how he'd stared across the Red Sea toward the Promised Land. Now she knew how Moses had felt. A flood of spit covered her nickel. She clutched it under her tongue as she swallowed.

A painful look crossed Mary's face, and she pressed her knees together. "I got to go!" She sounded like a frog. Trudy saw her tongue curled around her nickel. "Where's Mama?"

Trudy looked around and spotted their mother at the side of the store looking at flour sacks made from bright cotton prints of different colors and patterns. She pointed, and they ran over to Mama. Mary took her nickel out of her mouth with her free hand before they got there.

"Mama, I got to go!"

Her mother looked up and pointed to a wooden sign in the back of the store. Trudy read it, her lips silently forming the word. "Restrooms," it said.

Mary popped her nickel back into her mouth after their backs were turned to Mama. She grabbed Trudy's hand, and the two ran toward the sign. They pushed open the door marked "Ladies."

Inside, Trudy latched the door and stared at the toilet. She'd heard of toilets before, but had never seen one. Mary pushed down the handle. The water spun around, went down the hole, and then filled up again.

She pulled down her drawers, lifted herself onto the edge, and leaned forward so she wouldn't fall in.

When she finished, Mary wiped herself with white paper from a roll hanging nearby then stood up. Trudy stared at the ceiling as her little sister flushed the toilet. Something that glowed with a soft white light hung down in the center.

She hadn't seen an electric light bulb before either. It had a string hanging down from it. Trudy couldn't stop herself. "Look!" She pointed up and pulled the string. The room went dark. She pulled the string again. The light came back.

She spun around to look at Mary and saw those saucer eyes again. Mary's mouth hung open, and a confused look came over her face. It was followed by a look Trudy understood. Surprise, but in a bad way. Not like the good way when Mama gave them the nickels.

The nickels!

Mary stared into Trudy's eyes. No words were needed. Trudy knew what had happened. Her five-year-old sister opened her mouth again. She poked around the corners with her finger. But it was gone.

Trudy's eyes searched the floor, but she knew it wasn't there. She took the nickel out of her own mouth and began to laugh. She couldn't help it. Mary's lower lip trembled, and her eyes filled with tears. Trudy, still laughed, but she threw her arms around her little sister.

"It's okay, Sis. We'll share mine. Don't worry. We won't tell Mama."

Chapter Nine

Hush-a-Bye

Trudy poked Mary in the ribs. "Hey, don't say I didn't warn you. But you said you want to learn to drive. Pay attention." Mary pulled her eyes back to Trudy's hands and bent across to peer down at her feet.

"This lever up here on the right is the gas throttle. I lift it up all the way and that slows the engine down." She loosened her right hand on the steering wheel and eased the lever upward with two fingers. It clicked over the notches and settled into the top one.

"Then I have to put on the brake. See, my foot is pushing it down? And see, my left foot is holding the low/high pedal 'bout halfway. That's neutral. Now there's no gear moving the car forward." The Model T rolled to a stop.

"How long did it take you to learn, Sis?"

"Not that long really. Don't tell Joe, but I practiced without him sometimes. When he was gone to the fields. Gave me a chance to get a feel for it. It's nice being in charge of something besides what to cook for dinner, cornbread or biscuits."

"I can still hear the engine running. Don't you have to turn it off?"

"Sure do." She demonstrated the procedure, showing Mary how to lift the spark, set the parking brake, and turn off the ignition.

"Good Lord, that's a lot to remember. Are you sure you can teach me?" Mary looked at her with eyes full of doubt.

"Of course I can. After a while it's just a habit. Don't even have to think about it." Trudy braced one foot on the running board and pushed against the wooden steering wheel with both hands to ease her pregnant belly past it. She stepped down, and walked around the car.

Mary scrambled out her door and reached behind her to pull her dress loose from between her sweaty thighs. She stared around the camp again, swiveling her head around from side to side as far as it would go, then twisted her body to see further.

She looks like an old barn owl.

Trudy grinned. She put her arm around Mary's shoulder and pulled her baby sister against her then looked at the camp as if she were seeing it for the first time. Dust, disturbed by the car, billowed around them in the still, hot air. Bony stray dogs wandered, sniffing at piles of trash, looking for anything edible. Near the edge of the camp, a man with his back to them was urinating on a greasewood bush.

Don't be like me, Sis. Think twice before you jump from the frying pan into the fire. Compared to this, our house back home is a palace.

She bumped Mary's shoulder with her own and her grin grew wider. "Well, I told you it wasn't pretty. Let's go inside. At least it's clean in there."

Mary followed her through the flap, saying nothing. Inside she looked around. "This idn't so bad, Sis. Look, you got a radio! Does it work?"

Trudy snickered. "Yeah, believe it or not, it actually does. When we can afford the batteries."

"Is this where I sleep?" Mary pointed to the edge of her small pallet peeking out from under the blanket curtain.

"Yeah. It's not much."

"Well, it's not like I never slept on the floor before, is it?" Mary pulled the curtain aside and revealed a home-stitched quilt made of multicolored scraps. A small pillow lay on top. "Mama's?"

"No, Joe's mother's. I didn't take anything when I left. Didn't want Mama saying I was a thief as well as a loose woman." She told Mary the truth about the night she'd left Tahlequah. She hadn't told her in her letters for fear Papa might read them.

Mary stared at her, shook her head, and gave her sister a long, firm hug. "She can be a real bitch, can't she? I wondered. It was so sudden, and you'd never really seemed all that excited 'bout Joe. I'd a been too scared to do what you did, but I don't blame you a'tall."

"Well, it was stupid. In a way, I let her win. But since Willie's birth, I've got no regrets."

Mary dragged a chair out from under the table and sat down. "So where is that baby boy I keep hearing about?"

"He's with a neighbor lady. Wait here a minute." Trudy hurried to a tent nearby, thanked her neighbor, and collected her son. She started back to their tent with Willie on her hip. Willie pushed back against her elbow. She glanced up to see him eying her.

"Mama go bye-bye." He stared at her with brown eyes that didn't blink.

Trudy kissed his cheek. "Yes, sweetie, Mama went bye-bye, but she's back now. And Aunt Mary's here! She's gonna think you're a sweetie pie! You are, aren't you?" Willie frowned at her.

She stepped into the tent, and held him out to Mary just as the first serious labor pain gripped her. She almost dropped Willie. Mary grabbed the toddler. Her eyes grew huge, and she again looked like she had as a five-year-old in McAlester's. Trudy grinned despite her condition. She leaned forward and clutched the sides of her taut belly. The cramp receded. She plopped down on a creaky chair next to the table.

"Are you okay?" Mary held Willie with one arm and laid her free hand on Trudy's shoulder.

"Yeah, honey. I'm okay. I think I might be starting labor, though. I had some little ones before. I thought it was just false labor. Excited to see you, maybe. But that was a pretty good one."

"What should I do? What do you need?" Mary clasped Willie against her chest.

"Nothing yet. This part goes real slow. You never saw a baby born before, did you, Sis? We were too little for Mama to let us watch when she birthed Davy. They put us outside."

Mary shook her head. "No, I haven't. I'm a little scared, to tell the truth. I don't like to see you in pain. It hurts a lot, don't it?"

"Well, sure. It ain't easy. It's kinda like pushing an apple through a key hole." She laughed. "But just when it feels like it's gonna kill you, it's over. The baby comes, and the pain departs. Mostly." She grinned. "Don't want to lie to you, Sis." She inhaled and doubled over as another painful cramp hit.

At the same time, Willie put his hands against his aunt's chest and pushed himself away from her. He scowled as he looked her in the eye.

"Down," he said.

"Okay, Mister." Mary grasped him under the arms, and kissed his forehead. Then she lowered him to the floor.

He toddled over to his wooden toy box at the foot of Joe and Trudy's mattress, next to his pallet. He picked up a toy truck, dropped to the floor, and began rolling it around, sputtering to himself.

***

After sunset, Joe returned from the cotton field. Trudy lay on her side on the mattress. Her sister sat on the floor beside her, holding her hand, and Willie played nearby. Joe greeted Mary and moved forward as she released Trudy's hand and stood. He looked as if he might embrace her but extended his own hand instead. Mary shook it.

Boy, she looks relieved. I hope Joe didn't notice that expression.

Joe's eyes shifted to Trudy, and he dropped down to sit on the edge of the mattress, against her thighs. He mopped sweat, pushing greasy hair back off his forehead. He stank of perspiration.

No wonder she didn't want to hug him.

Trudy had washed her hair and bathed in their galvanized wash tub the night before in preparation for Mary's visit. She tried to bathe at least once a week, even though they had to haul water and heat pots on the Coleman if she wanted it warm.

She tried to remind Joe on Sundays, and he usually obliged. She'd forgotten last Sunday, so it had been over a week. She was more or less used to the smell but saw Mary wrinkle her nose.

"So it's your time. Do you need Sarah yet?" Joe rested a hand on her belly.

"Yes. I do."

"I'll go fetch her." He rose, left the tent, and returned five minutes later with the midwife. She and Mary put a pot of water to boil, and collected towels and a baby blanket as Trudy pointed to where things were kept.

A group of Joe's friends gathered outside the tent. Trudy could hear them talking and laughing as they waited for Joe to shovel down some cold beans and cornbread. He pecked Trudy on the cheek and left. The sounds of merriment faded into the night. Trudy resented that he didn't suffer along with her, or at least stay to listen to her complaints, although she was sure Mary was more comfortable with him gone.

"Wouldn't you think he'd want to stick around? In case I need something?" Trudy looked at Mary first, then the midwife.

"Why, he's no different from any other man," the midwife said. "They think they done their job, once't you got a bun in the oven. The rest is up to you. That's just the way a man is. A course, they enjoy their part more'n we do ours." She cackled, and Trudy noticed one of her front teeth was missing.

Mary spooned some leftover beans into an old cast iron skillet and topped them with cornbread. Striking a wooden match, she lit a burner of the Coleman and warmed the food up for herself and Willie. She picked Willie up and held him as they ate.

After rinsing the dishes, she coaxed the toddler onto her lap with his *Winnie-the-Pooh* book. They sat across the room from Trudy on Mary's makeshift pallet. Willie listened to her rhythmic, sing-song murmur for a while, then began to doze.

Mary eased the sleepy toddler onto her quilt and lay down beside him until he was sound asleep. Then she got up and returned to her sister's side.

***

Legs spread, Trudy gripped her raised knees with white-knuckled hands and grunted loudly. She gave one final tremendous push, and the infant's crowning head burst forth fourteen hours after she'd felt the first real pang. She fell back onto her elbows, exhausted, and watched as the midwife clasped her baby's upside-down upper body and let the rest, with a small additional push on Trudy's part, gradually slide out into her grasp. She turned the squalling infant over.

"It's a boy." She cut the umbilical cord with a butcher knife Mary had sterilized in the kettle of boiling water, tied it, and began to wipe the indignantly protesting baby with a ragged but clean towel.

Mary had risen to her feet in response to the din. She stood looking from the baby to Trudy to Willie. The toddler shifted and muttered in his sleep but didn't wake.

The midwife wrapped the infant in one of Willie's old blue flannel baby blankets and placed him in his mother's arms. Then she pressed firmly on Trudy's belly and tugged gently on the umbilical cord until the placenta slipped out. She wrapped it in old newspaper and put it next to the tent flap. Finished with the main event, she began to tidy up the tent. When things were back in place, she picked up the newspaper-wrapped afterbirth and left.

The baby calmed as Trudy held him to her chest. She rocked him gently side to side. The tent grew peaceful. He looked like a shriveled little red prune. Trudy turned him towards her sister who glanced at Willie. The child was sleeping soundly once more. Mary crossed the tent and sat back down next to Trudy. Trudy gazed up at her sister. Tears filled her eyes then overflowed as she smiled at Mary.

Mary's eyes shone with tears as well. She stared at her nephew then touched his miniature hand. His tiny fingers curled around hers. "He's beautiful. Does he have a name yet?"

"Robert Dalton. It's Joe's Grandpa's name. Bobby." Trudy bent closer to her infant as she whispered his name. The baby's dark eyes fastened on hers for an instant, then broke away and closed as his tiny face batted back and forth against her nipple. Trudy stabilized his chin with her forefinger, and he began to nurse.

Chapter Ten

What a Little Moonlight Can Do

Joe didn't get back 'til after one in the morning, about two hours after the birthing was over and everybody, including Trudy and the baby, was asleep. She woke as he collapsed on top of the far side of the mattress, still in his work clothes. He began to snore. He reeked of alcohol as well as sweat.

Drinking alcohol's against the law! Did he even stop to think 'bout what would've happened to us if he got arrested?

Joe still managed to get up before dawn. Trudy watched him through her eyelashes. Still angry about the drinking, she feigned sleep as he fixed himself a couple of sandwiches, licked the peanut butter off the case knife, and laid it on the table. Walking back to the mattress, he lifted the quilt over his sleeping son and stuck his hand underneath. Trudy could feel him fingering his son's toes.

Yeah, Joe, they're all there.

Then he pushed back the quilt, opened the baby blanket, and uncovered the baby's genitals. A smile crossed his face. He tucked the blanket back under the fussing baby, pulled up the quilt, and left.

Bobby had mewed and waved his arms and tiny fists as his father examined him then curled toward his mother. He rooted around for her nipple, and she pulled him closer. Soon he was asleep again. He snuggled under Trudy's warm armpit, against her soft breast, and napped and nursed for the next hour.

***

Trudy heard someone stir and looked over toward her sister. "Hey, sleepyhead."

Mary was climbing over her still sleeping nephew. She yawned and rubbed her eyes. "Hey, Sis. Where's Joe?" She looked around the tent. "Is he outside?"

"He left already."

"Oh, no. Am I in trouble?" Mary walked over, sat on the floor, and crossed her legs. She pulled the quilt down and looked at the sleeping newborn.

"No, I don't think he even remembered you being here." Trudy hesitated a moment. "He found some liquor someplace last night, so he was a little woozy this morning."

What's Mary gonna think? Mama would gloat if she knew.

"You mean he had a hangover?" Mary smothered another yawn, then rose and walked back to her pallet. She opened her suitcase and began to rummage through it.

"Is that the word for it? How'd you know?" Trudy frowned at her sister.

Mary looked up and grinned. "I expect things have changed a little since you left, Trudy. Back home, most of the people we used to know packed up and lit out for California. The ones that stayed, well, some go to church, and some get drunk. Everybody just tries to feel a little better. Moonshine is cheap."

"You don't drink it, do you?" Trudy's eyes examined her sister's face.

"Naw, Sis. I'd be scared to. One of the fellas offered me some at a barn dance once. I smelled it, but I didn't taste it." Mary paused, and her eyes twinkled. "Remember Betty?"

"Of course I do. She was my best friend, next to you. Why?" Trudy remembered how excited Betty had been about her elopement with Joe. "Has she found her Heathcliff?"

"Not exactly." Mary grinned. "She's got a baby now, too. But no husband. I heard it's 'cause she let some fella give her some moonshine." She laughed. "Can't trust them fellas."

***

Trudy caught the scent of lye soap when Joe returned later than usual that evening. Willie and his new brother were both sleeping, lying on top of their bed covers, though Bobby would likely wake soon to nurse. Mary had prepared supper and fed Willie earlier. Now she rose to dish up for the grown-ups as Joe seated himself at the table across from his wife. Trudy wore an old nightgown and perched on a pillow with a pair of threadbare towels tucked beneath her. She looked closely at her husband. The grease was gone from his hair, and he was clean shaven. Even his fingernails were clean.

He must have washed up at a friend's. He did notice Mary's expression.

Joe's head swiveled back and forth between them as the sisters ate and reminisced. A constant smile lit his face. He reminded Trudy of the rotating fan they'd had in their rental house. She longed for that fan, but with no electricity … still, the air had cooled somewhat after sunset. An errant breeze found its way through the raised tent flap and stirred the damp hair on the back of her neck.

Mary forked some fried potatoes into her mouth and chewed. Then she lifted her glass of warm sweet black tea and took a swallow. "Do you remember that kid that begged for our apple core walking home from school that day? We hadn't even took one bite when he started."

"Gimme yuh coah, puleeze! Puleeze gimme yuh coah!" Trudy wheedled in imitation, and they broke into laughter.

"His folks didn't have a lick of self respect. Maybe they was poorer than us, but they did have a well," Mary said. "They coulda took baths and washed clothes. But their kids was always dirty."

"Yeah, remember the snot running down his face?" Trudy said. There was a moment of silence.

"I'm glad we gave him the apple, though I did want it myself." Mary's face had sobered.

"Me, too. But he needed it more than we did. Remember how he ate it? Lord, I think he ate seeds and all." Trudy sighed.

"You know, I heard some women in the terminal yesterday, when you was gone to the bathroom. They were talking 'bout Okies. I couldn't hear what all they said, but I caught enough to know it wasn't exactly flattering. Do you think that's what they think we're all like? Like that kid's family?" The smile had left Mary's face. She looked at Trudy.

"I think they try to convince theirselves we're trash, that they're better than we are." She remembered the man from the A.J. Bayliss lot with contempt. "But I think it's really more 'bout jobs. Most of us *Okies* work hard, and we're willing to do whatever we have to. They don't wanna pick cotton, but I guess they're afraid if we stay, when things get better, we might take the jobs they *do* want."

They sat staring at their plates for a moment. Trudy glanced over at her still sleeping sons then continued. "Remember how Mama used to tell us stories 'bout the Klan? How they started up right after the War Between the States? If Republicans got equal rights for Negroes, Negroes might've taken poor white men's jobs. White folks couldn't have that, so the Klan stepped in to keep them in their place. Thank God, or maybe Papa, our family was never part of that."

"So, you're saying these people 'round here might start lynching us?" Mary winked at Joe.

Trudy knew her sister wasn't serious, but she did sense her underlying unease. "Not yet, Sis. The farmers need us too much. They got to get their damn cotton planted, watered and picked, and the weeds chopped. We're so desperate we'll take whatever they give us and work our butts off, just like the poor Mexicans." Trudy surprised herself.

When did I put all this together? But I know it's true. All most people care about now is the almighty dollar.

"Most people 'round here would starve to death before they'd work this hard and live like we do. We're no threat to them. Not now, anyways." She looked at her husband. "What do you think, Joe?"

"I think this country's gone to hell." Joe shoved his empty plate away, picked up the Zenith in one hand and his tin of Prince Albert, rolling papers, and a couple of matches in the other. He got up and ducked his head to step under the tent flap into the outside air. The sisters stared after him as he walked to the edge of the platform, sat down, and turned the radio on to the news. Trudy shrugged. Mary grinned.

***

The next morning, Trudy heard Joe get up an hour or so before dawn. When he left for the outhouse, she crawled across the floor and woke Mary. Then she crawled back to bed to nurse her baby. Mary got up, dressed and began to prepare a breakfast of Quaker's oatmeal on the Coleman. She and Joe ate in silence when Joe returned.

"How 'bout me, Sis?" Trudy said.

"Didn't know you was still awake." Mary handed her a bowlful, adding a splash of Carnation Evaporated Milk. Trudy nibbled it lying in bed.

Joe sat and watched as Mary made sandwiches with peanut butter on stale Holsum Bread, put them in a wrinkled paper bag, and brewed tea. She added large amounts of sugar, put the tea in two mason jars, and screwed on the lids. Then, after she made her own trip to the outhouse, she and Joe left for the cotton field on foot.

Mary returned in the early afternoon, and set the crumpled brown bag and empty mason jars on the table. She turned on the Zenith and set it to a music station. Then, chattering to Trudy, she lit the Coleman and started some beans.

But when "Forget Your Troubles Come on Get Happy" started to play, she swooped down to pick up Willie. She danced, spinning to the melody. Then, dropping the disoriented, giggling toddler onto the mattress where Trudy lay nursing Bobby, she made popcorn, cleaned up the tent, and prepared supper.

***

Trudy took over the housework and childcare completely after a week, and Mary began to work longer hours in the fields. She and Joe arrived every evening before nightfall, sunburned, hands and arms scratched by dried bristles despite the tattered gloves they wore. Trudy could read the exhaustion in their faces.

She'd picked cotton herself back home. She knew they were bone tired, especially their shoulders and necks, from the strain of bending over all day and dragging heavy cotton sacks up and down the rows. Before they went to bed each night, Trudy would knead first Joe's, then Mary's, neck and shoulders, until her fingers felt ready to fall off. Compared to them, she knew she had it easy.

But with two babies, what can I do?

***

They sat at the table forking beans, fried potatoes, and cornbread into their mouths. "Hey, Brother, Can You Spare a Dime?" played in the background. Willie chewed his last bite then wriggled off his mother's lap and ran to his toy box. He took out his blocks and began building a tower.

Joe reached over and switched to KTAR. After a brief patch of static, the local news came on and they sat listening to the latest developments in the Trunk Murderess case. Joe and Trudy had been listening to the ongoing saga for months. Mary leaned toward the radio. Her eyes widened, and Trudy smiled, although the story was nothing to smile about.

She's as easy to read as an open book. She should be in the movies.

"Exactly what did she do?" Mary said.

Trudy glanced over at Willie and lowered her voice. "Well, they say she was sleeping with this married man, and, for some reason, she decided a couple of her girlfriends was after him, too. So, 'in a fit of rage,' she shot 'em. Then she had to figure out how to get rid of the bodies. So she chopped 'em up, put 'em in trunks, and shipped 'em to California. But somebody saw blood leaking out of one of the trunks, so she got caught."

"Lord. Could a woman do all that by herself?" Mary's face crinkled in disgust and disbelief.

"That's the question, ain't it? They say she knew how to cut 'em up 'cause she was a nurse. But still. I think she had to've had help." Bobby began to stir and fret. Trudy rose, collected him from the pallet, and put him to her breast. She sat back down as Mary spoke.

"Maybe that married boy friend of hers?"

"Maybe. Maybe her friends were trying to blackmail him. But if he did it, he'll never get convicted. He's rich enough to buy everybody off, the bastard. I think Winnie Ruth's lawyer's going to say she's insane. That way, she won't get the electric chair, just sent to the State Hospital down on Twenty-fourth Street. Doubt a loony bin's much better than jail, but maybe it's better than electrocution."

"Shhh," Joe said. "The real news is coming on. I wanna hear it."

Trudy leaned over to Mary, cupping her hand around the side of her mouth. "What's really creepy is these murders happened in a duplex just a couple of miles from the house we was living in at the time. I remember seeing a pretty nurse in the Piggly-Wiggly once. It coulda been her."

Trudy and Mary stared at each other close up, their eyes bugged open. Then Trudy reached her arms around Mary's shoulders, hugged her, and grinned with her cheek against Mary's ear.

It's a horrible story, especially if Winnie Ruth is being framed for the murders. But I still like telling you scary stories and watching your face. It reminds me of home.

The world news began, and, inserted among stories of starvation in Russia, Japanese aggression, and mistreatment of veterans of the Great War, the bouncy music and optimistic lyrics of "Happy Days Are Here Again," Franklin Delano Roosevelt's campaign song, began to play. Trudy listened to his campaign promises.

Willie stacked his blocks, Bobby slept snugly in her arms, and her seventeen-year-old sister winked and then made a face at her.

So much could be riding on his promises. But even if FDR does win, he's just one man. Keeping his promises sounds even way less possible than Winnie Ruth Judd murdering two people, chopping them up, packing them in trunks, and hauling them to the train station by herself.

Chapter Eleven

Happy Days Are Here Again

It was Sunday, and Joe had left early to earn a little extra cash by helping a farmer repair a fence. Trudy and Mary sat on the mattress, folding laundry fresh from the clothesline that Joe had put up alongside their tent. The boys napped against the canvas on the far side. Pausing a moment, Trudy held a faded and stained but clean shirt up to her nose. She could smell the sunshine. In another life, she would have put it aside to iron later. She knew they could probably find an old fashioned flat-iron she could heat on the stove, but why? Joe didn't need ironed shirts for the kind of work he did now, and the tent was already too hot. The wrinkles could stay. She folded the shirt and set it aside.

Mary set a towel on a stack on the spare orange crate next to her and gossiped about an episode between two pickers that had occurred the previous morning. "I don't know how it started, but Lord, they was mad. They looked like they was gonna punch each other, but then Travis started teasing 'em, dancing around 'em like a boxer, making faces, and throwing fake punches. I thought they was gonna knock him out! Then all the fellas watching started laughing. Them guys musta felt stupid or got embarrassed or something, 'cause they picked up their sacks and lit off in different directions." She smiled.

"Who's Travis? You never mentioned him before." Something in her sister's voice and expression made Trudy suspect Mary wanted to tell her more about Travis.

"Well, that's probably 'cause he wasn't here before. He's this fella that showed up last Friday. I think he's alone. I guess he's a little older'n me. He's got red hair and freckles, and everybody likes him already. He jokes around a lot."

"I see. You like him, too, right?" Trudy grinned at her sister, got up and began to stack folded clothes into the orange crate dresser.

"He's all right, I guess. Kinda cute." Her sister winked and stuck out a pink tongue at Trudy as she rose to carry her few pieces of clothing back to her sleeping area, setting them on a towel at the foot of her quilt.

***

It was a Sunday morning near mid-October, but still warm although it had rained the night before. Trudy and Mary perched on the edge of the platform. Bobby nursed contentedly, and Willie, naked, squatted on the muddy ground in front of the tent making mud pies. A tub of water sat outside the tent flap. Mary would dip Willie in it to rinse him off before they went back inside.

Joe had hiked over to the Grand Canal to fish for carp or catfish with some other guys from the camp. If he caught something, they'd have fried fish for dinner, a nice change from beans. When Bobby fell asleep, Trudy passed him over to his aunt then rolled and lit a cigarette. Mary's eyes followed her movements.

Hope she's not thinking of starting.

Mary looked down at her bare feet, scratching the top of one with the sole of the other. "Travis told me 'bout his family. They live in Texas. He's got three brothers and a sister, but he's been on his own since he was fifteen. He says he didn't want his parents to have to support him, 'cause of the hard times and all."

"How old is he? Do you know?" Trudy looked at her sister. Mary glanced up briefly then returned to scratching the top of her left foot with the toes of her right.

"He's nineteen. He'll be twenty in December." She bent to brush the dirt off. "Do you think it'd be all right if he comes over for supper tonight?" she said, still not meeting Trudy's eyes.

"Sure. I'd like to meet him."

***

Trudy washed and rinsed the supper dishes while the young couple sat on the edge of the platform, talking quietly. Trudy heard her sister's soft laughter. Joe sat at the table, staring at his curled hands in silence. For once, the Zenith wasn't turned on.

"Trudy, I think it's time your sister went home." He turned his head and looked at her, eyes narrowed.

"Why, Joe? She brings in more than enough to pay her way, and it's nice having her company." She placed the last dish in the rack and turned to face her husband.

"I just think your Pa's got a right to know who she's seeing. This boy's got no prospects. He shares a tent with some other fellas, including this guy I know. Albert's pretty sure Travis stole three dollars he left in his pants' pocket the other night. He's too slick. I don't trust him."

You just wanna believe the worst 'cause you're jealous.

Bobby began to cry, and Trudy crossed the tent to pick him up before his brother, asleep on the pallet next to their mattress, woke up. She tucked her baby to her breast and returned to sit across from Joe. "So when did you ask Papa for my hand, honey? Mary's older than I was back then. Anyway, if Mary's getting serious about him, she'll talk to me first. I'll warn her to take it slow."

Joe didn't respond, except with a look of resentment. He rose and stepped inside the private space surrounding their mattress and Willie and drew the blanket closed. He was either sleeping, or pretending to be, when Trudy and their infant joined him shortly after.

***

Trudy could almost hear Mama's voice and see her told-you-so face. "It hurts when someone you care about just up and disappears without a word, don't it?"

That was different, Mama. You were glad to be rid of me. But I love Mary. She owed it to me to at least say goodbye.

When Trudy got up to make breakfast that morning near the beginning of November, the only sign of Mary was a note on the table. She and Travis had left during the night, and they weren't coming back. They'd run off to Nevada to be married and planned to return to Travis's parents' home in Texas afterward.

For the first time, Trudy felt a trace of doubt about leaving Mama as she had. Her anger was gone now, and she was beginning to realize the hardships her mother had dealt with. It didn't excuse Mama's harshness, but it did make it more understandable. She also worried about Mary. Travis seemed likable, and he had family to turn to, but, given the hard times, the couple would have a tough row to hoe.

But that's life now. Could she have done any better back home? At least she loves him.

She reread the final lines of Mary's note. "I'll write you first chance I get. I'm sorry I didn't say nothing. I was afraid you'd try to stop us. I truly love Travis. I love you too, Sis, and I'll miss you."

Trudy showed the note to Joe. He shrugged. He barely glanced at her then turned on the news again, leaning toward the radio as he gobbled his oatmeal. Finished, he grabbed his sandwich, gave her a peck on the cheek, and leaned over to kiss his infant son's head before leaving.

That afternoon, Joe thrust aside the tent flap earlier than usual. He spoke louder than usual, too. "Trudy, I just voted for President of the United States, and I voted for Franklin D. Roosevelt." He sounded defiant, and Trudy knew why.

"But, Joe, I thought you only voted Republican. Roosevelt's a Democrat, ain't he?" She smothered a smile.

"I *am* a Republican. But that don't mean I'm stupid. This country's gone to hell, and Hoover's gonna keep doing what got us into this mess in the first place. It's time for a change, and FDR might just be the man. I like what he's got to say. He sure couldn't be any damn worse, even if he is a damn Democrat."

The stubborn set of his jaw reminded Trudy of when he'd told her his plan to leave for California. She turned away so Joe couldn't see her grin. She knew women had had the right to vote for several years now. She was still too young, but it wouldn't have occurred to her to exercise it anyway. Politics was for men.

That night Joe listened to the election returns for a while before turning the radio off. "It's all just talk," he said. "Probably won't make a damn bit a difference either way." He scowled and went outside where he smoked a final solitary cigarette. Tobacco was as much a necessity as beans now.

Back inside, he crawled onto his side of the mattress. He turned towards the side of the tent away from Trudy without a word. Five minutes later, she heard him snoring.

***

The next day, when he got home from the fields, Joe told Trudy that Roosevelt had won. "It's all any a' them pickers can talk 'bout. Probably ain't gonna help, but we'll see." He sounded unusually cheery.

After supper that night, instead of turning on the news, Joe took a rubber ball out of Willie's toy box. As Trudy watched, he cupped the toddler's hands in front of him then dropped the ball into them. It rolled out. He did it again. Willie caught it.

Trudy sat at the table and washed, rinsed, dried, and stacked dishes. She twisted sideways then dragged her chair around to watch her husband and son as she worked. Joe tossed the ball from a little farther away. Willie missed the toss and ran after the ball on still chubby legs. Then, on Joe's third toss, the ball balanced in Willie's outstretched hands and allowed his small, already curled fingers to grasp it. He shrieked then hurled it back toward his father. The return throw was way wide of the mark. Trudy and Joe both laughed, then looked at each other, still smiling.

If things can just get a little better, maybe we can finally be a real family. Lord knows we've been through enough together.

But things didn't get better. Trudy watched Joe's initial optimism regarding FDR's ability to change the economy fade during the coming months to be replaced by his customary bitter moroseness. He retreated to the porch with his radio and tobacco right after supper, barely speaking to Trudy or his sons during the few hours he spent with them during that long winter and the spring and summer that followed.

***

Trudy and Joe sat at the table one Sunday evening about two weeks after cotton season had started the following autumn. They'd been living in the tent for more than a year, and Trudy fought to hold onto a faint hope that anything would ever change. The population of their Hooverville shifted constantly, but at least it was no longer growing. She tried to believe that was a good sign.

The radio was on, but Joe didn't appear to be listening. He stared into space and frowned. A mild wave of anxiety drifted over Trudy, as if she were watching storm clouds gather and hearing the rumble of distant thunder. The children slept. She was mending a tear in the back of one of Willie's well-worn shirts. It was almost too little for him, but Bobby could wear it.

Joe reached across and turned off the radio. "What do you do all day, anyway?" Before Trudy could reply, he continued. "How long can it take you to clean a goddamn tent, for Christ's sake? It ain't fair for you to sit on your butt all day while I'm out breaking my back. You're going to the field with me tomorrow. If your sister could do it, so can you."

Trudy started to protest. "But what about the babies? I can't pick cotton and carry Bobby."

Bobby was newly weaned. He'd been walking for a couple of months, saying a few words, and beginning to play with his brother. But she could not imagine even Willie following her up and down cotton rows for hours on end, let alone her younger son doing it.

"We can take the Ford. They'll stay in there. You work it out. Other folks do."

"Leave them in the car? By themselves? I know you're my husband, Joe, but they're just babies. This ain't right."

"Times are hard, Trudy. We all make sacrifices." He looked at her, his eyes as cold and hard as his words. "If I hadn't, I'd be in California right now." He stalked outside and disappeared into the darkness.

Trudy folded the tiny shirt and put it away then sat at the table, her head in her hands. John had given Mary bus fare to Phoenix. Trudy could ask him for enough money to bring her and the boys back to Tahlequah. But what then? She couldn't ask her brother or sisters to support them. She'd have to turn to Papa and Mama. She could feel Mama's contempt. What was worse, her children would feel it, too. She wouldn't put her boys through what she'd suffered as a child.

For better or for worse, she'd vowed. It was clear which it had turned out to be. But she was stuck. At least for now.

***

The following morning, they ate breakfast in silence. Trudy packed a piece of leftover catfish in a sandwich for Joe. She added a half sandwich and jar of tea for herself. Then she made two peanut butter and jelly sandwiches, cut them in half, and put the halves into a small paper bag. She stuffed the small bag, along with jars of water and some toys into a larger paper bag then added diapers and a washcloth.

She woke the children, dressed them, and took Willie to the outhouse. She explained on the way that they would be going to the cotton field that morning. She propped him over a hole, supporting him under the arms. "Are we gonna pick cotton, Mama?" Willie's eyes sparkled.

"No, sweetie. You and Bobby have to stay in the car while I help Daddy pick. Mama's counting on you to take care of your little brother. You can do that, can't you? I really need your help." Trudy bit her lip, and another wave of futile anger at Joe swept through her.

"Sure, Mama."

Back at the tent, as the boys ate their oatmeal, Willie pawed through the bag, inspecting its contents then hurried to their toy box for a puzzle his mother hadn't packed. He began to stuff it in the bag, but Trudy stopped him.

"No, honey. The pieces are too small. Bobby might choke if he puts one in his mouth." Her older son gazed at his baby brother with resentment. "Remember, he's your brother. You have to take care of him."

Willie looked at his mother and his expression changed. Suddenly he seemed older than his three years. "Okay, Mama. I will. I'll take care of him."

For an instant, Trudy felt she couldn't go on, but she was trapped. If Joe got mad enough to leave them, they'd be even worse off. Her anger flared again. She couldn't smother it, but she tamped it down. "Okay, Joe. We're ready."

Joe had been sitting on the edge of the mattress waiting and glowering. When Trudy spoke, he got up and went outside to start the Ford.

***

The boys stood on the front seat of the Model T parked at the edge of the cotton field. Joe went to pick up sacks for himself and Trudy. She waited beside the car while he was gone. After a moment, she laid a hand on top of Willie's head and ruffled his soft, brown hair.

"Willie, you're in charge, honey. Bobby's little. You have to take care of him. I'm depending on you, but if you need me, you honk the horn. But don't do it unless you really need to or Daddy'll be mad."

She showed him how. Ahooga! Pickers already in the field looked back over their shoulders to where she stood. She watched Joe approach, his sack slung over his shoulder, hers held by the shoulder strap, dragging behind. He scowled but said nothing.

"I'll be back to see how you're doing." She kissed them both then hurried over to where Joe had stopped.

She threw her sack over her shoulder and followed her husband to a pair of rows that weren't yet occupied by other pickers. She'd picked cotton back home, but it had been years ago. Joe handed her the shabby pair of heavy cotton gloves that Mary had worn, and she made her way down her row. She carefully separated the cotton from the bolls and tried her best to keep up with her husband.

Bristles penetrated the cheap gloves and pricked her hands. Dry branches caught at her wrists and bare legs beneath her dress, scraping her skin. As it filled, her cotton sack pulled at her shoulders and her bent upper back. The late summer sun beat down upon her. It drenched her in sweat and caused her scratches to sting and itch. But the ache in her heart grieved her more than any physical pain.

Two or three other old cars and trucks lined the edges of the fields, and Trudy saw little ones inside. Some, especially those of Mexican migrants, contained two or three children under five. Older ones followed their parents barefoot through the field, helping pick.

She stayed where she could look up and see the Ford and be in range of the sound of its horn. She abandoned one row for another as necessary and let Joe continue down his row without her. She returned to check on the children at least once every hour, dragging her sack behind her.

She made her way to a spot where Joe could see her when her sack was full, and waved him in to carry it to the weigh station. He returned it empty, and she continued until at last, when she could barely move, and the sun was sinking among the clouds on the western horizon, Joe decreed it was time to go home.

***

Trudy continued to pick alongside Joe as the season progressed. The boys waited in the car as they had that first day. Once, when Trudy returned to check on them, Bobby, almost as big as Willie now, sat in his older brother's lap. He'd been crying. Willie rocked him side-to-side, soothing him as he'd seen his mother do.

A lump rose in her throat, and she had to swallow her own tears, but, at the same time, pride in her older son brought a surge of comfort. She wrapped her arms around both of them, squeezing tight, kissed their foreheads, then returned to the field.

Then, one morning in late November, Trudy returned to the Model T to find her children standing in the seat bundled in all the warm clothing they owned and hugging each other tightly as they shivered. Their lips and tiny hands had gone blue with the cold.

Goddammit! This is the last straw!

Trudy dragged her half full sack back to the edge of the field, waved to catch Joe's attention, then climbed into the Ford and drove her babies home.

Joe entered the tent shortly after sunset. "Where'd you go?"

"Back here. It's too cold for the boys to wait in the car anymore this year." She could hear the distant coldness in her own voice.

Let this lie if you know what's good for you.

"Did you pick up my sack? It was half full." She took a drag on the cigarette she had rolled for herself. She smoked regularly now as did Joe, but it was no longer a companionable activity, just a habit.

"Yeah, I got it. Cashed it in. When you didn't come back, I thought maybe something'd happened. But I figured you could handle it, so I kept picking. Season's almost over. We need the money."

That was Trudy's final day of work in the fields that fall. The cotton harvest would be complete in a few days, anyway. Joe didn't make an issue of it.

Chapter Twelve

California Here I Come

In the late summer of 1936, more than three years after Trudy and Joe had listened to Franklin Delano Roosevelt assert on Inauguration Day that "The only thing we have to fear is fear itself," they heard on the national news that unemployment had finally dropped from twenty-five percent to fifteen. Trudy knew part of the reduced unemployment came from the CCC and WPA which put millions back to work. She'd heard about these programs from the President himself in FDR's *Fireside Chats* which Joe never missed. Before the election Roosevelt had said the government should put its faith once more in the forgotten man at the bottom of the economic pyramid. Trudy suspected that that phrase "the forgotten man" was what had won Joe's vote. She glanced at her husband who was intent on the voice of the news reporter.

Do you still feel forgotten, Joe? Then you know how I feel most of the time.

Trudy reached inside her apron pocket to touch Mary's latest letter. Her sister had written shortly after she and Travis eloped and they had resumed exchanging letters. Mary's news wasn't always good, but she was surviving, as all the family was, and she remained Trudy's anchor and confidant. Trudy also wrote other family members as often as she could persuade Joe to give her the additional postage, especially Papa. Trudy knew this included Mama indirectly since she was certain Papa read her letters aloud. She wondered if Mama was interested in news of her wayward daughters.

I'll never forgive you, but I'm starting to understand how you got to be what you are.

Cotton season began the next day, and they would be returning to the fields. Joe still managed, catch as catch can, during the other months of the year, but they saved as much as they could when they were both picking for the leaner times. Trudy knelt on the tent platform beside the galvanized wash tub, listening to the news as she bathed Bobby. Willie stood by, waiting his turn.

"Mama, we wanna pick cotton, too. Will you make us some sacks?" Willie looked at her, eager sincerity shining from his eyes.

"Yeah," Bobby said, adding his two cents. "We wanna pick cotton, too."

The boys had trailed after her for part of most days at the end of the previous season. It gave them a break from sitting for hours in the Ford, and Trudy had enjoyed being able to keep an eye on them. She knew they had seen some children, not much older than they, picking alongside their parents. The thought of those poor children having to pick cotton to help their families survive broke Trudy's heart.

This is different. It's just a game. It'll keep 'em entertained.

After both were bathed, with some misgivings, Trudy sewed straps on a pair of old pillow cases for Willie and Bobby to carry to the cotton field. She finished sewing and handed the miniature sacks to her sons, then suddenly wanted to grab them back, to rip them from their small hands and tear them apart. She closed her eyes and took a deep breath.

***

After they heard the encouraging economic news, Joe took to leaving Trudy and the boys in the field alone for a few hours each day to look for a job. About a month before the season ended, he returned before noon one day and, instead of picking up a sack and joining them in the field, stood next to the Ford and waved them over.

"Get in the car, boys," he said, opening the door. "Let's get away from this goddamn cotton!" The boys scrambled into the back seat.

"What happened?" Trudy rested her hands on the edge of the open passenger side door.

"I finally got a goddamn job, Trudy! That's what happened. Get in the car. I'll tell you 'bout it on the way home."

Trudy gestured toward her nearly full bag. "Wait for me to cash this in, Joe. Otherwise I wasted my time."

After she returned and climbed into the passenger's seat, they bumped back along the dirt road toward the camp. "It's a actual driving job, and it's full time. 'Member Ole Man Willis, the farmer that gave us the wood for the floor?"

"That fella that hires you every time he needs something done? Sure I remember him." Trudy pulled her unopened mason jar out of the lunch bag as she spoke, unscrewed the lid and took a long swig of the sugary tea, then passed it to Willie. "Give your brother some, too." She wiped her mouth with the back of her hand.

"Well, he heard 'bout this job through people he knows. He told me 'bout it, and he told 'em 'bout me. I'll be driving for Martori Brothers. It's a packing and distributing company. They buy citrus and vegetables from farmers here and in Salinas, California. They put all their stuff under the same label and haul it out to distributors in other states. Roll me a cigarette." He handed her his pouch of tobacco and a pack of papers. She did as he asked, rolling one for herself as well. "You know,

Trudy, there must a been at least thirty guys going for that job, and some probably got more experience than I do, but I got it. Know why?"

"Because you're a good, dependable worker?" She knew that was true, whatever his other faults.

He smirked. "That's true. I am, so I'll *keep* the job. But I got it 'cause a *who* I knew, and how *good* I can bullshit. That's what opens doors."

"Well, congratulations, anyway. When do you start?" Trudy leaned out the window, letting wind blow through her sweat damp hair as acres of cotton fields flowed past.

"Right away. I got to go down and renew my commercial license today. Then I'll start Monday." He shifted his eyes towards her then back to the road. "Trudy, it's long haul trucking. I'll be driving to other states, so I'll be gone a day or two at a time, maybe longer. I'll get one of the guys at camp to keep an eye on you and the boys. Is that gonna be all right with you? To have me gone part a the time?" He glanced sideways at her again.

She managed to keep a straight face. "Sure, Joe. I'm a big girl now."

Joe had spent his last day in the field, but Trudy and the boys continued to trudge up and down the rows. Joe wouldn't get paid for two weeks. Trudy couldn't pick nearly as much as he did, but at least she would be able to keep food on the table. The evening after he left on his first trip, as she dished up pinto beans for herself and the boys, it occurred to her that she hadn't asked how or what he'd eat on the road. But she wasn't concerned.

Probably something better than beans. He's always got money squirreled away.

***

Joe arrived home earlier than usual the Friday he was due to get his first paycheck. Trudy glanced up then continued to move back and forth between the rinse tub that sat on the edge of the platform and the clothesline a few feet away. Entering the tent, Joe dragged a chair out onto the porch. He sat down.

A pile of Joe's freshly laundered but still soapy work shirts rested on an orange crate. Trudy picked one up, dunked it in the tub, squeezed out as much water as she could, then stepped around Willie and Bobby who sat on the ground playing marbles, and walked over to the clothesline. The boys hadn't seemed to notice their father's arrival. Trudy wasn't surprised. He rarely paid any attention to them, either. With wooden clothespins from a bag tied around her waist she attached the shirt to the line.

"Well, I got paid today, so I guess we better move," Joe said and sighed. Trudy swiveled around to look at him, unable to believe her ears.

"I hate to have to start paying rent again. I rather save up the money. But if the guys I work with find out we're still living in a tent in this crappy place, they'd probably make fun a me, no matter how good a reason I got."

Trudy stood speechless, but inside, she fumed.

Oh, that's rich, Joe. Let's move so a goddamn bunch of strange men don't laugh at you. The hell with making things better for me and your sons!

She bit her tongue, and turned back toward the clothesline. She would never love Joe. She'd given that up. Sometimes it was a trial just to tolerate him.

If it wasn't for the boys ....

"But it's too expensive to rent a house. I been checking out a few furnished apartments the past few days, and I think I found us one." He paused. "Trudy, are you listening to me?" Impatience rang in his voice.

Afraid he might read the contempt she was feeling in her gaze, Trudy continued to face the clothesline. "Yeah, I hear you, Joe."

Only too well.

"It's cheap, and not too big, but it's got a separate bedroom for the boys and a evaporative cooler in the main bedroom window. I put down a deposit. We can move in this weekend."

You expect me to be so grateful to get out of this shitty tent that I won't complain that I never even seen the place. And you're right.

"Okay, Joe. That'll be good."

There's no point in telling you how I feel. You couldn't care less.

***

Trudy became accustomed to Joe's traveling over the next six months. He was often gone for three or four days at a time as he picked up loads of local citrus and other produce in Phoenix or Salinas and hauled them to wholesalers in neighboring states. Trudy didn't miss him. She'd long since stopped relying on him for anything other than financial support, and although the apartment was as cold and impersonal as the face of a stranger, it was peaceful. She kept loneliness at bay with the company of her sons and her books. Holding a small hand in each of hers, she'd finally caught a streetcar to the Carnegie Library and gotten a library card. She and the boys had even stopped at the S. H. Kress soda fountain. Despite everything, Phoenix was beginning to feel like home.

Joe had been gone for three days when Trudy heard the front door of the apartment bang shut, and he entered the kitchen where she was ironing one of his work shirts. The small rotating fan whirred in her direction from the table top. With an effort of will, she looked up and smiled. "Hello, Joe. Welcome home."

He grabbed her elbow as he came around the tip of the ironing board. His eyes shone. "Well, honey, we're finally on our way!"

Trudy carefully set the iron down on its end and stepped away from the board. She turned to face him, shocked by the term of endearment as rare now as snowfall in Phoenix.

"I asked the boss for a transfer, Trudy. We're moving to Salinas. I drive back and forth anyway, so it don't really matter where I live. He don't care. So we're finally going to California!"

She listened with mixed feelings. "So you already decided. Don't you think maybe you should've talked to me about it first?"

He looked at her as if she'd suddenly sprouted feathers. "Why? You know we always planned on going to California. What's changed?" He gave her a measuring look then stepped into the doorway to the living room. "Boys, were going to California!" She listened to her sons' squeals of delight and knew he was picking up one after the other and tossing them into the air above his head.

The next day Joe gave the minimum required notice to get back the security deposit on their apartment, and they moved to Salinas, California a month after he announced his decision to Trudy. He used the deposit money plus some additional savings to put a down payment on a small, two bedroom house on the outskirts of town. This was where he planned to stay. He'd selected it alone on one of his company trips, but Trudy hardly cared. She hadn't lived in a place she could think of as her home since she'd left Tahlequah. She tried to believe that living in a house they were actually buying might change that.

Joe continued his long haul trucking as before. If it had been a few days since he'd seen the boys, he kept Willie home from school to go for a picnic or visit the park for a game of catch. Trudy had mixed feelings about the practice. She knew her son needed time with his father, but felt Joe might be sending a message that school wasn't important. When she voiced this fear, Joe affirmed it.

"Don't worry about it, Trudy. Most a what they do in first grade is bullshit anyhow. 'Okay, boys and girls get out your crayons,'" he said, in a high pitched voice. "My boys are gonna learn to be men!"

Yeah, ignorant men, if you have anything to do with it.

Willie had started first grade at a neighborhood school five blocks from their house. Trudy and Bobby walked him there, and, after school was out, walked him home. He was doing fine, although Trudy got the impression he was more excited about things that happened at recess, than about the three Rs.

"Mama, Jimmy got punched in the nose today."

"My goodness. What happened?"

"Howie cut in line at the slide in front of Jimmy. Jimmy tattled to Mrs. Bouse. She made Howie eat lunch with her. Then at afternoon recess, Howie found Jimmy and punched him in the nose." He made a small fist and punched the air.

"Good grief. Did he get away with it? Did somebody tell the teacher?"

"Naw! Nobody had to. Mrs. Bouse saw Jimmy's nose was bleeding. She figured out what happened, and Howie got in trouble again. Just the same, I bet Jimmy don't tattle no more!"

"Willie, it's wrong for a person to break the rules, or push people around. Somebody *should* tell the teacher."

"I know, Ma, but fellas who tattle are sissies."

"Well, you better tell me if anyone pushes you around."

He looked at her like she was as distant as the stars.

Boys are definitely different than girls. I wish I could've had just one daughter.

Joe wore condoms religiously now, so that was unlikely to happen. She wished Betty, Mary's daughter, could be nearby, so she could see what having a little girl around was like. She only knew about her niece from Mary's precious letters.

The newlyweds had remained in Nevada about a year rather than joining Travis's parents in Texas. Travis had somehow found the means to support himself and his new wife. One day, he brought home a beautiful ring. Trudy could hear Mary's excited voice in her head as she'd read that letter.

"Trudy, I wish you could see it! It's got a little diamond in the center and tiny rubies in a circle around it. Travis swears they are real, and I believe him. He says he's been saving since we got here, but he must've started before then. He calls it a belated engagement ring! I never heard that word before, but it's plain what it means. Ain't he sweet?"

By the end of her first year of marriage, Mary had conceived her first child. "Travis thinks we would be better off with his parents when the baby comes," she'd written. "We're going to Texas now. I'm nervous about meeting his mother and father. I hope they're not mad we got married without telling them."

Mary gave birth to a daughter with a midwife and her mother-in-law standing by. Reading this news, Trudy felt a twinge of envy. She did not envy what Mary learned after meeting her in-laws.

Travis had been arrested as a juvenile for burglary. At age fourteen, after entering through an open window, he'd ransacked a neighbor's house. Then he bragged to the wrong classmate.

He'd served a six month sentence. He was still on probation when he left for parts unknown. The family considered it a childish prank, never to be repeated. Mary wasn't so sure. "Trudy, sometimes I look at my ring," she wrote, "and I wonder if he paid for it. When we were in Nevada, sometimes he worked at night. Or he told me he was working. Now I wonder if he was really climbing through somebody's window. He paid rent on our apartment and gave me money for groceries. I thought he was good at providing for us, but I never really understood how he did it."

Trudy felt more than doubt. She also felt guilt for not taking Joe seriously about the story of the disappearing three dollars back in tent city.

Chapter Thirteen

Over There

Over the next three years, Joe's job was steady, and with the country still in the throes of the Great Depression, that was about the most they could hope for. But Trudy knew Joe was still chasing his dream. Every evening he wasn't on the road, he sat glued to the radio, listening to the national economic news. Trudy listened with him. But she was more interested in what was happening in Europe.

In 1938 the British Prime Minister Chamberlain extolled the Munich agreement, stating, "I believe it is peace for our time." But immediately afterward, news reports indicated that Hitler had begun to press Czechoslovakia for ever greater concessions.

Then, at the end of August of '39, Der Fuhrer staged the Gleiwitz incident as propaganda to justify the invasion of Poland. On September 3rd, England and France at last entered the conflict in defense of their ally. Europe was at war.

The possibility of a second worldwide Great War hung over Trudy like a dark funnel cloud from her childhood. The United States might not be able to hide in the cellar forever. Then her younger brother, Davy, now eighteen, would probably enlist. The thought of that gentle boy in a muddy trench froze her heart.

FDR had reiterated the nation's policy of neutrality in his *Fireside Chat* on the day Great Britain declared war on Germany and its allies. But a year later, he stated in a press conference, "from a selfish point of view of American defense … we should do everything to help the British Empire to defend itself."

His proposed Lend-Lease program circumvented rather than changed the U.S. cash-and-carry policy. In the same press conference, she and Joe heard him compare lending military equipment to Great Britain to loaning a water hose to a neighbor whose house was on fire. He affirmed that the neighbor shouldn't have to buy the hose, but would be expected to return it. It was unsaid, but obvious, that the practice might also keep the fire from spreading.

The day after the press conference was broadcast, Trudy listened to the response of Robert Taft, an isolationist Republican Congressman who retorted, "Lending war equipment is a good deal like lending chewing gum. You don't want it back."

Three months later they learned that Congress had approved seven billion dollars in funding for the Lend-Lease Program. When he heard the news, Joe slammed his fist on the table. "Trudy, do you know what this means for the economy?"

Trudy just shook her head. "No. But I think it means we're that much closer to being in the war."

"I don't know 'bout that. You worry too much, Trudy. If it happens, it happens. We'll kick some kraut butt." He frowned at her, then his face brightened again. "This is good news for jobs. They have money to hire people to make all that military stuff. People are gonna have more money in their pockets. You just wait and see. Things are gonna get better."

It's all about money for you, too, ain't it, Joe? But then, you'd never have to see combat, would you? And you don't give a damn about the people who might.

From the economic standpoint at least, she soon had to admit he was right. Things did get a little better. Joe got a small raise and gave Trudy enough household money to buy the boys a few new pants and shirts. Trudy was especially happy for Bobby. He'd been raised in Willie's hand-me-downs which had already been used when Willie got them. A couple of times when Joe was on the road Trudy even managed to pinch enough pennies to take the boys to a Saturday movie matinee downtown at the Crystal Theater.

***

One Wednesday morning between trips a few months later, Joe sat looking through the paper. Trudy knew he was checking trucking business for sale ads. He always did. She'd walked the boys to school earlier and was washing the breakfast dishes.

Joe slammed his half full coffee cup down on the table so hard that coffee sloshed over the side. He tore something out of the business pages and dropped the paper on the table, jumped up, and left the house without a word to Trudy. She blotted up the coffee and sat his cup in the sink, unimpressed by Joe's dramatics. The distance between them was so unbreachable by now that she had little interest in what he did unless it impacted her sons.

He returned two hours later, and Trudy could hear the suppressed excitement in his voice. "This could be it! I'll let him wait for a while, think this fish ain't biting."

"What are you talking about?"

"I found an old guy wants to sell his trucking business. He really wants out. Looks 'bout ninety. He's been advertising for a few months now. I seen his ad before, but I never went to talk to him. He wanted cash, and it's more than I got saved. I thought I might dicker a little, but then decided to let it go. It was just too much. I don't want to go to no bank and have to pay interest and all. But he's been advertising so long I thought it might be worth taking a look. Thought he might be desperate by now. And he is." Joe rolled a cigarette, then paused to light it, taking a deep drag.

"Did you buy it?"

"Not yet, but I might! He's willing to carry the balance I can't pay him outright. I'll make payments to him. No interest. But he's still asking too much. I'll wait a few days then go see if he'll come down. If he don't, I might just do it anyways. I'm tired a waiting." This was an extremely long speech for Joe.

Trudy didn't bother to inquire about the asking price. She knew he didn't want to give her any clue about how much money he'd put away, and, as usual, he wasn't interested in her opinion.

A week later Joe made a final offer and the owner took it. In addition to the buildings, land, and business name, the small trucking outfit included a modest fleet of three lightly used Ford flatbed trucks. Joe began transporting building materials from local suppliers to construction sites.

Trudy did feel a certain reluctant respect. But it was *his* success, not theirs, although her sons might benefit. Trudy and Joe didn't share anything but the boys. Joe had taken to coming home late some evenings. After the children were asleep, Trudy often sat outside, smoking and looking up at the stars as she had on the old tent platform with Joe years ago. Any hope of even that companionship was gone now.

***

It was December 7, 1941, and the newscast poured forth details of Japan's stunning attack on Pearl Harbor. Trudy sat on the living room couch beside Joe and stared at the radio, unable to comprehend what she was hearing. The broadcasters sounded horrified and disbelieving, too.

Why'd they do this? Do they want us in this damned war, the crazy sons of bitches?

The sun rose the next morning, and Joe left for work. Trudy kept the news on in the background all day and found herself wandering over to sit transfixed, eyes locked on their new Philco as if it were a live person delivering a shocking tale. She learned that President Roosevelt had asked Congress to declare a state of war. In the face of Japan's infamy, not even the most ardent isolationist could oppose. Much as she hated this outcome, even Trudy realized it was inevitable.

FDR appealed to the American people for support in his *Fireside Chat* the next evening. He said, "It is not a sacrifice to do without many things to which we are accustomed if the national defense calls for doing without." Trudy might have laughed if circumstances had been less dire.

If there's anything Joe and me know how to do, it's do without.

He also asserted that, "It is not a sacrifice for any man, old or young, to be in the Army or the Navy of the United States. Rather is it a privilege." The only person Trudy loved who might engage in battle was her younger brother, Davy, and that milk had already been spilled.

A letter from Papa, shortly after England entered the war, had brought the news that Davy had hitchhiked across the Canadian border to train for service in the RCAF. After training, he'd been transported to England as a pilot to serve in the First Eagle Squadron, comprised entirely of U.S. volunteers. The U.S.'s entry into the war would put him at no more risk than he'd already been in voluntarily for the past year and a half.

Trudy fretted over mounting U.S. casualties during the months following Congress's official declaration of war. Joe appeared to be more interested in the economic boost the war was giving his trucking business.

"See, Trudy? Now everybody's got jobs. And a lot a that government money is going into construction. Military production plants, training camps, even civilian housing for the workers. Them contractors doing all that building need me to bring in their materials. It's the law of supply and demand. Things get better for everybody, 'specially when you own your own business."

Trudy detected a positive note, not only in Joe's voice, but in the voices of the newscasters, and even parents she spoke with on the way to and from school with the boys. A new sense of purpose electrified the air. Trudy found it ironic how something so horrible, that resulted in slaughter, actually made some people feel better.

Chapter Fourteen

Honky Tonk Man

Joe pulled the Ford into the driveway as Trudy sat on the porch smoking. He was even later than usual. The ember of Trudy's cigarette brightened in the darkness as she took a final drag before crushing it out. She watched him as he climbed down from the car. He stumbled as he stepped off the running board and grabbed the door to regain his balance. He closed it with great care, using both hands, then made his way toward her, with slow, deliberate steps.

Is he sick?

"Are you okay?"

He stopped about five feet away, swaying like an oak sapling in a breeze. "I'm a whole lot better'n okay, sweetheart. I'm a boss man. Just hired me a guy to help out 'round the yard. I'll still do the driving. He'll keep the trucks loaded and keep track a supply orders. But if things keep going the way they are, I'm gonna hafta hire me somebody to help deliver, too." The instant Joe opened his mouth, the scent of alcohol floated across the still air into Trudy's nostrils.

"Joe, you been drinking." Trudy spoke without thinking. She could hear the accusation and disappointment in her voice. Caution struck too late. She should have waited to talk about this when he was sober.

"Hell, yeah! You hear what I said, Trudy? Don't that sound like something to celebrate? That kid I hired is the nephew a one a my customers. His uncle bought me a couple a beers for giving the kid a chance. What's wrong with that? Never hurts to get friendly with customers. 'Sides, in case you ain't heard, FDR ended Prohibition." He glared at her as if daring her to say more.

The contempt in Joe's voice and eyes reminded Trudy of their hard early years. Lately, their relationship had been so distant that little emotion of any kind passed between them. She shivered, remembering. She didn't want more of that.

Joe waited for her to speak. When she didn't, he gave her a final look, his upper lip raised in a sneer, and entered the house. Trudy remained on the porch. She smoked another cigarette slowly, hoping he would be asleep when she went inside. He was.

Trudy continued to refrain from saying anything about the incident the next day. Joe rose and went to work as usual, as he'd done after

Bobby's birth in tent city. When he came home sober before she and the boys ate supper, she began to relax a little.

***

"When's Poppa getting back? He promised to take us to the park to play ball today." Bobby regarded her with innocent, coffee-brown eyes. At eight, he looked like he'd inherited all of Mama's Cherokee blood, but his cheerful, childish good humor was Papa's. Trudy saw none of his father in him.

Thank God.

"Something must've happened that he needs to take care of, honey. Go get your brother. I'll take you."

"But what if Poppa comes home, and we're not here?"

She saw the disappointment and concern on her son's face. Joe had left for the truck yard at seven that Saturday morning. He'd told Trudy he had to check on a few things, but would be back before lunch. When he wasn't back by two, Trudy had begun to worry. It wasn't like Joe to disappoint his sons.

Probably some business thing he had to handle. Hope it's not serious,

"I'll leave him a note. I'll tell him to come meet us when he gets home." She forced herself to grin at her younger son. He tilted his head and grinned, too, then ran to find Willie.

Joe never joined them. The boys were asleep, and Trudy was waiting on the couch trying to read *The Postman Always Rings Twice* when he finally came home. He staggered as he entered the living room carrying a six pack of Coors beer. He paused to look at her. Trudy kept her eyes fixed on her book. After a moment, Joe walked into the kitchen, and she heard him place the beer in the ice box. Then he returned.

"I met with some customers. You know, a *business* meeting." Sarcasm dripped from his voice.

"Okay, Joe." Trudy kept her voice soft and non-committal. Her eyes remained on her book.

"Okay, Joe." His mocking tone reminded her of an irritable old parrot she'd seen in a cartoon when she'd taken the boys to see *Stagecoach* back when Joe was still driving interstate. She refused to react or to take her eyes off her book.

Finally, Joe left the room. An hour later when she came to bed, he was snoring. She lay awake in the darkness trying to decide how to handle things the next day. Joe never worked on Sundays. Even in tent city, he'd spent most Sundays fishing or sitting on their platform listening to the Zenith and talking to co-workers who dropped by.

I'll talk to him. When he's sober, he'll know this is not right. He loves the boys. He can't treat them like this.

***

Although Trudy had gone to bed after Joe, she rose before him the next morning. The first thing she did was take the beer out of the ice box, wrap it in one of Joe's old shirts, and put it in the trunk of the Ford.

When Joe entered the kitchen the boys were outside playing cowboys and Indians. Trudy could hear Bobby's war cries through the screen window. She scooped still warm eggs, bacon, and biscuits onto a plate and set it in front of her husband, then handed him a cup of coffee. He took it without speaking, and she saw him wince at a loud shriek from his younger son. Then he looked down at his plate.

Probably got a hangover. That's what it's called, right, Mary?

She smiled with a trace of bitterness, remembering the conversation in tent city when her sister had taught her that term. She turned her back before Joe could see her expression, poured herself fresh coffee, added canned evaporated milk, and sat down across from him. She kept her face blank and waited for him to speak. She wanted to test the water before diving in.

Joe sat in silence. He nibbled a few bites of egg, then tasted the bacon and set it aside. Finally, he pushed the plate away and concentrated on sipping his black coffee.

"We got any a that orange juice left?"

Trudy rose, stepped to the ice box, and retrieved a glass bottle half full of juice. She set it on the table and moved to the cupboard for a glass. By the time she turned around, Joe was gulping the juice directly from the bottle. He drained it, set the bottle down, and leaned back in his chair.

"I ain't gonna apologize for yesterday, if that's what you're thinking. A man's got a right to do what he wants on his own time."

Trudy bit her tongue. She was sure it was callused after all these years. She took a deep breath. "I'd never try to tell you what to do, Joe. I know I can't. But please think about the boys. I know you was raised like I was. I can't have drinking in this house. They're too young to be exposed to that."

Joe stared at her in silence.

"I know you can go out with your friends when you want to. That's your business. Just please don't bring it home, and please don't let the boys see you when you been drinking. For their sake, not for me." Trudy kept her voice soft. She knew she was walking a tightrope, but hoped he was too under the weather to react.

"All right, Trudy. I guess you're right. I can't imagine getting much of a party going 'round here, anyhow." Trudy read the scorn in his eyes. He rose and walked to the ice box. "What'd you do with my beer?"

"It's in the truck of the car."

"Good. I thought maybe you drunk it. No, that's right, you're Miss Goody-Two-Shoes." He cackled, and looked around as if he wished he had an audience to appreciate his wit. The Charlie Chapman look-alike back in tent city flashed through Trudy's memory.

Has Joe really changed that much? Do I even know him anymore?

***

By the end of the year, Joe had hired a total of four employees, including a foreman who could basically run the business. He went to work every day, and Trudy knew he kept a shrewd eye on everything, but she suspected most of his time was spent courting new customers and having *business* meetings at local bars. When by chance she saw him after noon he was rarely sober but seemed to control his drinking enough to function during the day.

When he came home early one afternoon after school was out for the summer, Trudy smelled beer, but other than looking unusually good-humored, he seemed in control.

"Where're the boys?"

"They're in the backyard. Joe, are you okay?"

He gave her a dismissive glance. "I'm fine." As he stepped out the back door, Trudy hurried after to watch through a window. Bobby dropped his baseball glove and ran up to his father.

"Poppa, you're home!" Joe grabbed his younger son under the armpits and lifted him into the air, as Bobby grinned with happiness.

"Yeah, I thought maybe we could go to the park. Would you fellas like that?"

"We sure would," Bobby said. Willie nodded and approached his father and brother, a look of puzzlement on his face, but then he grinned, too.

You know something's strange, but you're too young and naive to understand why. Thank God! But how long 'til you figure it out?

As she watched, Trudy wondered, not for the first time, what had caused the change in Joe. Her first guess was that finally achieving his dream had taken the challenge out of his life, and he was bored. But Papa preached that alcohol was the Devil's trap, so, she decided, maybe it was that simple. Joe had fallen in and couldn't get out. She couldn't bring herself to feel sorry for him.

You dragged me and your boys in, too. Besides, you enjoy it.

A few days later when she was sorting the laundry Trudy noticed a red stain on a pair of his jockey shorts. When she examined it more closely, she could see that it was lipstick, cherry red and smeared, but obviously lipstick, near the fly.

Her lip curled in contempt, but she didn't really care. If he had other interests, it might take the burden of having sex with him off her shoulders. She tossed the shorts with the other whites into the old Maytag that sat on their back porch and added a little extra bleach.

***

Trudy jerked awake when the front door slammed. Moments later Joe appeared in the doorway of their bedroom. Trudy lay in bed and watched as he swayed from side-to-side. "I'm hungry. Get me some breakfast!"

"Get it yourself, and keep your voice down. You're gonna wake up the boys. You want them to see you like this?" The words were out of her mouth before she took time to think, but she didn't care. She glanced at the bedside clock. It was a little after three in the morning.

Suddenly he loomed over her. "You bitch!" He punched the side of her face with his fist hard enough to stun her and cut her upper lip.

Trudy touched her throbbing face with her fingertips and regarded her husband through slitted eyes. She didn't hesitate. There were lines she would not let him cross, whatever the cost. "If you ever do that again, you'd better kill me, or I'll kill you." She meant it with all her heart.

Joe gazed at her for several moments, still weaving back and forth, then broke eye contact and looked away. He turned and left the room. Moments later Trudy heard the front door slam again. She lay awake until the alarm went off, then rose to make breakfast for herself and her sons and get them ready for school. She hoped the boys wouldn't notice the bruise on her jaw and her cut lip, but Bobby did.

"What happened to your face, Ma?"

Her mind raced. "I tripped coming in from the backyard in the dark last night. I bumped into the side of the door."

Bobby fingered her bruise. "That's a dandy. Looks like you been in a fight." He grinned at her.

Trudy smiled at him. "Girls don't fight." Willie gave her a skeptical look, but said nothing.

Could he have heard something? God, I hope not.

She didn't see Joe until that afternoon. He returned home in time for supper, ate, asked the boys about school, and played catch with them, avoiding Trudy's eyes. They exchanged less than a dozen words. He left without a word to her as soon as his sons went to bed. Trudy stayed awake waiting resolutely for whatever might occur when and if he returned. Finally, exhausted from the night before, she fell asleep lying across their bed in her bathrobe.

The next morning, she found Joe asleep on the couch in the living room. After a few days of this routine, she woke to find him in bed beside her. A week later, near dawn, his hand began stroking her breast. He scooped his arm under her waist and pulled her against him. She submitted, struggling against her instinct to pull away.

If I refuse, things will only get worse. I can bear this for the boys.

Indifference would have been a blessing now, but lack of feeling had been replaced with contempt that verged on hatred for Joe and shame for herself.

He never even said he was sorry. He'd probably do it again if he thought he could get away with it.

Chapter Fifteen

Blue Moon

The days slipped by. Willie's eleventh birthday came, reminding Trudy, as it always did, of the early days of her life with Joe when she'd still had hope that she could make her marriage work. She wondered if things might have been different if the rug hadn't been pulled out from under the U.S. economy and they'd made it all the way to California then, while they were young and hopeful. Still, the past couldn't be undone, and the boys were all that mattered. They were the center of her life.

What will I do when they're gone?

The thought occurred as Trudy was drying dishes the next morning. It both saddened and intrigued her. She'd gotten so used to living day to day that the future was a blank page. A knock on the back door brought her back, and she hurried to answer it. She expected to find Tony, the iceman, but it wasn't him. A tall, lanky man with deep blue eyes and sandy blond hair stood on her doorstep. He wore a crisply ironed white shirt and navy trousers and carried a block of ice balanced on his left shoulder.

"Hello, Mrs. Dobson. How are you this fine morning?" the man said. "Your regular guy, Tony's, got a new route, so I'll be your iceman from now on. My name's Karl."

"Call me Trudy, please"

Don't remind me I'm Mrs. Dobson.

"Okay, Trudy." He smiled at her and thrust out his right hand. She took it. His grip was warm and firm. Following her into the kitchen, he inserted the block of ice into the top shelf of her icebox, smiled again, then turned and left the house.

Joe could at least buy us an electric refrigerator. God knows he can afford it. Thank goodness one of his customer's sold him that old Maytag, or I'd still be using my scrub board.

Salinas was cooler than Phoenix, but ice melted fast, and without it milk soured and food spoiled, so a fresh block was delivered every other day. Karl usually showed up around eight in the morning, but one day a couple of weeks after he'd taken over the route, he didn't arrive until late afternoon. When Trudy answered his knock, she noticed he looked disheveled. His normally pristine shirt had rings of sweat under the arms, and a lock of damp hair lay on his forehead. He even seemed a little flustered.

"Mrs. Dobson—Trudy, I'm sorry. I hope you didn't have to wait around for this. I'm sure you've got other things to do. I never mean to hold up my customers." He grinned. "I mean keep them waiting, not rob them." He looked flustered again. "Sorry, dumb thing to say."

Trudy laughed. "It's okay. It wouldn't be worth your while anyway. You might find a few cans of green beans, but that's about it. What happened?"

He shifted the ice resting on his broad shoulder and started to speak, but Trudy interrupted. "I'm sorry. Karl. That must be heavy, and cold. Let's put it in the icebox. Then you can tell me what happened, if you have time. I imagine you have other customers waiting." She smiled and stepped aside.

He carried the ice into the kitchen then returned. "No, actually, I don't. You're my last customer, and they won't expect me to come back to the ice house this late. What happened was my truck broke down. I thought it was a flat, but the axle was broke, so I had to call someone to fix it then wait around 'til they got there. It threw my schedule way off."

"That's okay. I'm here pretty much all the time. I don't really have a schedule, and the ice box is still cold." Trudy held the door open, but Karl paused as he stepped onto the porch. "I couldn't help noticing your garden. I haven't seen okra growing since I was a kid."

"Yeah, I'm not even sure I like it all that much, but I ate a lot of it as a child every summer, so it takes me back. Reminds me of home. And I feed it to my kids. Maybe it'll tie them to their Okie roots. When it's ready I'll give you some if you like. Ever have it fried?" She grinned at him.

"Only way I'll eat it." He grinned back, then stepped off the porch and walked back to his truck.

Trudy trailed him as far as her garden and turned to watch as he drove away. She'd enjoyed the exchange. Conversation of any kind with an adult had become rare for her. His comment about robbing customers showed he had a sense of humor, and he'd recognized the okra. Trudy wondered if he was from Oklahoma. She turned back into her empty house.

Trudy's loneliness was self-inflicted. Over the months, watching Joe slide into a pit of alcoholism, she'd taken refuge in her sons, but they were in school most of the day or playing with friends. So when she finished the housework, she escaped in reading; Raymond Chandler and other mysteries now, not the Brontë sisters. She no longer believed in romance. She couldn't discuss her life with anyone, so real friendship was impossible. Even Mary didn't know the worst, although Trudy had confided some of her troubles in her letters.

***

At first Trudy and her iceman chatted about the weather and current events. Since Trudy was his last customer, he was never in a rush. Trudy did ask if he was from Oklahoma. He wasn't. He was from Texas. Then Karl began to tell Trudy stories about his job or other customers. His stories were often funny. Trudy's sense of humor had long been limited to sharing child limericks and jokes with the boys. It was a treat to laugh with another adult.

As Karl began to linger, they shared family histories. When Trudy told him her father was a preacher, Karl said, "Well then, you must know my friend, Gladly, the cross-eyed bear!" It was painfully corny and his shame-faced laughter showed he knew that, but she hadn't been able to refrain from laughing as she shook her head.

Karl was a year younger than she, and had been on his own since age sixteen. The son of German immigrants, he'd left Texas near the beginning of the Depression. That reminded her of Travis. She wondered if Karl knew him. She asked.

"No, I never heard of anybody by that name. Texas is a big state, biggest in the Union. Do you know which city?"

"Austin, I think. At least that's where his parents live now." Trudy realized it was silly to think the two might have met.

"I never even passed through Austin. Rode a lot of freight trains, but they were all headed west from Sweetwater. I enjoyed the adventures, but I'm too old for that now. I'm glad things are more stable."

"You rode the rails?" Memories of making sandwiches for drifters in their rented house in Phoenix flooded Trudy.

"Sure did. Only way a kid could get anywhere without money. My folks didn't want me to leave, but they were barely making it, and there were no jobs in Sweetwater. Only thing I regret is not finishing my last year of high school. Didn't matter back then, but it would help now."

Trudy looked away. "Mama took me out of school before I started fifth grade."

When she looked up Karl was staring at her. "You're kidding me. You're so smart and you know so much about what's happening in the world. I thought you at least went to high school, probably graduated."

Trudy grinned and pointed at the radio. "I listen to the news and read anything I get my hands on. Maybe that helps."

***

Trudy had held her red-and-black checkered dress with the white collar up in front of her. This would be the dress she'd wear tomorrow for the first day of fifth grade. Mama had made it, with some help from Millie, late last spring. The only place Trudy had worn it so far was church. She grinned in anticipation, then looked up to see Mama standing in the bedroom doorway watching her. She hung the dress back in the closet then turned as Mama spoke.

"Trudy, I made up my mind. You ain't going back to school this year."

"What, Mama?" Frozen, she stared at her mother.

"I said you ain't going back to school. You don't need no more book learning, and there're things you need to learn 'round here. Besides, you need to help me and your sisters with the housework, the garden, and the other chores. Everybody needs to do their fair share."

"But, Mama, school don't even last all day. I can help when I get home and on Saturdays. I promise I'll do more. I'll do whatever you want me to. Just one more year." Trudy fought to sound calm and reasonable, but heard the tears in her voice. She hoped Mama didn't.

"I didn't go to school at all, and I do just fine. You can read the Bible. That's all any woman needs." Mama's dark hair was parted in the middle and pulled back in a bun away from her forehead and high cheekbones. Her nearly black eyes glittered. She was part Cherokee, and sometimes, like right now, arms crossed under her bosom and the corners of her mouth turned down, except for the headdress, she looked like the carved cigar store Indian Trudy had seen downtown.

Trudy stared back in silence. Evelyn stepped through the bedroom doorway with baby Davy on her hip, took one look at the two of them, and scuttled back out. Mama turned and followed. The discussion was over.

When Mama went out to hoe weeds and water the long rows of ripening corn, Trudy sought support from Papa, but when she saw the sadness in his eyes she knew it was useless even before he spoke.

"I know how much you love school, honey, but there *is* a lot of work to do 'round here. 'Sides, your mother wants time to teach you to cook and sew. A woman needs to bring those gifts to her marriage. I know that seems like a long time away." His voice faded out, and he cleared his throat. "But she's your mother. She knows best."

And who are you?

Trudy walked back to the bedroom without another word. When she glanced back, Papa was stroking the cover of his ever-present Bible as he gazed into space. Trudy knew her schooling had ended.

***

That night she lay crying in the bed she shared with Mary. Mary patted her shoulder, but that didn't help much. Trudy heard the springs on the other bed creak. She looked across the room and saw moonlight reflected in Evelyn's open eyes.

"Evie, did you know Mama wasn't going to let me go back to school?" She sniffled and cleared her throat.

It was quiet for a minute. "Yeah, Sis, I knew."

"How'd you know?"

"Millie and me heard her talking to Papa while you and Mary were out in the woods this afternoon."

"I knew she'd talked to Papa before I did! What'd she say?" She saw Millie's shadow as she raised herself up on her elbow to join the conversation.

"You can probably guess," Millie said before Evelyn could speak. "She don't think you need to learn any more than how to read and do a little 'rithmetic. She told Papa you already read the Bible as good as he does. Which is true. And she said you know how to add and subtract, so nobody's gonna cheat you at the store."

"What'd Papa say?"

"Well, he wanted her to let you keep going. He knows how much you love school, and you know he don't like to see your feelings get hurt," Evelyn said. "But Mama wouldn't have it. She said you need to learn to bake pies, sew, milk the cow. You know, all the things that wives do. The things Millie and me learned already. She made us quit after fifth grade, remember? Not that we cared that much."

"How soon does she think I'm gonna get married?"

"Not soon enough for her!" Millie cackled, then covered her mouth.

"So Papa let her have her way, like he always does?" Trudy felt a rush of anger, followed by resignation. She couldn't stay angry with Papa.

"You know you're his favorite, but he can't stand up to her. You do more'n anybody. Even if you don't say nothing, we all see it in your face. She sees it, too. Why do you think she picks on you? Besides her being jealous that Papa thinks you're so special, that is?" Millie said.

"He thinks I'm special, but he don't stick up for me. Mama rules this roost.

**

Karl's exotic life intrigued Trudy. He'd ridden the rails, slept in Hobo Jungles, and done odd jobs for food during the Depression, like the vagrants she'd met in Arizona. Then, when President Roosevelt had signed the Selective Service and Training Act, he'd registered for the draft.

"I thought about enlisting right then and there and making a career of the military. But I wasn't sure I could handle all those rules. I like change. I like adventure." His words resonated with Trudy's long suppressed and almost forgotten yearnings. The strains of "Far Away Places" played inside her head.

"The idea of boot polishing, and checking the folds at the corners of my bunk to be sure they're straight, and 'Yes, sir, no, sir,' didn't appeal to me. But on the other hand, you don't have to worry about where your next meal's coming from." He grinned at her and his blue eyes reminded her of Papa's. "So I was thinking about it."

Pearl Harbor had made the decision for him. He rushed to enlist voluntarily, as so many other patriotic Americans had. Stationed in the South Pacific, he'd not yet seen battle when he was kicked in the head by an army mule.

"I guess I shouldn't have walked up behind the stupid thing. I was just bringing it a bucket of grain. I still wonder if it got fed after it kicked me." His grin was contagious.

You can laugh at yourself. How I've missed that!

"You're a farm girl. You know about mules, Trudy." He looked at her and tilted his head. "Do you think it might have decided kicking me was worth losing its dinner?"

"Probably." She laughed. "They *are* pretty ornery." She suddenly realized that he'd been hurt, maybe badly. Trudy put her hand over her mouth. But when she met his eyes, she saw he was laughing, too. "How bad was it?"

"Well, I guess I was out long enough to worry them. When I did come to, I couldn't remember how to talk right for a couple of weeks. I used words wrong, and even when I started getting the words right, I must have said some crazy stuff for a while. I was in the hospital for five weeks. By then I was all right, but they were still cautious that I might relapse, so they sent me home. Unfit for military service, my discharge papers said. That sounds derogatory to me, but that's the army for you. I guess I should just be grateful I got out of the war alive. Some of the guys I knew didn't, and some are still over there fighting."

***

As the weeks passed, Trudy found herself looking forward more and more to Karl's arrival. Her growing friendship with him was a patch of sunlight shining through the dark clouds of Joe's drunkenness and bad temper, and the boring sameness of her days. She put aside her fear that she might be leading Karl to expect more than friendship and conversation. She could never be an adulteress.

How Mama would gloat over that!

As time passed, she began to tell him more about her family, the events that had led to her need to escape, her reckless elopement, and the hard times that had followed. Eventually, one morning she even told him about Joe's drinking and infidelity.

"Why do you stay with that bastard?" His eyes bored into hers. She could feel his underlying fury at Joe, and sadness for her in the question and in his eyes.

She considered her response. It had never occurred to her to that there might be other options. The boys were in school, and more and more women had been working since the beginning of the war. "I don't know." She shook her head. "Maybe I won't." Mama's stubbornness surged through her, and the blank pages of her future were suddenly filled with possibilities.

Karl swept her into his arms, kissed her, and obliterated all doubt about his feelings. They clung together, and he kissed her face, her neck, her hair.

Maybe some of what I read in those library books might be true after all.

Chapter Sixteen

Taking A Chance On Love

Trudy was thankful she'd let Mama and Joe teach her one thing: be frugal and squirrel away some money, just in case. Joe still controlled their finances. But after their circumstances had improved Trudy began to exaggerate the amount she needed for household expenses. It wasn't by much, and Joe never questioned. By then, his attention was mostly elsewhere.

She tucked the extra cash away in a Folgers coffee tin. She wasn't sure why, but she liked knowing it was there. It gave her a rare sense of control, of freedom, as learning to drive the Model T had done so long ago. It had gradually become a decent nest egg.

Now Trudy cracked it open and used those savings to retain a lawyer and pay first month's rent on a run-down apartment on the other side of Salinas for herself and her sons. She didn't want to fight over who stayed in the house she'd shared with Joe. She just wanted out. It had never really been her home. It didn't matter to her.

She made her preparations behind Joe's back. If she confronted him, sparks would fly, and she didn't want her sons caught in the middle. In truth, she was afraid for herself as well. Joe's potential for drunken violence had been tempered by her threat, but if his pride was challenged directly, she feared he might snap. When she was ready, she left a note, picked the boys up from school, and disappeared without a forwarding address.

Willie and Bobby seemed subdued, but not all that surprised that their mother didn't want to live with their father anymore. They'd seen less and less of Joe as his drinking increased, and Trudy knew they were old enough to know there were problems. Losing their friends through the move would be harder.

They'll make new ones, and they can visit Joe sometimes after he cools off. They're better off not having to live with him.

The following week Trudy, by way of her new lawyer, sued Joe for divorce on grounds of mental cruelty. She hadn't wanted to blame him despite having some good reasons. Marrying him in the first place was the original mistake, and that, she knew, was her own doing. She just wanted to walk away. But the law wouldn't let her.

She refused Karl's offers of help and managed to subsist on the remainder of her savings, supplemented by the court ordered temporary child support from Joe. As she waited for the decree to be finalized, Trudy knew one thing: this wasn't about Karl, although he'd opened her eyes. Whatever happened between them, she would never go back to Joe. She hoped she and Karl had a future, but if not, she would find a job and somehow make a life of her own.

One afternoon, a few weeks after she'd left the house, she and Karl bumped into Joe as they walked down a street in downtown Salinas. He stood in their path and fixed red, watery eyes on Trudy. He never even glanced at Karl. "Where do you think you're going, bitch? It's time you come home!" Staggering, he grabbed at her arm.

Karl flattened him with a hook to the lower jaw. "Don't you ever touch her again."

Joe pulled himself erect, gave Trudy a brief stare of accusation, and stumbled away without looking back. Trudy gazed up at Karl's clenched jaw and felt safe for the first time since Joe's drunkenness had begun. She took a deep breath and blinked away tears.

Later that night, she and Karl danced to the strains of Jimmy Dorsey's "Blue Moon" in her barren apartment living room. As Karl's kisses and caresses became more intense, she pulled away.

"Please don't. I can't. I hope you can understand." She glanced towards the door of the bedroom where her young sons slept. Her eyes returned to his and pleaded with him.

"That's all right. You're worth waiting for." He stepped back and looked at her. "I love you."

Trudy cupped her hands around the sides of his face, bending it down to hers. She kissed him until she was breathless then stared into his eyes. "I love you, too. With all my heart."

"I don't have a ring yet. I want you to pick it out. I was going to wait 'til your divorce was final, but I need to know." His eyes searched hers. "Will you marry me?"

Trudy threw her arms around him and kissed him again with a fervor she'd dreamed of and done without, as she had so many other things, all those long, hard years.

***

Trudy had to find a way to break the news of her engagement to the boys. After school, she sat them down at the kitchen table with glasses of milk and a plate of peanut butter cookies. Willie looked at her as if he knew something was up. Bobby's attention fixed on the cookies.

"We need to talk, boys.

"What, Mama? I'm all ears," Willie said, glancing sideways at his brother. Bobby giggled and cupped his hands behind his ears, bending them forward.

Trudy looked at them until Bobby dropped his hands and Willie stopped grinning. "You know we're never going to live with your father again. But he is your father. You can still do things with him. Go places with him." Both boys looked down at the table. It had been a long while since Joe had spent much time with them.

"Your daddy loves you. He's just been really busy lately." She could tell neither believed her. Sometimes she, herself, wondered how much they mattered to him. "Anyway, I want to talk to you 'bout Karl." She hesitated. "Do you like him?"

Bobby widened his eyes, tilted his head, and shrugged his shoulders. He said nothing.

Willie narrowed his eyes and looked at her. "He's all right, I guess. Why?"

"I think we might be getting married." Trudy looked from one to the other. "How would you feel about that?"

"It's up to you, Mama." Willie said. "If that's what you want." His voice sounded older than his twelve years, and more distant than across the table. Bobby picked up a cookie and broke it into small pieces. When he finished, he began eating it one crumb at a time.

Well, that's done. You'll get used to the idea, and Karl will be a better father than Joe ever was.

***

When the divorce was final, Trudy and Karl married in a civil ceremony, the only witnesses, Will and Robert. Karl had purchased a small Kodak box camera for the occasion and took several pictures. He posed Trudy carefully on the front steps of the courthouse. Adjusting the wide brim of her hat, he placed both her hands around the stems of the bouquet of yellow roses he'd given her. Then he showed her how to position her feet, one at an angle to the other, in her fashionable high heels.

"These are the first pictures for our family album, boys." The boys glanced at each other and said nothing. He posed one on either side of their mother. "Say, cheese!" After that, he showed Willie how to aim the viewfinder and snap the shutter, then hurried to pose beside Trudy.

***

They all moved into Karl's one-bedroom apartment while the couple planned their next steps. Trudy had decided she wanted to return to

Dorelyn Kunkel

Arizona. After the boys were asleep on their pallet in the living room, she and Karl lay in bed and discussed it.

"It's not too far from here," Trudy said. "The boys could visit Joe once in a while. He's a jackass, but he *is* their father. But I don't want them around him all the time, so it would be good to be farther away. Out of this state. If he only sees them once in a while, maybe he'll make an effort to stay sober for the occasion. You'd have to find another job. Do you think that would be a problem? We could live on my settlement money 'til you do."

"I imagine they must need ice delivery men in Arizona, don't you?" Karl grinned up at her as she propped on an elbow to lean over him, intent on the discussion. "I've got recent experience. It shouldn't be too hard."

"It may sound strange, but Phoenix still feels more like home to me than California does. Even if we did live in a tent most of the time. I love that greasewood smell, and it's a dry heat." Trudy stuck a Lucky Strike into her mouth, lit it with the lighter Karl had given her, and grinned around it. Then she removed it with her index and middle fingers. "Besides, it's where the boys were born." Her voice grew softer as she searched Karl's face. She knew he had passed through Phoenix and stayed a few days when he'd rode the blinds during the Great Depression.

"I wish I'd met you then. I'd have gotten you out of that goddamned tent." His arm folded on the pillow under his head, he stared into her eyes.

It felt like he was reading her mind. "Don't know if I could've hopped a freight train nursing a baby and carrying a two-year-old. But if anybody could've made me try, it'd've been you."

She leaned over and gave him a long, slow kiss, relishing the tingle that had returned after all those years. He responded as she'd known he would. She reached behind her to crush out her cigarette in the ashtray on the bedside table.

***

Karl and Trudy purchased a small house in Sunnyslope, a suburb north of Phoenix. It was far from the neighborhood where Trudy and Joe had rented their first house, so it felt like a fresh start. With the proceeds from Trudy's divorce settlement, they were able to buy the house free and clear. Joe had given her three thousand dollars in cash, and had signed an agreement to provide a modest monthly amount for child support. His business was booming, and Trudy knew he'd gotten off easy, but all she'd cared about was her freedom.

102

She stood in their front yard the day they moved in and gazed around their new neighborhood. It was basically a desert with one and two bedroom houses sprinkled here and there among cacti, greasewood, weeds, and dry, barren earth. The hot sun beat down on everything, just as she'd remembered.

But once the monsoons start, it'll smell wonderful.

Arizona was nothing like the home she'd known and loved as a child, but it was the home where she'd come of age. Phoenix held her memories of both hard lessons learned and the incredible joy of becoming a mother. Trudy still missed the Tahlequah forests, and she told herself that she would see them again one day. She closed her eyes and imagined the breeze as she had swung through green oak branches on a possum grape vine.

We'll go back for a visit. After we're settled. I have to see Papa again before it's too late.

But the past had taught her nothing if not to live in the present. Some houses, like theirs, had deep green oleander hedges at the sides and back. There were few trees within sight except a handful of palo verdes. She'd learned that name and its meaning, years before. She smirked at them with good-natured skepticism.

Green sticks, not really trees. But pretty in a way.

She looked around to find her boys. They were picking up small stones from the dirt road and flinging them to bump along the ruts. Then they argued about whose had gone the farthest. Karl bent over at the side of the house, inspecting a water faucet. He looked up and smiled at her.

This is my home now. Our home.

Chapter Seventeen

On the Sunny Side of the Street

Karl found a delivery job at the nearby Mission Dairy. His new job was pretty much identical to the old, except he now delivered bottles of milk instead of blocks of ice. Trudy got up in the wee hours of the morning to fix him breakfast and kiss him goodbye before he left for the dairy. She couldn't let him go without saying goodbye. He always kissed her first thing when he returned.

Trudy enrolled the boys in the neighborhood elementary school. Willie asked if he and his brother could walk the half mile along the Arizona Canal to the schoolyard alone. Trudy figured he was old enough now to be embarrassed by his mother's hovering, so she gave her permission. Then one afternoon Bobby arrived home soaked to the skin.

"Honey, what happened? How'd you get wet? Where's your brother?" Panic flooded Trudy.

"Willie wanted to stay later to try out for the baseball team. I didn't wanna wait. You know I know how to walk home by myself, Mama," he said, wiping his dripping curls back off his forehead. "But when I was 'bout halfway, some older guys come by on their bicycles. They was talking, and laughing, and looking at me. Then, they stopped, just dropped their bikes, and grabbed me. One grabbed my hands and 'nother one grabbed my ankles, and they swung me back and forth.

"I tried to fight, Mama, but it weren't no use. They was too big. I did hit one in the eye pretty good before they grabbed my hands. When I got high enough, they let me fly into the canal."

"But, baby, you don't know how to swim! That canal is deep, and there's a strong current! Did they pull you out?" Trudy caught his face between her hands and stared intently into his eyes. He twisted away, obviously embarrassed by her concern.

"Naw, they rode off. I got out by myself. When I hit bottom, I got my feet under me and jumped hard as I could. I breathed when my head come up out of the water, and then held my nose when I went down. Next time I jumped, I seen where the edge was, so I jumped toward it. The current kept pushing me sideways, so it took a while, but I made it. There's grass on the bank so I climbed out easy. Got kinda muddy, though." He brushed at a streak of mud on his shirt. Trudy listened in horror, stricken by how vulnerable motherhood made her.

I could have lost you! How can a mother ever recover from that?

That evening she made both boys promise they would stay together as they walked to and from school. If Willie stayed to play ball, Bobby would stay also. She made them swear.

***

Every Saturday morning, Trudy made her sons write letters to their father, although he seldom bothered to answer. After they finished this task the Saturday following Bobby's misadventure, Karl took them both to the canal and taught Bobby to swim.

Trudy sat on the sidelines and watched as her husband and younger son walked out into the canal. When the water came up to Bobby's shoulders, his stepfather turned to face him. Slipping his hands under Bobby's armpits, he pulled him into deeper water.

"Now when I let go, I'm going to step back. Just a little ways. You'll go under. Jump up with your feet, like you did before, then kick and pull with your arms like I showed you. I'll be right here. You'll be fine."

Bobby *was* fine. He caught on quickly, and by the time the lesson was over he was laughing and talking with Karl. Trudy watched, smiling herself, as her husband encouraged her son.

He'll be a father to them if they just give him a chance.

As they returned to the bank, Karl ruffled Bobby's hair. The boy looked up at him and smiled. Willie paddled around at a distance from Karl and his brother. Joe had taught him to swim before his drinking had begun. When he saw the others climbing out, Willie turned and swam back. He scrambled out and sat down next to his mother.

***

Karl had been in the backyard trimming the oleanders since right after lunch. Bobby and Willie were at Saturday baseball practice, Bobby tagging along even though he wasn't on the team. But they would arrive home any minute. Trudy couldn't wait any longer.

"Honey, could you come inside? The boys'll be getting home soon, and there's something I want to tell you."

"Can't you just tell me, Trudy? I've only got a little of this left. I'd like to finish up before I come in the house, so I can take a shower." He held the shears in one hand, and wiped sweat off his brow with his free arm.

"I could ... but I think maybe you better be sitting down." She couldn't hold back her grin.

Karl dropped the hedge trimmers and stared at her. "Are you saying ...?"

Trudy could only smile wider and nod her head, as tears filled her eyes. Karl ran to her, lifted her into his arms and twirled her around. "Be careful! I'll throw up on you!" Pure joy rang in her laughter.

After a year and a half of hoping, Trudy was finally pregnant. She'd expected to either conceive right away, as she had with Joe, or not at all. After all, she was almost thirty-two, a little old to have a baby. But then she remembered that Mama had been ten years older when baby David was born.

Unfortunately, she also remembered an Oklahoma neighbor in her late thirties who had given birth to a retarded child. But this would be Karl's first and possibly only child and would complete their family. So she tried to put aside her worry and let herself be happy. As her pregnancy progressed that became easier.

***

The night she went into labor, Karl drove her to the Good Samaritan hospital, a few blocks from where she and Joe had lived in their first rental home. As they drove through the area, familiar buildings, including the neighborhood Piggly-Wiggly where she had shopped, loomed unchanged. Between contractions, Trudy was filled with an eerie sense of deja vú.

I wonder what ever happened to Winnie Ruth?

After Willie's birth at home and Bobby's in a tent, she had been doubtful about a hospital birth, but Karl had insisted. He and his brothers and sisters had all been born in hospitals. So Trudy put herself in the hands of nurses and a physician. They handled everything, including administering anesthetics.

The medication not only took away her pain, but also left her with only foggy memories of the birth itself. She felt a strange sense of loss. It also worried her when they took her long-awaited daughter away to a nursery and told her they would bring Molly to her every three hours or so for feeding.

"She'll want to nurse more often than that!"

The nurse smiled, and spoke as if she were talking to a whining child. "That's all she needs. You don't want to spoil her, now, do you?"

They allowed Karl in to see Trudy just before the first feeding. The nurse brought in Molly and fetched a vase for the bouquet of yellow roses he'd brought. As soon as they were alone, her husband leaned forward to kiss her furrowed brow. "Why are you frowning? Is something wrong?"

"Why can't they just leave her with me? If they think she's not safe in my bed, they could put a bassinet right next to me. Then, if she cried, I could nurse her."

Karl smiled and ruffled her hair. "Worry wart! She's fine in the nursery. They're professionals. They know what they're doing. This way you can get some rest. If she needs feeding, they'll give her formula." Trudy knew she would find no support there.

Professionals! How many babies have they raised? Mama was a professional.

At last, four days later, a nurse wheeled her out to the curb with Molly cuddled in her arms. Karl walked beside her, carrying the wilting roses he'd brought to her room on his first visit. At the car, the nurse handed her formula samples and pamphlets on bottle-feeding. She took them to be polite.

My breasts still work fine and I'm not gonna be leaving her.

***

Trudy threw the Nestle samples away as soon as they got home, then sat down on the couch in the living room with Molly and introduced her to her brothers. Bobby sat next to her, stroking Molly's tiny fingers with his own, a grin on his face. Willie stood in front of her.

"Can I hold her, Ma?" Bobby held his arms poised over his sister. Trudy pushed him back.

"You can hold her, but you can't pick her up yet. Scoot back." Bobby did as he'd been told, and Trudy turned to place Molly in his arms.

"She's so little. Was I that little, Ma?"

"Not quite, but almost." Trudy remembered his little prune face. "Do you want a turn, Will?" Willie nodded and sat down on her other side as Karl watched, smiling, from across the room.

Trudy wanted to keep the baby near her, but was uncertain about bringing her into bed as she'd done with her sons. Karl had been raised differently than she and Joe. He was a city boy. She doubted that city people slept with their babies.

That night, Trudy lay Molly on their bed then removed the clothing from the deep middle drawer of their bedroom dresser and stacked it on a shelf in the closet. She opened the drawer halfway. It remained stable.

Good. If I had to put it on the floor, spiders might climb in. Daddy-Long-Legs are everywhere!

With a pillow and baby blankets, she prepared a tiny bed then tucked Molly inside. Her daughter began to wail. Trudy lifted her out, nursed her, burped her, and, swaying side-to-side, rocked her to sleep. She put her back in the drawer. Molly wailed. Trudy tried once more, gave up, and got into bed, tucking the child in beside her. Molly thrust her face against Trudy's breast and fell asleep at once.

Karl entered the bedroom. He leaned over to kiss his wife's forehead, then, without comment, climbed into bed on the opposite side and draped his arm over his wife and sleeping infant. A wave of pure contentment carried Trudy into sleep.

***

Trudy stood in the backyard with Bobby. She held Molly, the infant's head bumping against the top of her shoulder. Karl was at work, and Willie hadn't yet come home. Bobby put his hands around his sister's waist, and Trudy released her to him.

Bobby and Willie had found Molly to be a source of entertainment since she'd begun to hold her little bald head erect. Now Bobby placed her on his shoulders, grasped her tiny wrists in one hand, and tucked her feet under his armpits as her small body curled forward. Her chin rested on the top of his head. "Look, Mama!" Grasping one wrist in each hand and gripping her feet with his armpits, he began to trot around the backyard with his baby sister.

Trudy watched. "Be careful!" Molly's small head wobbled in time to Bobby's steps. At first Trudy had worried, but she'd gotten used to seeing this by now. Bobby paused near the oleander hedge, and, after a couple of minutes, returned and handed Trudy the perfectly placid baby, with pink oleander flowers tucked behind her ears.

Chapter Eighteen

Come Rain or Come Shine

As they slipped into adolescence, Bobby and Willie sometimes reminded Trudy of young Billy goats, constantly spoiling for a fight. She hadn't had brothers so close in age, but she knew boys were more competitive than girls, so maybe rivalry between male siblings was natural. But if her sons ever had to face a common enemy, she knew they would be united. That was the meaning of *family*. So she didn't consider their combativeness to be serious.

After watching them quarrel one afternoon, Karl went to a sporting goods store. That evening, hours after their dispute had ended, he surprised the boys with boxing gloves. They grinned and put the gloves on. They boxed a couple of rounds with Karl's coaching.

Trudy could see they liked the competition. "What a good idea, honey!" She linked her arm around her husband's and smiled up at him. "Maybe they can let off some steam this way."

The next afternoon when Bobby's bike had a flat tire, he borrowed Willie's bike to deliver newspapers to customers along his new paper route without asking his brother's permission. When he returned the boys began to argue. Karl brought out the gloves. Trudy stood in the backyard watching, her nose itching from the pungent odor of the blossoming oleanders.

"Put them on, boys." He handed a pair to each of them. Frowning, they did so, watching Karl.

Are you sure this is a good time, Karl?

"Go on, Will. Punch him. Get it out of your system. You hit him, Bob. You'll both feel better." He circled them like a referee at a boxing match. Both boys stood in silence, gloved hands at their sides, and glared at Karl. After a few moments of silence, shoulders slumped, Karl returned to the house. Trudy heard the screen door slam behind him.

The boys dropped their gloves on the ground and walked over to their bikes. Willie went into the house and came back with a repair kit as Bobby removed his punctured tire. Together they began to repair Bobby's flat. Trudy walked over to them. "Karl was just trying to help. You could've humored him." She picked up the gloves and dusted them off.

"If I'd wanted to punch Bobby, I wouldn't have stopped to put on those stupid gloves. Karl needs to mind his own business. That was between me and Bobby."

***

The following afternoon, Trudy stood next to the kitchen counter peeling apples. The front door slammed, and she looked up as Karl strode through the kitchen doorway. He stalked across the room without speaking, threw open the back door, and stepped off the tiny concrete porch into the backyard.

Trudy glanced at the delicate gold watch he'd given her for their second anniversary. He was more than two hours early, and he'd never failed to greet her before. Dropping the apple into a bowl of water with the others, she followed him outside. The dry spring heat engulfed her.

"You're early, honey. Is something wrong?" The unfiltered sun made her squint, and a moment from her years with Joe flashed in her memory.

Oh, no. Something's wrong at work!

"Well, I guess I won't have to get up early tomorrow." Karl glared down at a red ant. It was struggling to move a desiccated grasshopper. He lifted his foot and stomped on it.

"What happened?" She was afraid she already knew, but couldn't believe it without his confirmation.

"I tried to tell Larry a better way to set up the routes, and for some reason he decided to take offense." He glanced at her then looked away. "He wouldn't even listen. Told me it wasn't my business. I'm the one that knows this damn town like the back of my hand. He's the one that sits on his fat ass in his office, answering the phone. Besides, he's not too bright." He glanced up and away again. "The owner would be better off if I was in charge. I guess I told Larry that. Anyway, he let me go. You have to be careful, Trudy. People that know less than you do, or know that you're smarter than they are, are always out to get you. Don't worry, I'll find another job. A better job. Where people respect me." He frowned and clenched his jaw.

Trudy knew he expected a response, but she couldn't think of a thing to say. She'd never heard him talk this way before. For an instant the years slipped away, and she was back with Joe. She shook the feeling off. Karl was nothing like Joe. That just wasn't possible.

Still stunned, she returned to the kitchen and began to slice the apples into the bottom pie crust. When Karl didn't follow her inside, she sprinkled the apples with sugar, spices, lemon juice, and butter and attached the top crust. Then, after pricking the crust, she slid the pie pan into the oven and walked over to the door. Peering through the window, she saw Karl pushing the lawn mower back and forth over the sparse Bermuda grass patches. That was the boys' job, but they'd neglected it lately.

The boys! After that thing yesterday there's already tension between them and Karl. This won't help.

She replayed the scene with Karl, remembering how he'd smashed the ant. The front door slammed. Bobby was home from school. She hurried to catch him before he went to his room. "Hi, kiddo. How was your day?"

"Okay, I guess. It was school." He grinned, teasing her, then started to step around her.

"Wait. I need to talk to you about something." He stood waiting. "For one thing, how come you don't have any books? Don't you have homework?"

"Aw, Ma." He evaded her eyes. "Just a little 'rithmetic. I can do it in the morning before the bell rings." He sat down on the couch and looked at her.

She came over and sat beside him. "Karl's in kind of a bad mood, Bobby. He lost his job. Just leave him be for a while, okay?" Bobby's mouth twisted as if he'd smelled something disgusting. "Look, after the way you guys treated him yesterday, just give him some peace, huh?" Trudy frowned and stared at him until his mouth relaxed, and he lowered his eyes. Then she had an idea. "I need to talk to both of you in private when Will gets home. Tell him for me, okay? Not about Karl. Something else."

"Okay, Ma. I'll tell him."

Molly wandered into the living room, her face flushed from sleep. Bobby scooped her up onto his lap and started to tickle her. Molly pushed at his hands. She looked as if she were about to cry. Trudy lifted her away from her brother. "She just woke up, big brother. She's not ready for that." She carried the toddler back to the kitchen.

***

Willie got home as Trudy was finishing frying chicken for supper that evening. By the time she'd put the food on the table, he and Bobby were seated, ready to eat. Bobby played peek-a-boo with Molly who giggled in her high chair next to him. Karl came in from the living room and sat down, and they began dishing up their food. Trudy added shredded chicken and broccoli to Molly's tray, sat down, and began to prepare her own plate.

After several minutes of silent chewing, Karl spoke. "I lost my job today, boys. I'll get another one soon, but 'til I do, I won't be able to give you your allowance, Bobby. I'm sorry." His smile contradicted his words.

"That's okay," Willie said. "I got some money from my job. I can give some to Bobby." Chin up, he challenged his stepfather with his eyes.

Trudy got up abruptly. "Would anyone like some apple pie? Karl?" She leaned in front of him and blocked his view of his stepson.

"No, thanks," he said. He got up and headed for the living room. "I'll be checking want ads. By the way, I mowed the backyard today. I guess you boys forgot."

Trudy gave Willie a stern look. "You two stay here. I want to talk to you."

"Yeah, Bobby told me. Can we get some of that pie first?" Willie slumped in his seat and watched her.

She dished up thick slices of apple pie for each of them, then sat down. "It's been three years since you saw your dad. I know he's finally started writing you more than once a month. What's going on with him?"

The boys exchanged glances. "Well, he's gonna have a baby. Or Patti is." Willie grinned.

"A baby? I didn't know he got married."

I hope. He's a bad enough example as it is.

"Yeah, a few months ago. Guess we didn't tell you. Didn't think you'd be interested." Willie looked at her, a question in his eyes. She had a question, too, but he wouldn't know the answer.

Is it that woman with the cherry lipstick?

"Sounds like things are going good with the business, too. He had to hire more workers," Bobby said. They sat in silence for a couple of moments.

"Has he ever mentioned you guys coming to see him?" Trudy knew asking was a risk. She didn't want to see their hurt if he was still indifferent.

But if they could get away until Karl finds a job ... and it would give everybody a chance to cool off.

The boys exchanged glances again. "As a matter of fact, he did. He was thinking maybe this summer, after school is out. I told him that don't matter to me, since I don't go to school anymore, but Bobby graduates this year."

"It don't matter none to me, neither. I ain't going to high school, so I don't need no dumb eighth grade diploma." Bobby looked at his mother. Defiance shone in his dark eyes.

Trudy shook her head. "Why won't you even consider high school? You could get a better job." If she tried to push him it would backfire as it had with Willie. Mama had forced her to quit school, but she couldn't force her sons to continue. It was another of life's many ironies.

"Dad didn't even finish grade school, and he makes more money than Karl ever will," Willie said. "I do pretty good, too. Just wait 'til I turn sixteen."

Trudy knew her older son did do well for a fifteen-year-old. Tall and muscular, he could always find under-the-table work by just showing up at construction sites. He'd hung sheetrock since he'd been dropped from high school the previous fall for ditching.

Maybe their contempt for learning makes this easier.

"Do you think your father might want to come get you now? Maybe you could stay for a month or two. Give Karl time to find a job." Her voice trailed off. She hated the thought of being without them, even for a week. But she could see the excitement in their eyes.

"We can write him. Find out." Bobby crammed the last piece of pie crust into his mouth, and he and Willie rushed out of the kitchen. The next morning Trudy found a letter in a sealed envelope addressed to Joe on the kitchen table. She put a stamp on it and stuck it in the mailbox.

***

Joe's letter telling them he was coming and approximately when he'd be there arrived four days later. He pulled up in front of the house the following afternoon and honked the horn. The boys raced to get their suitcases.

Trudy walked out to the car. She wanted to see him, to get an impression. She'd decided to cancel the trip if she caught even a whiff of alcohol. Karl was in the house. He'd back her up, and she knew Joe wouldn't challenge him after their last encounter.

"Hello, Joe." She stood beside the car with Molly on her hip. He sat with his elbow on the frame of the open window. Trudy could see his scalp through thinning hair and a pattern of fine red veins criss-crossed his blunt nose. He looked older but perfectly sober. She caught the scent of a spicy aftershave, nothing else. His fingers strummed the roof of the car. It was a brand new Ford.

She didn't begrudge him his success. She was glad he'd gotten what he wanted. She had no urge to share it. Seeing him brought everything back, and she smiled more in relief that it was over than at him.

"Hello, Trudy. I'm glad you come out. I wanted to give you this." He handed her a slip of paper with a phone number on it. "We got a phone now, so if you need to reach me, 'bout the boys."

'Bout the boys. Do you seriously think I'd call you for any other reason?

"They should be out in a minute. They're almost ready. They're excited about the visit." Trudy smiled again, deciding to let bygones be bygones. Joe was her sons' father, and it was clear they would never let Karl fill that role.

Joe nodded then stared past her. He obviously didn't want to chat with her, and that was fine with Trudy. She turned to leave, then stepped back to wait as the boys bounded out of the house. Joe greeted them then handed Will the car keys. They stuffed their suitcases into the trunk, returned the keys to their father, and turned to their mother and sister.

"Bye, Mama," Willie said, putting his arms around her and Molly, and kissing both their cheeks. "Tell Karl bye."

Bobby hugged both of them, too, then bent to look into his sister's face. "You be good, you little brat! Don't you forget your brothers."

God, you won't be gone that long. No more than a month or so at most. She won't forget.

Both boys climbed into the back seat. Joe had the car running, and pulled away as soon as the back door slammed. Her sons continued to wave until the car turned the corner and disappeared from sight. Tears blurred Trudy's vision. She turned and walked back to the house.

Chapter Nineteen

Thanks for The Memories

Trudy missed her boys and worried about finances while Karl sought a new job. One night a week after her sons had left, she couldn't sleep. When she did fall into a light slumber, a nightmare woke her. She'd dreamed about Bobby. Something had happened to him, but she couldn't remember the details of the dream. Tossing and turning, she tried without success to shake off the feeling and go back to sleep. As soon as it was light out, she drove to a payphone and called her ex-husband. Joe's new wife answered the phone, and Trudy identified herself.

"Hi, Trudy. I'm glad you called. I'm Patti, but you need to talk to your son." There was a pause then Trudy heard Willie's voice.

"How'd you know, Ma? You couldn't have gotten the letter yet. I don't think the mailman's even picked it up."

"What letter? What's happened to Bobby?" Her older son didn't sound upset. A wave of relief swept through her, but the hand holding the phone still trembled.

"His arm's broke, but the doctor put a cast on it. He'll be okay." Willie almost sounded amused.

"When? What happened?"

"We was down at the truck yard with Dad yesterday. He was showing me some new equipment he'd bought, and Bobby was watching a guy load lumber onto one of the trucks. Guess the guy aimed too low or something. Anyway, the forklift knocked the load off balance. Most of it fell off the truck and knocked Bobby down. A couple of four by sixes landed on his arm right below his elbow. He's a little bruised and scrapped up on that side, but most of them four-by-sixes missed him. Good thing. If he'd been a little closer and they'd hit his head—" He chuckled. "—he might be even dumber than he is now. But he's all right."

"Oh, God!"

"Wanna talk to him?"

Of course she did. When Bobby came on the line he sounded almost proud. "Hi, Mama. I got a big plaster cast. Me and Willie drew some pictures on it. Pa wrote you last night, but the letter's still in the mailbox, and you ain't got a phone. He said he'd've sent a telegram, but it wadn't that bad. How'd you know?"

Trudy couldn't explain, but she had known. She recalled when he'd almost drowned.

He draws trouble like a trailer court draws tornadoes. And I'm not around to watch out for him.

***

To fill her days and distract her from the uncertainty of their future, Trudy focused on Molly. The toddler was an easy child. Serious but pliable, Molly didn't protest when Trudy dressed her in frilly, pink dresses. She would sit quietly for long periods while her mother fussed over her wispy blonde hair. Trudy tied ribbons and clasped barrettes that would slip out almost immediately.

After three weeks of scouring want ads, Karl found another job. This time he was driving for a local bakery. Relieved but cautious, Trudy decided to wait until after he'd received a couple of paychecks to bring the boys home. According to their letters, things were fine at their father's.

The Saturday morning after his first payday at the new job, Karl took Trudy and Molly out to breakfast at MacAlpine's. As they waited for their food to arrive, he spread a copy of the real estate section of the Arizona Republic on the table and tapped an ad. "Trudy, this house is just down the street from us. Do you see what they're asking for it? They'll probably get it, too. Places around here are selling like hotcakes." He grinned at the waitress who had arrived with their waffles then picked up the newspaper, folded it, and put it in his lap.

"Are you saying you want to move, Karl?" Trudy wasn't sure what to expect, but hoped that wasn't true. Their lives were unsettled enough already.

"No, Trudy." He looked at her as if she were a foolish child. It was a look he'd been giving her more and more lately. It was starting to make her uneasy. "What I'm saying is that house prices are going up, and smart people are investing in real estate. One of my bakery customers is a realtor, and I've been talking to him about doing it. We could buy a house, or maybe a couple of houses, rent them for a while, then sell them when the price is right."

"But, Karl, we don't have enough savings to do that. We used up a lot when you weren't working." Trudy looked at her second husband and thought about her first. Making money had never seemed that important to Karl. Had she been wrong?

"I know that, Trudy." He smirked at her, and her unease increased. "But we could get a mortgage on our house. This guy said it's gone up in value since we bought it. We could get money out for a down payment on another one, and rent it. Then, when we can make a profit, we could sell it, and get another. It could snowball. Lots of shrewd millionaires got started in real estate. So could we."

"But, Karl, if something happened, and we couldn't make payments on the mortgage we might lose our home!" Thoughts of living in the tent flooded Trudy's memory.

"I guess I thought you were willing to take some risks, Trudy. Don't you trust me?" He looked at her for a moment, then picked up his fork and concentrated on his food. They ate in silence for a few minutes.

Suddenly Trudy felt ashamed. She remembered their conversations when he delivered her ice. He'd inspired her with his sense of adventure. Maybe that's what this was about, not money. She didn't want to be a wet blanket. "I guess I was just thinking about Molly, but if you think it's the right thing to do, of course I trust you." She swallowed her doubts along with her breakfast, chasing them with a long swig of coffee.

A week later Karl mortgaged their home with the help of the realtor he'd talked with. He invested part of the proceeds in a small rental, also with a mortgage. Trudy insisted on saving the remainder. Then, just when she was going to contact Joe about bringing the boys back, Karl lost his new job. A customer had complained about rude behavior. Trudy wrote to her sons and asked if it was all right for them to stay a little longer with their father. She walked out to the road, stuck the letter in the mailbox, and stood for a moment in the hot sun wiping her eyes.

Dear God, what is happening to Karl?

Her husband was becoming more and more of a stranger to her. When she asked him about the incident that had cost him his job, he looked at her with a flash of contempt. "Are you implying it was my fault, Trudy? I'd expect you to know better than that." He stepped into the backyard, and she didn't follow. A few moments later, when she looked through the window, he appeared to be talking and gesturing to himself.

Karl's next job took longer to find and paid less. Fortunately they'd managed to install a renter in the new house. The rent payment was slightly more than the cost of the mortgage payments on their home. They used the income to make those payments, but struggled to make the ones on the rental without dipping into their savings. Trudy tried desperately to avoid that. Then Karl lost his most recent job, for a total of three jobs in less than six months.

During the years since their marriage Trudy had tucked away most of Joe's child support payments in a savings account for the boys, thinking her sons might need the money someday. She also had the funds she'd stashed away from their mortgage proceeds. And they received money from the rental. But as months slipped away, so did their savings. Karl spent less and less time searching for a job each day. Trudy didn't question him because recently he had begun to talk to her about God in a way that was not really reverent, but rather strangely personal.

She'd been finishing the breakfast dishes one morning when he stepped up behind her. Startled, she almost dropped the cup she was drying. "Trudy," he said, "do you know God hears everything we say? He even knows what we're thinking. I'm sure your father told you that. God told me you thought it was my fault I lost those jobs." He stared at her through narrowed eyes. "Those people were stupid. They were out to get me because they could see that I'm more intelligent than they are. The Lord knows that, and He said you should know it, too. I *did* tell you."

She was still struggling for a response when the suspicion slipped from his face.

"Say, honey, have you seen my screwdriver? The wheel on the lawnmower's a little loose. I need to tighten it before I mow." He smiled, his eyes crinkling in the way that was so familiar, but that now only added to her growing unease.

***

Four months after Karl had received his final paycheck, Trudy sat at the kitchen table completing a money order for the last mortgage payment that she would be able to make on the house that had been their home. Joe had stopped his support payments as soon as the boys had gone to live with him, and since Trudy and Karl were no longer paying the mortgage on the rental, they'd just received a foreclosure notice on that property.

Desperate, she considered looking for a job, but she had no real marketable skills, and working would have meant leaving Molly with Karl. The mere thought frightened her. She kept remembering her husband's time in the army hospital and his discharge.

Did that mule do some permanent damage to his brain?

Then, in the midst of their troubles, Trudy discovered she was pregnant again. She had no choice but to turn to Karl's family for help. Right after their marriage, Karl had told his family about Trudy in letters. Frieda, his sister, wrote back directly to her new sister-in-law and welcomed Trudy and her two sons into their family. Trudy responded, and the two began exchanging occasional letters. Frieda lived in Big Spring, Texas. Now Trudy wrote Frieda detailing their situation as best she could and pleading for help to convince Karl to return to Texas.

A few days later, Trudy found a letter to Karl from Frieda in their mailbox. She looked at it doubtfully, hoping her sister-in-law hadn't given her away. She was tempted to steam it open as characters in the mysteries she read did, but instead carried it into the living room where

Karl sat skimming the want ads. "You've got a letter, Karl. It's from Frieda."

Karl opened the letter, scanned it, then handed it to Trudy. Frieda had given no indication in her letter that she'd heard from Trudy. Their father's health was failing, she wrote. They needed Karl. Could he and Trudy please come to Texas to visit?

"If your father's ill, we have to go, Karl." Trudy held her breath.

"Of course we do." He looked at her impatiently. "Do you think you have to tell me that?"

"No, Karl, I just meant that I understood you'd want to be there for your family."

He took the letter from her hand and stuffed it back into the envelope. Folding the envelope twice, he reached into his pocket for his wallet and tucked the letter inside. "I'll keep her address handy, so I can find her house. I haven't been there since they first discharged me from the army. That's been a few years." He stared into space for a moment. "Where's the tablet? I need to write her we're coming."

They began to plan for the trip. Trudy easily persuaded Karl to sell the house. They couldn't keep paying the mortgage anyway, and they needed money. Home values in Sunnyslope had gone up, and they sold it in less than two weeks for a couple of thousand more than the mortgage. Trudy reflected that Karl had been right. Under different circumstances, there *was* money to be made in real estate. They sold the furnishings as well, though they didn't bring in much additional cash. With their future so uncertain, Trudy wanted to carry as few belongings into it as possible.

Before leaving, Trudy walked around the small backyard with Molly, picturing her boys as they'd trotted around with their baby sister back when times were good, and she'd known happiness for the first time in many long, hard years. She struggled with limited success to focus on those memories as fear of what the future might hold threatened to overwhelm her.

She picked a final pink oleander blossom and put it behind Molly's ear. Then she stepped a few feet away from her toddler, and, fighting back tears, she snapped Molly's picture with their Kodak. Blinking in the bright sunlight, her daughter reached one small arm out toward Trudy just as the shutter clicked.

Chapter Twenty

Fools Rush In Where Angels Fear To Tread

Karl placed their suitcases in the trunk and got into the Chevy on the driver's side the next morning. Trudy wracked her brain for a way to convince him that she should drive but could think of nothing. Taking a deep breath, she climbed in on the passenger's side and lifted Molly onto her lap.

They stopped in Globe before noon for a bathroom break and gas. Minutes later, on the highway east of the town, Karl's eyes shifted to the rear view mirror and excitement lit his face. "Trudy, look in the backseat!" He swiveled around and pointed. "My guardian angel is traveling with us!" He tilted his head. A look of concentration furrowed his brow. "Wait!" He put the palm of his right hand against the side of Trudy's head and blocked her instinct to turn.

"He says he doesn't want anybody but me to look at him. He's brought me a message from the Lord. It's private. You're not supposed to hear it, so he's speaking into my mind." He gazed at her with a suspicious look that was becoming too familiar.

Trudy froze, Molly asleep in her lap. She watched the car veer, first toward the verge, then, over-corrected, across the edge of the opposite lane toward oncoming traffic and the cliff beyond. She saw no other cars. Her left hand moved to the steering wheel and stabilized it.

I have to get him off the road before he kills us!

"Well, honey, if he has a message for you from God, don't you think it would be more respectful to give him your full attention. We can pull over. You can get in back with him. I can drive for a while." Trudy fought to keep her voice calm as she kept her eyes on the road and the steering wheel under her control.

Karl looked at her. He frowned. "I'm always respectful of God and His angels. You're the irreverent one, Trudy." Then his face changed, and he turned toward the back seat again. "That's a good idea! Honey, let's pull over. I want to be able to concentrate on what he says. My angel thinks it's a good idea, too. Yes, she was." He stared into the back seat and nodded his head in agreement. "He says I should tell you you were wise to suggest it. But please don't look at him!"

Trudy wouldn't have dreamed of doing so, but the hairs on the back of her neck stood on end, and she had an almost irresistible urge to turn around. With Trudy's hands still on the wheel, they pulled off the road. Karl set the brake, got out, and climbed into the back seat. Trudy eased Molly off her lap and onto the seat as she scooted across to the driver's side. Molly slept through it all.

***

Whenever Trudy looked into the rear view mirror the remainder of that afternoon, Karl appeared to be engrossed in a silent conversation. He gestured, frowned, nodded, and stared, but never uttered a word aloud. Apparently he and the angel communicated by telepathy. Trudy was purely grateful.

When she glanced back and Karl appeared to be asleep, she pulled off the road, climbed out of the car, and circled to the passenger's side. She roused Molly and lifted her out, then carried her daughter behind some bushes. After they had relieved themselves, they returned to the car. Trudy gave Molly a peanut butter sandwich and cautioned her to be quiet. "Daddy's sleeping. He needs his rest."

"Okay." Trudy retrieved Molly's crayons and coloring book from under the passenger seat and lifted the toddler into the car. She climbed in herself and continued the trip. She stopped at a diner late that night long enough to refill her empty coffee thermos. She left Molly sleeping in the car with Karl, but took the keys. She knew she'd had too much caffeine already.

But, God knows, I need to be alert.

She smothered a hysterical impulse to giggle. She had to hold herself together, for Molly's sake and for Karl. It occurred to her that she was retracing the route she had traveled with Joe a lifetime ago. She was glad it was too dark to see the interminable plains of eastern New Mexico drift past. She didn't need that desolate view in her current state of mind.

Karl woke at dawn, as they crossed the border into Texas. "Trudy, pull over and let me drive." He sounded rational, though subdued. "Did you stop to sleep at all?"

"No, honey, I just didn't feel sleepy," she said. That was true. She hadn't felt sleepy, couldn't have slept, in fact. But she was bone tired, in body and soul.

"Where are we?" Karl's eyes searched the landscape.

"We're about two hundred miles north of Big Spring. We should be at Frieda's by around noon, maybe before." She pulled over and parked the car.

Will Karl's angel say this is wise?

Molly stirred. Trudy picked her up and slid back to the passenger's side of the car. Karl pulled Frieda's letter out of his wallet to look at the address, then stuck it back in. The rest of the trip passed without incident. A little before noon, Karl parked the Chevy in front of his sister's house.

Frieda met them at the curb. A tall, stately woman with sandy hair mixed with gray, she had Karl's dark blue eyes. She greeted him with a long hug. Then she turned to Trudy. They'd never met and knew each other only through their letters.

Trudy saw an undercurrent of unspoken questions in her sister-in-law's eyes and knew her return gaze held only sadness and despair, no answers. Frieda hugged her and patted her back as Karl took their suitcases out of the trunk. Molly stood next to Trudy and held onto her mother's skirt with one hand until her aunt bent down to look her in the face.

"Why, Karl, she looks just like you in your baby pictures. That hair and those eyes!" She smiled, her own eyes crinkled like her brother's. She reached for Molly's hand. Molly put her hand inside her aunt's and followed Frieda into the house. Trudy came after. She looked over her shoulder to make sure Karl was there. He walked a short distance behind, a suitcase in each hand.

The house, bright with fresh paint, had a wide front lawn, garage, and a covered porch that extended the width of the front. Padded antique rockers sat on either side of the double-door entry, and potted palms and other plants graced the remainder of the porch. Despite her anxiety, Trudy could see that their stay wouldn't be a burden for Frieda and her husband. She felt relieved.

Karl dropped the suitcases on the carpet, and shook hands with Raymond, Frieda's husband, as they entered the living room. Raymond returned to his armchair, and Karl sat down on the sofa. Frieda picked up the suitcases as she introduced Trudy and Molly to her husband. Then she passed one to Trudy, took Molly's hand again, and led them down the hall to a guest room leaving the two men engaged in conversation.

Trudy wondered what Karl was saying. "I hope you warned Raymond about Karl, or he could be in for a shock," she said. Frieda glanced at her, but remained silent as she opened the bedroom door, and they stepped inside.

Then they put down the suitcases, and she turned to face Trudy. "So tell me, what's going on?"

Trudy glanced down at Molly who stood between the women and stared up at them. Frieda followed her look. "Just a minute," she said. She left the room and returned in a few moments with a small box of toys, and a black and white cat. "This is Bootsie," Frieda said, "and Bootsie, this is Molly." The toddler's eyes widened, and she reached out to touch the cat. It began to rub itself against her legs.

"These were my children's toys. When they were little. I know they'd be happy to share them with you." Frieda carried the toys to a corner of the room, trailed by Molly and the cat. Molly sat down on the floor and began to sort through the toy box.

Frieda returned to Trudy. Trudy lowered her voice and told her sister-in-law what had happened on the trip. Karl's sister listened, frowning. "He seemed fine just now," she said.

"Sometimes he is, then something sets him off. I never know when it'll happen, but it's getting to be more often." Trudy's voice began to crack, and she bit her lip. She struggled, determined not to cry in front of Molly.

Frieda looked at her, brow furrowed. "You need some rest. Molly, will you help me feed Bootsie? Let's bring your toys. We can play, or I have a coloring book. Do you like to color?" She walked over to stand beside her niece. Molly nodded. Frieda picked up the toy box and reached for Molly's hand. She paused at the door to call the cat. Bootsie meowed and raced out in front of them. Frieda closed the door.

Trudy collapsed across the bed and let go. She buried her face in a pillow to smother the moans of anguish she could no longer contain. She felt like she'd been struggling against the current forever. Now she was finally drowning.

It's too much. It took me so long to find you, Karl. If I lose you now, I'll just give up.

Then she heard Molly's laughter from the living room. Trudy missed her sons beyond measure, but at least they had their father. Molly had no one but her. She had to be strong for Molly.

She clung to that thought as sleep engulfed her.

***

Trudy stared around the room, disoriented. She ran her hand across the floral print bedspread beneath her, Frieda's bedspread. Everything came back. The house was quiet. She rolled to the edge of the bed and stood up. Emerging from the bedroom, she crossed the silent hall, and entered the living room. Molly ran to her and grabbed her around the knees. "Mommy!"

Trudy stumbled but recovered her balance. "Whoa!" She laughed and bent to swing her two-year old onto her hip.

"Careful." A frown of concern wrinkled Frieda's forehead. Trudy could see Karl sitting on the couch beyond. He held a coffee cup in his left hand. A newspaper lay across his lap.

"It's okay." She met Frieda's eyes and smiled to reassure her. She knew her pregnancy showed, but she wasn't yet far enough along for her to feel clumsy. "What time is it?"

"It's nearly four, but you needed the rest," Frieda said. Her eyes darted to Karl, then back to Trudy.

"Hi, sleepy head," Karl said. He set the coffee cup on the table next to him and picked up the newspaper. "I was reading Frieda this article 'bout Truman's speech yesterday. I know all about this." He tapped the paper with his forefinger.

"The communists are taking over this country. That's what my angel told me yesterday. They're printing secret messages to their *comrades* in our newspapers. My angel gave me the code. Of course, most damned reporters are already communists." He smirked with a condescending air of superiority that Trudy had learned to recognize and dread. She glanced at Frieda who stood staring at Karl.

"Truman can send money and troops to Greece and Turkey to try to stop it. He's a fighter. But it'll be too late unless we get people to see what's happening. I'm part of God's plan for that. My angel hasn't told me what I'm supposed to do yet, but He will anytime now."

"Honey, aren't you tired? Maybe you could use a little nap, too? It was a long trip and you've been under a lot of strain lately." Trudy set Molly down and watched her husband, hoping he would take her suggestion. He didn't seem to have heard.

Molly cocked her head to one side and stared at her father. "An angel talked to you, Daddy?" Her father didn't respond. He was buried in the newspaper again.

"Could you give me a hand with something in the kitchen, Trudy?" Frieda moved past her into the hallway.

"Sure. Be back in a minute, hon." She looked at Karl. The newspaper was lying on his knee. He picked up a pencil from the table and began to circle words. Raymond was nowhere in sight.

He probably went back to work. Lucky him.

Trudy reached for Molly's hand. She wanted her close by. In the kitchen, the two women held each other in silence for a moment until Molly pushed herself between them. Trudy released her sister-in-law and bent to pick up her daughter. "How long's he been like this?" She held Molly close and swayed back and forth.

"Most of the afternoon, Trudy. He's hallucinating. I'm pretty sure. Sometimes he stares into space and nods, or frowns and shakes his head like he's listening to something we can't hear. Sometimes he looks like he might be seeing something, too. And he keeps talking about *you know what*." She nodded toward the back of Molly's head.

"Yes. His messenger." An infinite despair nearly paralyzed Trudy. Molly wriggled in her arms, and Trudy set her down. The child ran over next to the refrigerator where Bootsie nibbled at something in a white china bowl.

"He's got to be seen by a psychiatrist." Frieda spoke firmly. "It's too late today, unless we go to the emergency ward. I'm not sure it's an emergency exactly. I'd rather not do that unless we have no choice."

Trudy had to sit down. She pulled out a tall wooden stool from the work island in the center of the kitchen and climbed onto it. "What if he tries to leave?"

Frieda looked down then raised her eyes to Trudy's. "Then I guess we'd have to call the police. If we can't talk him out of it. I'd rather do that than try to hold him by force, even if we could. I talked to him about going to see Dad in the morning, since that's supposed to be the reason I asked you all to come. Daddy really is getting a little frail, but I don't think Karl even remembered what I wrote.

"I'll tell Karl I want to introduce him to the people I work with, the doctors and other nurses. That'll give me an excuse to stop by my hospital on the way. I'll call ahead. They can arrange to have a psychiatrist there to evaluate him. I don't know if he'll be rational," she said and shook her head, "but, they have attendants who can subdue and sedate him if it's necessary."

Trudy hunched her shoulders and closed her eyes, fighting a wave of dizziness and nausea. She felt Frieda's hand touch her back.

"Trudy, I'm so sorry, but I just don't know what else to do. Something like this happened when he was in the army, too." Trudy opened her eyes and twisted to look at Frieda. Her sister-in-law didn't meet her gaze but looked away. "I'm sorry I never mentioned it, but we honestly thought it was all over."

Trudy brushed the air with one hand and straightened up. "You mean that thing with the mule and his discharge? He told me 'bout it a long time ago, before we got married. I thought it was just temporary. I don't blame you for thinking so, too."

"Well, we were worried for a while. If it was bad enough to warrant a discharge," Frieda's voice trailed off. "But it's been years." She turned away. "Maybe we better check on him." They returned to the living room, but no one was there. Molly dropped to the floor next to a coloring book and picked up a crayon. Frieda hurried down the hall, calling Karl's name.

Trudy discovered him in their room, again apparently engaged in a silent conversation with an invisible partner. He glared at her from the corner of his eye, like a dog protecting a bone. She shivered, turned, and left the room to give him and his angel privacy.

Back in the kitchen, Trudy heard the front door close, and Raymond called out from the hallway. "Where is everybody?" Frieda hurried down the hall and Trudy heard muted voices, then silence.

Well, I guess if you missed the drama before, you're learning 'bout it now.

That was painful in a way. For some reason, the more people who knew about Karl's condition, the more real it became.

***

Trudy and Frieda spent the early evening preparing dinner. They exchanged words solely as related to meal preparation, each ensconced in her own private thoughts. Trudy returned to the guest room to bring Karl a tray of food. She found him asleep. He'd undressed before climbing into bed. Neat, as always, he'd left his clothes hanging on a chair next to the wall.

Frieda and Raymond, who had reappeared for dinner, said goodnight and went to their room a little after nine. Trudy carried the toy box and then her sleepy little girl into their room. They got ready for bed. Karl did not stir when Trudy lifted his daughter and held her over him to kiss his cheek.

"Night-night, Daddy," Molly said. Trudy carried her over to the pallet that Frieda had prepared earlier. Half-awake, Molly murmured the prayer her mother had taught her. "Now I lay me down to sleep. I pray the Lord my soul to keep. If I should die before I wake. I pray the Lord my soul to take. Night-night, Mommy." She kissed her mother and yawned.

Trudy sat and rubbed Molly's back until the child fell asleep. Then, resigned to sleeplessness, she edged into bed beside Karl. She lay motionless for a while, listening to her husband's breathing. The sound was so familiar, so comforting. She managed to spoon herself against his back without waking him and placed her arm around his waist. She kissed the back of his neck and laid her cheek against it. He was safe beside her. She slept.

Chapter Twenty-one

That Old Black Magic

Trudy awoke early to a silent house. Eyes still closed, she reached out for Karl. Her fingers touched an empty mattress, and her eyes flew open. Karl and his clothes were gone. Pulling her gown over her head, she threw on the same underwear and dress she'd removed hours earlier. After glancing into the dark, empty living room and kitchen, she twisted open the front door's thumb deadbolt, opened the door, and peered outside. The Chevy was in the same spot where Karl had parked it the afternoon before.

At the other end of the hallway, the back door was locked with a keyed deadbolt. Raymond's study door stood open. Trudy stepped inside. A large, casement window revealed the backyard, vacant except for a willow tree, bushes, and wicker lawn furniture.

Back in the living room, she perched on the edge of a rocking chair. Her feet pushed against the floor with a will of their own, rocking her back and forth as she fought to calm herself.

Was the bathroom door closed?

She got up and rushed down the hall to the bathroom. She knocked then pushed against the door. It was ajar and swung open. No one. She came back through the living room to the door that must lead to the garage at the side of the house. Locked. She glanced up. Frieda, still in her bathrobe, stood in the hallway. Their eyes met. "Karl's gone."

"What happened?" The trace of sleepiness fled Frieda's eyes.

"I don't know when he left. I just woke up." Trudy ran her hand over her face. "I should have stayed awake."

"Are you sure he's not outside? Did you check?"

Trudy nodded. "I looked. Maybe he took a walk. He walks around the neighborhood at home." She bit her lower lip and tasted blood.

"Let me dress and get my keys. We'll drive around, see if we can spot him." Frieda started back toward her room.

Molly opened the guest room door and entered the hall, rubbing her eyes. Bootsie darted past Trudy, ran up to the child, and began to wrap herself around her legs. "Bootsie!" Molly collapsed to the floor, legs crossed. The cat climbed into her lap and thrust its head against her chin. She giggled.

Frieda returned, dressed in khaki pants and a yellow blouse. "Let's go."

Distracted as she was, Trudy registered the unusual attire. She'd only seen a few women in pants before. Frieda looked strong, competent. That was reassuring. Trudy scooped her daughter into her arms.

The doorbell rang as Frieda took out her key ring. She crossed to the front door and opened it as Trudy peered over her shoulder. Two police officers stood on the porch. Frieda collapsed against the door. Her hands clutched the knob from both sides.

"Excuse me, ma'am, we're looking for a Frieda Carson. This is the address we have." The shorter one held out an envelope addressed to Karl. He pointed to her return address in the corner. Frieda released the handle as Trudy yanked the door open and stepped around her onto the porch with Molly perched on her hip.

"Karl's my husband. What did he do? Is he under arrest?" The policemen exchanged glances.

"What's happened?" Frieda stepped forward to join Trudy on the porch, grasping her sister-in-law's elbow, steadying her. "Yes, I'm Frieda Carson. Karl's my brother." She placed her hand on Trudy's shoulder. "This is my brother's wife. What's happened? Is he hurt?"

"No, ma'am. But there's been an incident. May we come in?" Frieda moved back, and they entered.

***

Trudy stared at the card the policemen had given her. It had the number for Big Spring State Hospital written on the back.

After entering and checking Trudy's driver's license, the officers had told her that Karl had been taken to the hospital for observation. The police had been notified when a desk clerk at a hotel near the Big Spring business district had seen a man—Karl—grab a passerby by the arm. The gentleman tried to pull away as a crowd gathered.

"When officers arrived, your husband was behaving erratically. No one was injured, but, technically, your husband committed assault. The person involved is not pressing charges, but we are required to have this type of behavior evaluated to determine the subject's risk to himself or others." After an awkward pause, they handed her the card and left.

"We need something to eat. Then we'll decide what to do. A few minutes won't make any difference now," Frieda said and walked into the kitchen.

***

They sat at the kitchen island. Trudy stared at the toast and sunny-side-up eggs, then pushed the plate away and reached for a cup of black coffee. She felt its acidity churn in her stomach, and picked up her discarded toast. She managed to swallow a few bites before it caught in her throat. Gagging, she grabbed for a glass of orange juice, and, as she sipped, she began to sing softly. "I know an old lady who swallowed a fly."

Frieda stared at her wide-eyed. Molly looked up from her breakfast and grinned. "I don' know why she swallowed a fly," Molly sang back at her mother.

"Perhaps she'll die." They sang the line together, and Molly burst into giggles.

Poor Frieda. You have enough to contend with without this silliness.

Trudy wanted to hold onto the moment's reprieve, but felt it slip away. She picked up the cup of coffee again. Raymond appeared dressed for work and, after a quick conference in the hall with Frieda, ate a hasty breakfast, then left.

When the flash of humor, or whatever it had been, passed, it was replaced by an overwhelming depression. Frieda rose to gather up dishes. Trudy placed a hand on her arm and her sister-in-law paused. "I need to see Karl. I don't want to talk to some stranger on the phone. I need to see with my own eyes that he's all right." Trudy's face crumpled, and she struggled for control, glancing at Molly. The toddler was pushing a piece of bread crust through a puddle of egg yolk, oblivious to her mother's pain. "Well, I know he's not all right, but I have to see him, to see how they're treating him." Images of Bedlam flickered through her mind. She pushed them away.

"Are you sure you don't want me to come with you?" Frieda's concern lined her face.

Trudy shook her head. She looked at Molly, and tears rose in her eyes. "No, she's better off here with you. Can you stay with her? What about your work?"

"I called in. I'm taking a couple of days. I'll look up the address in the phone book and draw you a map. If you're sure you're all right to go alone?"

"I'm sure." She couldn't remember when she'd ever felt so alone. A memory of Mama on the railroad tracks surfaced, and Trudy remembered how her childhood self had longed for Papa's comfort.

Not even you could make this better, Papa. I have to face it myself.

***

The Big Spring State Hospital sprawled behind a manicured lawn and pristine, hedge-lined sidewalks. It looked even more dignified than Good

Samaritan, but Trudy regarded it with suspicion and drove by twice before getting up the nerve to pull into the parking lot beside the main building.

The red brick edifice with double rows of clean, white-trimmed windows had a gentrified look, but this appearance didn't reassure Trudy. She'd read several stories about loony bins. Inside, pathetic, howling freaks might be chained to the walls, rolling around in their own poop, or strapped to beds as surgeons removed random parts of their brains.

God only knows what they might do to Karl if I don't stop them.

The hysteria she had somehow tamped down almost bubbled up through the cracks in her precarious self-control. She could barely hear or think anything containing the word *God* in her present state without hearing echoes of Karl's rants. She sighed.

A portico with a row of white classical columns marked the entrance to the administration building. After Trudy identified herself and asked to see her husband, a white-coated attendant led her through a locked door and down a long, quiet corridor.

On one side at the end was a large window with what looked like chicken-wire embedded in the glass. Beyond, she could see Karl, his eyes closed, apparently asleep. Straps around his wrists secured them to the sides of the bed. A tube trailed from a bag suspended above the bed to the bend of his right arm.

"What is that they're putting in his arm? Are they drugging him?" In the hospital for Molly's birth, she'd floated away on the drugs. She'd been a helium balloon, tethered to reality by a slender thread. She almost felt that way now.

"I'm sorry, but I can't really discuss that with you. You can talk about it with the doctors. I'll take you to their office," the attendant said.

You're just a cog in this big machine.

She followed him back down the corridor, through the locked door, and into an office where she waited for the next half hour. The receptionist glanced at her from time to time then wound another form into her Remington and resumed typing. Finally she motioned Trudy into the inner office.

The two psychiatrists shook her hand and introduced themselves, then invited her to sit down on the narrow sofa across from the desks. The taller, balding man with heavy dark-rimmed glasses was Neumann. The older one with white hair was Levinson. After introductions, Dr. Neumann spoke.

"Your husband exhibits the symptoms of paranoid schizophrenia, Mrs. Krause." Trudy had never heard the term before. She looked from one to the other. Each leaned against a desk and stared back at her for a second before Dr. Neumann continued. "He is suffering from delusions. He believes God and angels speak to him. He also believes he has enemies who plot against him. That is the paranoia aspect. He has auditory and visual hallucinations." He peered at her above his glasses, raising his eyebrows. "He hears and sees things that aren't there."

This was nothing Trudy didn't already know. She disregarded Neumann's superior attitude, although she immediately disliked him. There were more important things on her mind. "So, he is insane?" It was difficult to put into words. It felt like it had been stuck in her throat for a long time.

Neumann regarded her without emotion. "Schizophrenia is regarded as a form of insanity, yes."

"The nurse took me to see him before he brought me here. I saw a needle in his arm. What are you giving him?" She regarded Neumann, expecting him to answer, but the older doctor spoke for the first time since he'd introduced himself.

"He was extremely agitated. He's been under sedation since shortly after he arrived, but we observed and spoke with him before it was administered. For our initial diagnosis. It will be discontinued after a few hours."

"What happens now? Can you help him? Will he get better?" She looked at one then the other, feeling her heart pound, wondering how much she could trust whatever they said.

Dr. Levinson leaned forward, reached out, and took her right hand in both of his. "I can't promise you, but I think we can. We have treatments that sometimes show remarkable results in these cases."

"Can he come home with me? I can bring him back for the treatments." She struggled to keep her voice unemotional. She didn't want her question to sound like a plea.

Dr. Levinson released her hand, stepped to the desk, picked up some papers, and turned to face her. "I'm afraid he must stay here a minimum of three days for observation. This is a legal requirement to determine if he is a risk to himself or others. Then, if it is decided that he is, the court will require a longer commitment."

Trudy stared into his eyes. She knew her fears were written in her face. He looked down at the papers in his hands. "But there is nothing to indicate that yet." Before Trudy could ask who would make that decision, Levinson continued. "In the meantime, we have temporary commitment papers we would like you to sign. These will allow us to begin treatment right away. This would be in your husband's best interests." He held Trudy's gaze. "I believe you know that what is wrong with Karl won't cure itself. Something must be done to help him."

Dear God, but what? Is this the right thing? Do I even have a choice?

"We also have some questions for you about the onset of your husband's symptoms, what you noticed and when."

"How much will this cost? We don't have much money. Karl's been out of work for a while."

"Has your husband ever served in the armed services? Considering his age and the recent war, we thought perhaps ..?"

Trudy wondered why they were asking this. "Yes. He was in the Army. He got an early discharge. A mule kicked him in the head. He told me he said some crazy things back then, but stopped after a while. But when this started happening I kind of wondered could it have anything to do with that? That mule?"

The psychiatrists exchanged looks. "We'll look into that," the older one said. "In the meantime, you don't have to worry about medical bills. Your husband's health care costs are covered by the Veteran's Administration. The hospital staff will handle the paperwork."

He handed her the sheaf of papers and indicated where she should sign. She glanced through them, signed, and handed them back. She was pretty certain she wouldn't have understood all the details even if she'd read them, and what was the point? She had to trust these doctors. There was nothing else to do.

"I think I noticed some changes in Karl about seven months ago, a little before he lost his first job." She described how Karl had changed over the months, his growing distrust and contempt for other people, including her, his suspicious expressions and strange mannerisms, his references to God, and, finally, his conversations with his guardian angel. Dr. Levinson led the questioning. Trudy could barely look him in the eye and admit she had seen signs that long ago. She'd covered her eyes, ears, and mouth like one of those silly little monkey statues she'd seen in Woolworth's: see no evil, hear no evil, speak no evil.

I should've done something sooner, but what?

When they finished, Dr. Levinson rose. He took Trudy's elbow to help her to her feet. As if he'd read her mind, the doctor continued to hold her arm after she rose. "The change was gradual. You couldn't have foreseen it, or known how serious it might become."

"When can I see him? When will he be awake?"

"I'm afraid you won't be able to see him for a while. It might upset him, and we need to keep him as calm as possible. Here's my card. You can call my nurse to discuss his progress. She'll tell you when he can have visitors."

Trudy returned to the car and drove back to Frieda's. She had no idea what her future held, but at least she had somewhere to go, where someone needed her.

Chapter Twenty-two

Pick Yourself Up

"I know you're worried, Trudy. We all are. But you have to believe that Karl's in good hands now. All those old horror tales about loony bins aren't true anymore. Big Spring is one of the best state hospitals in the country. It's no loony bin. Why, it was built less than ten years ago. It's completely modern and up-to-date with top drawer psychiatrists. You know, psychiatry got a lot more attention after we entered the war."

Frieda, I wish I could believe you, but I think you're just whistling past the graveyard.

"I went to a mental health workshop at the hospital last fall." Frieda stopped and turned to face Trudy. "Did you know draft boards had to label a million draftees Four-F because of their mental state?"

Trudy shook her head, pretending to pay attention to Frieda's lecture. In other circumstances it might have been interesting, but right now she had to concentrate on putting one foot in front of the other.

Stay in the present and don't think. Just survive and wait for whatever comes.

It was the day after Karl's commitment, and Frieda led Trudy and Molly toward a neighborhood park. It was old, but well maintained. She'd brought her own children there when they were small. "That pushed the government to establish the National Institute of Mental Health." Frieda turned back around and continued walking. "It's only been been in operation for about a year, but it's helping already. And, as I said before, Big Spring Hospital's one of the best. Karl'll come home. He beat this thing the first time, in the army. He'll beat it again. We just have to be patient, wait it out."

Trudy bit her tongue. *If he'd beaten it that first time, he probably wouldn't be in the hospital now.*

They paused at the edge of the park. "Sometimes it's good to get out of the house, get some fresh air," Frieda said. "It helps put things in perspective."

"Yeah, it is good to get some fresh air." Trudy looked sideways at her sister-in-law. "Karl's gone. Is he somewhere inside that raving lunatic that sees things we can't see and talks to angels? Will they be able get him back? Right now that feels like a fairy tale. That's hard to put into perspective."

Speechless for once, Frieda took Molly's hand and led her to the children's play area. Molly had never been to a park playground before. At the slide, her aunt showed her how to climb up the ladder. She balanced at the top for an instant then flew downward, her back curved against the force of gravity. She swept into Frieda's outstretched arms, and began giggling.

"Again!" She ran back up the ladder.

Next, Molly ran for the swing set. Trudy taught her to pump her legs, and she caught on fast. She soared higher and higher. Trudy finally jumped off her own swing to catch her daughter and slow her down. Molly giggled again. Trudy knew her daughter was teasing but couldn't help responding.

If you hurt yourself, on top of everything else ….

She remembered her own childhood when she'd swung unsupervised from high oak branches on wild grapevines and tried to tell herself that children have a self-preservation instinct. Her unborn child gave her a solid kick as they all walked back to the house, and she thought about her sons in California with their father, growing into men without her. She sighed and squeezed the hand of the little girl who was there.

***

Trudy called the psychiatrist's nurse every day. Finally, about two weeks after Karl had entered the hospital, the nurse told her she could visit him, but she would need to get there within the next hour. Raymond hadn't gone into the office that morning, so she was able to leave Molly with him despite the short notice.

When she arrived, the attendant from her first visit led her to a ward where Karl waited, standing beside a bed. He wore a loose-fitting white shirt and trousers. She could see he had lost weight. Her lower lip trembled as she smiled at him. He glanced at her then looked away.

Only one of the other three beds in the room was occupied. The patient in it slept with leather straps clasped around his chest and thighs. The man's arms were invisible, folded across his stomach in a garment that enclosed his hands as well.

Trudy noticed the straps that hung from the sides of Karl's bed. A picture of Karl, tied down and raving, rushed into her mind. She shoved it away and focused her attention on his face.

He spoke without raising his eyes to her. "Hello, Trudy."

Trudy started to move toward him then stopped. "Hello, Karl."

The attendant stepped between them. "Let me take you to the visitor's room." They followed him down the hallway to a room with a row of windows on the wall that faced the hall. A table with three wooden chairs sat inside. The attendant unlocked the door and stepped aside for them to enter. He closed it behind them and stationed himself outside.

Karl stepped around Trudy without touching her to sit at the far side of the table. His arms rested on the table top, and his eyes were fixed on his fidgeting fingers as if they belonged to someone else. "I'm sorry," he said.

Trudy's hands shot across the table and clasped Karl's fingers in her own. They felt like ice. He finally lifted his head and met her eyes. She squeezed his hands. "You've got nothing to be sorry for. This's not your fault. It's probably that damn mule's! I hope they shot it! But you're better now. That's all that matters. How do you feel?"

"I sleep a lot. There are holes in my memory. Big gaps. I don't think they're telling me everything." He released her hands and leaned back in the chair. He regarded her through narrowed eyes.

Oh, no.

Trudy glanced behind her, making sure the attendant was still there. Then Karl's face relaxed, and he moved forward. "How's Molly?" Karl smiled as he listened to tales of Molly at the playground. Just before the attendant took him away, Karl took Trudy into his arms. He didn't hug her tight, or for very long, but at least he held her.

***

She was not allowed to see him again for more than two weeks. Trudy plunged into despair. She completely lost her appetite but forced herself to eat because of the baby. The hazel eyes that stared back at her from the mirror were developing dark circles underneath.

Life with Frieda and Raymond had assumed a routine. Frieda had returned to work, and Trudy and Molly spent their mornings at the park. Their afternoons were spent doing housework and coloring in a new Mickey Mouse coloring book that Raymond had brought home. Trudy taught Molly new nursery rhymes and songs. When Trudy took to preparing the family dinner as Molly watched, they sang or recited together.

After the first week, Trudy began paying her in-laws a small amount for room and board. Although they clearly didn't need the money, she insisted, and they accepted. Mama had taught her not to accept charity, but she was struggling to plan what she would do if Karl didn't recover by the time her meager savings ran out.

After the two-week hiatus, the doctors allowed her to visit Karl twice a week. During their meetings, suspicion crossed his face less and less often. He said nothing unreasonable. Trudy began to relax in his presence. Still he refused to discuss his treatment with her.

Trudy didn't press him, but steered their conversations toward news of Molly and life with Frieda and Raymond. Karl's responses were so normal, she began to wonder why they were still keeping him. It had been nearly three months now. Then one morning the nurse told her that Karl's psychiatrists would like to meet with her.

Both were smiling when she entered the room, though Dr. Neumann's smile looked somewhat forced. The papers he held in his hand drew Trudy's eyes. They were releasing Karl. She had to sign the paperwork, more legal formalities.

"There are never guarantees," Dr. Levinson said. "Episodes sometimes reoccur. But we're hopeful. Your husband has responded exceptionally well to treatment, particularly EST, and we've seen no signs of regression. He seems to have stabilized."

What's EST, some kind of drug? Can he get a prescription, if he needs it?

She would ask later, but she had other concerns to clear up first. "He's said there's a lot of things he can't remember. Not just the things he imagined when he was sick. Things that happened when we first got married. Do you know why? Will his memories ever come back?"

She saw the psychiatrists glance at each other, and then Dr. Neumann spoke.

"Karl's condition was extreme when he entered this hospital. As a result we were required to administer several electroshock treatments before he had a break through. Memory loss is an unfortunate side effect of that therapy. But considering the alternative, it's well worth the cost. With time, some memories may return."

"What?" A wave of horror engulfed her. Suddenly she remembered. She'd read about it. EST, Electroshock Therapy!

The first time she'd spoken to him after his hospitalization flooded her memory. The beds with the leather straps. Trudy stared aghast at the psychiatrist.

"The procedure involves passing a mild electric current through the patient's brain. Patients are sedated throughout the procedure. It's perfectly safe, and often very effective. In your husband's case, we've seen remarkable results." Dr. Neumann's chin jutted forward as he stared back.

You electrocuted Karl like a condemned murderer! Just not all the way. That sounds more like torture than treatment to me. This is top-drawer psychiatry, Frieda?

She took a deep breath and pulled herself together, struggling to reserve judgment. "Exactly how does it help?"

"The exact mechanism that creates the therapeutic effects of electroshock therapy is not fully understood at this time. Schizophrenia is sometimes caused by unknown biological abnormalities in the brain. By some interaction within the brain, electroshock cures these biological anomalies." Dr. Neumann sounded as if he were reciting by rote.

"So, in other words, you don't know what was wrong with Karl's brain, but you believe sending electricity through it cured it? But you don't know how?" Trudy struggled to keep her tone of voice mild, merely curious. She visualized painted witch doctors dancing around a fire.

Despite Trudy's tone, Dr. Neumann frowned. "Science is advancing at an extremely rapid rate. One day we will have a better understanding. In the meantime, we treat our patients with what has been shown to work. EST has given you back your husband, Mrs. Krause."

Dr. Levinson looked into Trudy's eyes. His held a sad tiredness. Trudy wondered if he might retire soon. "If you're ever concerned, you have my number. Don't hesitate to call. Good luck, Trudy." He used her first name for the first time.

A gaunt Karl waited in the hallway with a uniformed attendant Trudy hadn't seen before. Trudy looked into her husband's eyes and waited for a sign. He smiled and reached for her hand. "Let's get out of this place, sweetheart," he said.

She stepped forward to kiss him. "Yes, let's," she said against his lips. She squeezed his palm and fought to cast her doubts aside as they walked out of the loony bin together.

Chapter Twenty-three

Swinging on A Star

"There was a little man. He had a little gun. Its bullets were made of lead, lead, lead. He went to the brook. He saw a little duck. He shot it through the head, head, head." Molly walked around and around the kitchen table, chanting the lines her mother had taught her while Trudy made salami sandwiches for lunch.

Trudy smiled as she listened to her daughter recite the final four stanzas of the dark little poem. It had a happy ending anyway. The duck was shot, but the drake flew away with a quack, quack, quack, escaping with its life. Trudy set the sandwiches on the table with a pitcher of sweet iced tea. Karl would be home any minute. He didn't have deliveries on Saturday afternoons.

Raymond had used his connections to get Karl a job delivering milk for the only dairy in Amarillo, Texas. Trudy suspected Frieda's husband was relieved to have found Karl a job that got them out of Big Spring, and, in truth, so was she. They needed a new start, close to his family in case of an emergency, but not too close. They'd found a cramped upstairs apartment for five dollars a month less than their old mortgage payment.

At first Trudy had held her breath, waiting for a suspicious look, a reference to God or angels, an air of superior knowledge. But weeks had passed into months. As fear waned, she fought to accept how much the man she loved had changed. It wasn't only his memory. It was as if the adventurous spirit that had first attracted Trudy had been welded to his madness. Now both had disappeared. He was rational. She knew she should be grateful for that, but she mourned the man she'd married every time she looked at Karl.

When he stepped into the apartment, she placed her hands on his waist and stretched over her protuberant belly to kiss him as she'd greeted him every day in those early years. He responded as if he were playing a part, but as she released him, his smile crinkled the corners of his eyes as it had in Salinas when he'd first entered her life, bringing a burst of sunshine into its darkness.

Give it time. He's been through so much.

***

The last days of Trudy's pregnancy passed slowly. She couldn't allow herself to think about the uncertain future, about when she would ever be able to see her nearly grown sons, about Papa growing old. So she distracted herself as she had done when her boys had first left for California: by focusing on Molly.

As the three of them sat around the apartment one Saturday afternoon, she decided to give her daughter a permanent wave. Using a Tonette children's home permanent kit she'd bought at the local drugstore, Trudy wound tissue wrapped sections of Molly's fine, wispy hair up on dozens of small rubber curlers. Then she applied the curling lotion. A stinky chemical odor permeated the apartment.

Molly's eyes watered, but she didn't stir. When the curling lotion dripped down the back of her neck, she started to scratch it. Trudy caught her daughter's hand and rubbed the lotion off her neck with a cloth.

Karl sat on the couch as his women completed the beauty ritual. Then, with an exaggerated look of disgust, he gripped his nostrils between his fingers. "Pee-hew!" He looked at Molly. She giggled and got off the chair. She approached her father on tip-toe with slow, deliberate steps. As she got closer, he drew back and grabbed his nose again.

"Pee-hew!"

She darted past him giggling. This simple little game between father and daughter filled Trudy with an almost absurd happiness. It was so normal, but so special. She allowed herself to release her doubts for the moment.

When they finally rinsed Molly's hair in the sink, it was less curly than Trudy had hoped, but it was pretty. When it dried the barrettes stayed in. They were still in when the three of them drove to St. Anthony's hospital later that same evening. There, Trudy gave birth to Karl's first and her third son.

***

Frieda was there to help when they brought Martin, named after Karl's father, home from the hospital. But her and Trudy's child rearing practices clashed from the beginning. Frieda protested the fact that Marty shared Trudy and Karl's bed and nursed whenever he felt like it.

"Trudy, aren't you worried you might roll over and smother him?" A concerned frown lingered on Frieda's face.

"No, Frieda. I always know he's there. I don't sleep that sound. All my babies slept with me when they were little. It's less trouble than putting them in a crib, and they're happier. They sleep better, so it's easier for us. He'll be fine, I promise."

"Don't you think you might spoil him if you just let him nurse whenever he likes instead of keeping him on a schedule?" The look of concern remained.

"He's too little to spoil. I want him to know his momma would never let him go hungry. That just seems mean to me. Molly nursed whenever she wanted to. Does she seem spoiled?" Trudy knew it was a good argument, but she also knew it wouldn't change Frieda's opinion.

The two women were very different. They came from different backgrounds, and Trudy knew they would never be especially close, but they had Karl in common. In that regard, they would always be allies. Frieda stayed for less than a week.

***

Marty was fussy that morning, and the usual methods hadn't worked, so Trudy resorted to the stroller Karl had bought while she was still in the hospital. Molly led the way downstairs. Dragging the bouncing stroller behind, Trudy followed with Marty clutched in one arm.

The stroller bumped over sidewalk cracks and stuttered over inscriptions in the cement that read WPA 1941. They wheeled Martin, quiet now, his huge blue eyes staring at the outside world, to the drugstore where Trudy had purchased her daughter's Tonette. The drugstore had a soda fountain, and when Martin tolerated a pause in motion, Trudy and Molly sat on stools at the counter and sipped root beer. Molly chewed her straw until bits of paper came loose on her tongue. She spit them into her hand as her mother tore off the soggy tip so the sweet liquid could flow again.

After Marty was asleep, they strolled back to their apartment building. As they entered the courtyard, an elderly man stepped out of the ground floor apartment. "Here," he said, "let me help you with that."

Trudy smiled and picked Martin up. "Thank you."

Lifting the stroller, the neighbor followed Trudy and Molly up the stairs. He set it down just outside the apartment door, then sank down to Molly's level. "I'm Mr. Schumacher," he said, "What's your name?"

"Molly Krause, 602 Main." She recited the address of the apartment building as her mother had taught her.

Mr. Schumacher chuckled. "Pleased to meet you, Molly. How old are you?" Molly held up two and a half fingers. Trudy smiled at the exchange. Then she introduced herself and shook hands with Mr. Schumacher.

"My wife and I been watching you struggle up and down with that stroller. It'd be a lot easier if you stored it downstairs with us. You could knock anytime you need it. We're always there, at least one of us. We're retired."

"Thank you. You're sure it wouldn't be a bother?"

"No bother a'tall. That one," he pointed at Molly, "reminds us of our granddaughter. She's a little older now, but we have a grandson 'bout the same age. We don't get to see them very often. Maybe you, and Molly, and the baby …?" He looked at Trudy with an unspoken question in his eyes.

"Marty." Trudy smiled.

"Maybe you could come down for tea and cookies sometimes. My wife loves to bake, and we never eat 'em all."

"Thanks, we'd like that." Trudy watched the elderly man pick up the stroller, turn, and go back downstairs. Tears filled her eyes.

Papa, are you and Mama lonely, too? You've never seen any of my children even once. Will I ever see you again? At least you have Evelyn nearby. I'm glad for that.

***

The Schumachers became Molly's substitute grandparents. They stuffed her with cookies, and encouraged Trudy to share details of everything she did. The first time Molly sat in their living room, reciting the words of a Little Golden Book as she turned the pages, they stared at her, eyes wide. "Is she reading?" Mr. Schumacher gawked at the less than three-year-old child.

Trudy shook her head and smiled. "She's memorized the words. The pictures remind her what words are on that page."

"Are you sure?"

"Yes. I showed her the words on a piece of paper. She couldn't read them. She's just got a great memory, and she loves pretending that she's reading."

After the Schumachers offered to keep a close eye on Molly, Trudy let her go downstairs to play in the small fenced yard in front of the couple's living room windows. She dressed her daughter carefully in one of her frilly dresses before she left the apartment. Molly returned a short while later, still clean, except for a circle of mud around her mouth.

"What've you been doing?" She didn't really need to ask.

"Eating doit."

Trudy couldn't help but smile. She turned away so Molly wouldn't see. She knew children often ate dirt; she'd tasted it herself as a child. Molly clearly enjoyed the taste. Trudy enjoyed the child's guileless honesty.

When the Schumachers' daughter and her family came to visit and stayed for a week, Trudy often found her daughter and Danny, the

Schumachers' grandson, playing side-by-side but separately. He pushed his toy cars and trucks along roads in the dirt, while she mothered her baby doll. The day before the visit ended, Trudy heard a pounding at the apartment door. She opened it, and Mr. Schumacher stood on the stoop. "Trudy! Come quick! He scurried back down the steps, nearly tripping. "I'm so sorry!" He yelled over his shoulder. "Lucky Amanda looked out the window!"

Trudy followed. Mrs. Schumacher was wiping blood streaked shaving lather from Molly's face. Several shallow scratches lay beneath the lather on her cheeks and chin. Molly sat frowning, as everyone gathered around her. Danny sat on the ground next to his grandfather's razor and can of shaving cream. He stared, round-eyed, at the commotion. Trudy could see the wounds weren't serious. Molly wasn't even crying, just frowning at Mrs. Schumacher.

They were actually playing together! Good thing it wasn't a straight razor!

She kept Molly in the apartment for a couple of days so the dirt she might eat in the yard wouldn't get into her scratches until they healed. They read books together, and Trudy sat on the floor coloring blue skies and pretty little houses surrounded by green trees and pink and purple flowers. Molly sat beside her mother coloring the opposite page of the coloring book. She held the crayons firmly in her small fingers, and all the colors stayed inside the lines where they belonged.

***

"It's over, Trudy," Karl stood across the room from her, still in his pajamas. "The End of Days is here. The Lord can no longer tolerate the sin and stupidity of the human race. But He knows who the righteous are. I am one of his lambs. He told me so. Are you, Trudy? I'm not so sure."

Bitter, agonizing anger struck like lightning. Before she had time to think, she flung the pan she was about to scramble eggs in straight at Karl's head. He dodged the missile with the smug smile she remembered so well. The pan clattered against the wall. Then unbearable pain struck.

At that moment, Molly walked into the kitchen rubbing her eyes. She crossed the worn linoleum to her mother, wrapped her arms around Trudy's legs, and laid her head against her mother's thigh. Trudy swallowed her tears and forced herself under control with a gargantuan effort of will. She laid her hand on her daughter's shoulder, pressing her close. Molly looked up at her with sharp, inquisitive blue eyes. A fading pink scar ran from under her left cheek bone to near the corner of her mouth. "Would you like some toast, baby?"

Molly nodded. Trudy heard Karl give a snort, heavy with contempt.

She glanced toward him and saw him turn and go back to their bedroom. She lit the oven pilot light and put a slice of bread on the broiler plate, turning the broiler to low and sliding the bread under the flame. She loosened Molly's grip on her leg, led her to the kitchen table, and poured her a glass of milk. Then she buttered the toast, placed it on a saucer with a picture of Chicken Little, and put it in front of Molly.

When her daughter became absorbed in picking off the crust, Trudy crossed to the bedroom door. Karl hadn't closed it completely. She peered through the opening between the door and frame. He was sitting on the side of the bed in his pajamas. The newspaper she had brought inside earlier was spread across his lap, and he appeared to be engaged in a silent discussion.

The sight brought everything back. Her eyes searched for Martin. He was sleeping near the top of the bed, on the far side from Karl. She opened the door enough to ease through, and then walked quickly past the end of the bed to where her infant lay. Karl seemed unaware of her presence. She picked Marty up and walked back toward the door. Her husband glanced sideways at her and sneered as she passed then turned back to his paper. She ignored him, and closed the door, all the way this time.

Molly still nibbled the remnants of her toast. Trudy found her daughter's fuzzy blue house slippers, and, holding Marty, bent down to slip them on Molly's dangling bare feet. "We're going to see Mr. and Mrs. Schumacher." Trudy spoke in a whisper.

"Why?" Molly said, in a voice that was loud in the silence.

Trudy searched for a plausible answer then whispered again. "Ms. Schumacher made some special coffee this morning. She wants to give me a cup."

"Okay." Molly whispered in return, then giggled as if it were an enchanting game. She hopped off her chair and started for the door. Trudy followed, carrying Martin. In the living room, she paused long to slip her purse on her arm then followed her daughter down the stairs.

When Mrs. Schumacher opened the door to let them in, Trudy stared into the woman's eyes, hoping she had some mind reading skills. "I told Molly you made some special coffee this morning and were going to give me a cup," she said, never breaking eye contact. Mrs. Schumacher nodded.

"Yes. We haven't had the coffee yet. Let's warm it up." She took Molly's hand and led them toward their kitchen, looking back over her shoulder at Trudy.

"I'll explain later," Trudy mouthed. Martin was beginning to whimper and paw at his mother's breast. Molly walked over to a shelf on the far kitchen wall and began to examine the tiny porcelain figures that sat there. "Could I use your phone?"

"Of course."

"Could you keep an eye on the stairs? If you see Karl come down, please tell me."

Mrs. Schumacher stared at her then crossed to the window near the door. Trudy glanced at her daughter. Molly had taken down several of the small figurines, and was engaged in a game of pretend with Mr. Schumacher who had just appeared looking fresh from the shower. If he was surprised to see them, he didn't show it.

Trudy slipped out of the kitchen and into the living room. Sitting in a chair next to the telephone, she freed her breast. She turned Martin's face toward her nipple. He latched on and began to nurse as she fumbled through her purse for Dr. Levinson's card.

She spoke to a nurse who put her through to the doctor. She told him what had happened, although she left out the part about the frying pan. She could hear the disappointment in his voice as he told her he would contact the local hospital. They would send an ambulance to pick Karl up. The attendants would sedate him and take him to await transfer to Big Spring. Dr. Levinson would arrange the transfer as quickly as possible. Trudy hung up the receiver.

What have I done? But what else could I do? The children come first. I have to keep them safe, at whatever cost.

She sat, shoulders hunched, and stared into space as Marty nursed himself to sleep and Molly played pretend in the kitchen.

I'll just have to find a way to live with it.

***

Trudy spread Marty's blanket on the floor and put her sleeping baby down. She returned to where Mrs. Schumacher stood keeping an eye out for Karl. Trudy had never shared the details of her husband's history with her elderly neighbors. They had not pried. They were decent people who would never poke their noses into something that wasn't their business. Now she wished she had revealed more.

She didn't know where to start. "Remember when I told you 'bout Karl's breakdown?" Mrs. Schumacher nodded, watching her intently. "I didn't tell you how serious it was. They put him in the hospital. A mental hospital." Trudy struggled for control. Her neighbor pulled her into her arms and held her for a minute as Trudy fought not to cry.

"He's not in his right mind this morning. It's like that other time. I called his psychiatrist. An ambulance is coming to get him, to take him back there. I don't know what'll happen, what he'll do when it gets here."

Mrs. Schumacher took her husband aside and conferred with him briefly. Mr. Schumacher walked over to Trudy, put a hand on her shoulder, and lifted her chin to face him. "Don't worry about Marty. I'll keep an eye on him." He turned and went into the living room.

Mrs. Schumacher interrupted Molly's play. "Molly, let's go to the bakery. I want some donuts to eat with our special coffee. You can help pick them out. You know the kind your momma likes, don't you?"

"Yes." Molly took Mrs. Schumacher's hand and they left. Trudy followed them out front to wait for the ambulance.

Chapter Twenty-four

Ac-Cent-Tchu-Ate the Positive

When the ambulance arrived, one of the attendants approached Trudy. "We've had a request from Big Spring State Hospital, a Dr. Levinson, to pick up a patient, Karl Krause, at this address?"

"Yes, I'm his wife. I called Dr. Levinson." She crossed her arms, wrapping her cold hands above her elbows.

"We understand he's hallucinating?" Trudy detected a hint of doubt in his voice. Had he ever been sent on such a mission before?

"Yes. He is." The certainty in her voice must have reassured him. The tone of his next question was more business-like.

"Is he violent?"

"No, no, he's never been violent." A memory of flinging the frying pan flared like lightning, and she burned with shame. "He's upstairs, apartment 2B. The door's unlocked. He was in the bedroom when I left. Can I wait down here?"

"Yes. That's probably best. Sign this for me, please." He handed her sheets of paper attached to a clipboard.

Trudy frowned. "These aren't commitment papers, are they? I want to talk to Dr. Levinson first."

"Just temporary, to take him for observation and evaluation. Seventy-two hours."

Trudy looked the papers over, signed, and handed them back. The attendants hurried up the stairs and returned shortly. They held Karl between them. His arms were wrapped in the same sort of white garment Trudy had seen on his roommate at Big Spring. The ends of the sleeves were tied behind his back. The attendant who had spoken to Trudy cupped a bloody cloth to his nose with his free hand.

Karl's glistening stare captured Trudy as they approached. He cursed them all, calling God's damnation down on their heads. As they passed, he twisted his neck to look back at her. He continued to incinerate her with his eyes as they took a stretcher from the ambulance, lifted him onto it, and strapped him down. Trudy couldn't bear to watch any longer and turned away. She heard them drive off as she re-entered the Schumacher apartment.

***

Mrs. Schumacher and Molly returned, and Trudy forced a glazed donut down her tight, dry throat for Molly's sake. Afterward, she gave Mrs. Schumacher a quick hug, grasped Mr. Schumacher's hand, then picked up her still sleeping son. The Schumachers watched her with identical troubled frowns as she, Martin, and Molly went back up the stairs.

After a while, Trudy numbly prepared canned tomato soup and crackers for lunch. She dreaded explaining the situation to her daughter. Molly dipped a corner of a saltine into her soup and nibbled the soup-soaked cracker.

"Daddy's gone to the hospital for a while, Molly."

"Is Daddy sick?" Molly placed her cracker on the table. "Is he going to die?" Her voice trembled, and tears filled her eyes. She and her mother had recently discussed the concept of death since it often popped up in her fairy tales.

Trudy stood next to Molly's chair. She bent her knees until she stooped at eye level with her child. "No, sweetheart, no. It's not that kind of sickness. It's just his mind's not working right. It's called *mental* illness. He's got to stay in the hospital again, like that time we stayed at Aunt Frieda's. The doctors will keep him safe 'til he gets better."

"Will he be home soon?"

"I don't know. We'll just have to wait and see." She rose, lifted her daughter out of her chair, and held her close.

"Will you read me a story, Momma?"

***

Karl was transferred from the Amarillo hospital to the Big Spring State Hospital two days after the ambulance took him away. The morning after he arrived there, Trudy called the psychiatric facility from the Schumacher's apartment and identified herself. The nurse she spoke to had a voice engraved in Trudy's memory but didn't seem to remember her.

"Mrs. Krause? I understand your husband has been hospitalized here before?"

"Yes, less than six months ago."

"Then you know the visitation rules. Delusional patients can't receive visitors, even immediate family members, until their condition has stabilized." She sounded like she was repeating a memorized script.

"But, you see, I don't know what his condition is. That's what I'm trying to find out. Could I speak to Dr. Levinson, please?" Trudy sensed she would learn nothing from this woman. *Just another cog in the machine.* That had become her mantra in situations such as this.

"Dr. Levinson is not available at the moment. All I can tell you is that Mr. Krause arrived late yesterday afternoon and is currently under heavy sedation."

Trudy remembered the first glimpse she'd had of him in the hospital the day after they'd arrived in Big Springs. The brief time since melted away. "When am I supposed to come in to meet with the doctors to sign the commitment papers and talk about his treatment?"

"Oh, you don't have to sign anything, Mrs. Krause. He is being committed involuntarily. Dr. Levinson began the process yesterday. The hospital has the authority to do that in certain cases."

"What? What cases? What do you mean?"

"When the symptoms are severe, and they have evidence that the patient might be a danger to himself or others. You'll have to discuss the reasons for their decision with the doctor. They'll contact you after they develop a treatment plan and prognosis."

Trudy hung up the phone, stunned. She remembered the ambulance attendant's bloody nose. Was that enough to make Karl a danger? Had she lost all control over his treatment?

Oh, Karl! What have I done?

***

The following day, Trudy decided to demand an appointment with Karl's psychiatrists. To her surprise, when she called the nurse informed her that the doctors wanted to meet with her, too. "Can you be here at nine tomorrow morning?"

Outside Big Spring, the Chevy's right rear tire collapsed. Trudy climbed out, leaving the children inside, and opened the trunk to check the spare. It was flat. She'd relied on Karl to maintain the car. A realization swept through her. It would be hard for her to rely, not just on Karl, but on anyone but herself, from now on.

Can I do this? I have to.

She opened the passenger side door and lifted Marty out. Molly held onto the back of the passenger seat and bounced up and down on the rear floorboard. "Mommy, Mommy, can I get out?"

"Not yet, honey. It's safer for you in the car. Be patient." With a baby on her hip, Trudy waved down a Ford pickup then returned to the car to let Molly out. The elderly driver parked the truck and got out.

"Need some help?"

"Yes. I guess my husband forgot to check our spare. Could you please give us a lift to a service station?"

"Sure." Their rescuer walked around the truck to open his passenger door, as Trudy opened the left rear door of the Chevy and Molly bounced out. The man strode over to where they stood, picked up Molly, and lifted her onto the bench seat of his truck. Trudy squeezed in beside her with Marty in her arms.

He let them out at the nearest Texaco station. Trudy called Frieda and waited for Raymond to pick her and the children up. Over Trudy's objections, Raymond paid to have the car towed and the tire and spare repaired. He would bring her back to get it the following day. She made a silent promise to herself to somehow pay him back.

They arrived in Big Spring in time for a mostly silent supper. Molly's excitement at seeing Bootsie again was the only bright spot. Trudy glanced up from her plate and caught Frieda watching her. She wasn't sure what she read in her sister-in-law's eyes.

Do you think I could have kept this from happening? Could I have?

Instead of staying on the pallet Frieda laid for her, Molly climbed into bed with her mother and baby brother and fell asleep. Trudy lay awake between her sleeping children and worried. She had to find a way to pay Raymond back for fixing the tires and paying for the tow. Thinking about that opened a can of worms. One after another wriggled out.

I'll have to catch a cab to the hospital. How much is that gonna cost? I can probably buy enough food and pay rent one more month. Then what?

Trudy had no faith that the doctors would be able to cure Karl. She wasn't sure it was worth the pain of his treatment to even try.

They'll put him through hell again, so he can walk around like a zombie for a few months until his "angel" comes back.

Sometime in the morning hours, the last worry inched away, and she fell into an exhausted sleep.

***

Molly followed her mother around the bedroom as she dressed the next morning. "Momma, can I go?"

Trudy considered. This meeting was going to be difficult. She was leaving Marty with Frieda, but Molly's presence would be a comfort. "Sweetie, we can't see Daddy. I have to talk to the doctors. You'd have to be quiet while we talk. Could you do that?"

Molly nodded. Trudy knew Molly could be good; she was always good, and although she was smart, this conversation would be far over her head. Having her present would anchor Trudy. She couldn't let herself fall apart with Molly there, and that might give her the endurance she needed to deal with whatever Dr. Levinson told her.

"Okay. Get your coat. Get your crayons and coloring book, too." Molly hurried off. Frieda, armed with a bottle of extracted breast milk, held Martin. She looked doubtful, but no longer tried to question

Trudy's child-rearing decisions.

Rain was falling, and a brisk breeze blew when the taxi arrived. Molly trailed Trudy out to the street, clasping her mother's fingers in one hand. She gripped her crayons and coloring book against her chest with the other. The wind whipped cold, stinging rain into their faces.

When they got to the hospital, the rain had stopped, but the wind swept around them as they raced up the sidewalk. Molly halted and turned to face the wind. She closed her eyes and grinned as her fine hair flew up and away from her face. Trudy smiled then tugged her daughter through the hospital entrance and up to the reception desk. She gave her name and said she had a nine o'clock appointment.

The receptionist stared at Molly then Trudy. "Do you have someone to take care of the little girl?" Molly looked up at her mother.

"No, she'll go inside with me." Trudy smiled at Molly, then looked back to the receptionist.

"I'm not sure that's a good idea," the receptionist said. "Maybe I can find a nurse who's available."

"She'll go with me. If there's any problem, I'll bring her out. But don't worry. She won't be any trouble." She pointed to the coloring book and crayons Molly clutched. "She'll color." She smiled, knowing her resolution was reflected in her eyes.

The receptionist gave her a frosty look. "I'll tell the doctors you're here."

Both the psychiatrists who had worked with Karl before were there. Dr. Neumann glanced at the little girl who held Trudy's hand then looked away. Dr. Levinson caught Molly's eye and gave her a quick wink and a smile. Then both doctors turned back to Trudy.

Each offered his hand. Trudy took them in turn then sat down next to her daughter on the small couch. The psychiatrists pulled chairs around to face her. Dr. Levinson leaned forward, his elbows on his knees. "Trudy, there are several things we need to discuss today. I know your first concern is Karl's well-being. He is well physically. There are no concerns in that regard. Although his response to treatment lasted a shorter time than we'd hoped, he did respond. It will definitely take longer for him to stabilize this time than it did the last time, possibly much longer. But hopefully the effects will be more permanent."

"Why don't I have to sign commitment papers this time?" The receptionist had told her, but she wanted to hear it directly from the psychiatrists.

Dr. Neumann responded. "We've already handled that. There was no need to involve you. We have the authority and the responsibility to ensure that patients with severe mental disorders are off the streets, for their welfare and that of the public."

"The nurse told me. Why do you consider Karl a danger to himself or others? What's he done but the word you used, hallucinate?"

"The hospital attendants who collected him from your apartment filed a report. He resisted with force and injured one of them. That provides adequate cause for civil commitment." Trudy read smugness in both his tone and expression.

"He was confused! He was defending himself!" Surely they couldn't equate self-defense with violence, could they?

Dr. Levinson held his hand palm out toward Dr. Neumann. "Trudy," he said in a calm, patient voice, "that's the point. Karl's extremely confused and afraid. In this state he may lash out at anyone. You know that."

"Maybe he's right to be afraid. Are you going to electrocute him again?" Trudy kept her voice calm. She was sure Molly didn't know that word. Why would she?

Dr. Levinson sighed. "If you're referring to electroshock therapy, yes. We will be administering that. It's the only treatment he has responded to."

"If he'd responded, he wouldn't be back here, would he?"

Dr. Levinson took a deep breath and leaned back in his chair. "I know you're disappointed, Trudy. So are we. I told you there are no guarantees." Dr. Neumann shook his head, gathered up some papers, and left the office.

"Dr. Levinson, I want those treatments stopped. They changed him. Even when he was rational, he wasn't the same man I married. If I have to sign something, I will. Let him keep talking to angels. I know I've lost him. Just, please, don't put him through that anymore." She cleared her throat then glanced at Molly who had moved from the couch to the floor where she sat coloring. Molly looked up, grinned then went back to her picture.

The psychiatrist didn't speak for a time. Suddenly he looked very old, and extremely tired. "Trudy, the state has placed the responsibility for Karl's treatment in my hands. It isn't easy, but I must do what I think provides the best chance to rehabilitate my patient." He stared at his hands then changed the subject. "The last time Karl was hospitalized, you mentioned an incident in the Army."

"The mule." Trudy nodded as numbness crept through her. Karl's treatment was out of her control. Her mind swirled with confusion, but she couldn't think about it now.

"Yes, the mule. Your husband's condition is complex. Research continues, but it indicates so far that schizophrenia combines several factors. Some are hereditary. But heredity alone doesn't determine the onset. There is even research to suggest that this hereditary link often skips a generation. Grandchildren are slightly more at risk than children, for both schizophrenia and a related condition known as autism." As far as Trudy knew, Karl's parents had never experienced such episodes.

Did his grandparents? He's never mentioned it. Neither has Frieda. Will Molly's children be at risk? God, no!

"There are other factors, environmental factors," the psychiatrist said. "Many patients with Karl's condition have experienced a traumatic childhood which tips the scale. Cold, rejecting mothers are a common factor. These patients almost always show symptoms in their late teenage years or early twenties." He paused, and Trudy sensed he was reaching the heart of his lecture. "Another precipitating factor is brain trauma. We know of no episode that predates your husband's Army injury. So my colleagues and I have concluded that that was the precipitating factor in Karl's case." Dr. Levinson smiled.

Trudy frowned. "What difference does it make? Do you treat him different? Does he have more or less chance of getting well?"

"Trudy, I know this situation has been hard for you. You were worried about medical costs and were unaware that the Veteran's Administration would cover those. I suspect that there are other benefits you may not know about. There is something called the War Risk Insurance Act. After WWI, Congress amended it to establish a presumption of service connection for two illnesses: tuberculosis and psychosis. Even if there weren't a presumed connection between Karl's service and his illness, the mule incident shows a clear one."

Trudy stared at him. "So does this mean Karl's got more medical insurance? I thought his expenses were already covered."

"They are. This is different. This is disability insurance. Our staff has completed the paperwork for you, except for a few details. We are certifying that your husband is one hundred percent disabled. Of course, we hope that will change. But in the meantime, as his wife you will receive a monthly government disability check. The amount should be approximately a hundred dollars." Trudy heard herself gasp.

"Trudy, where were you and your husband married? Here? In Texas?" Dr. Levinson said.

"No, we got married in Salinas, California." Trudy fought to comprehend. A faint light in this long tunnel of darkness.

"Karl can't file a disability claim himself, obviously. But, as his wife, you can file the paperwork for him. But you need proof that the two of you are married. Do you know which county Salinas is in?"

"Yes, Monterey. I have my marriage certificate, Doctor. Do you need it?"

"Just a moment." Dr. Levinson stepped into the doorway and spoke with his receptionist then turned to Trudy. "I'm getting the address of the

Monterey County Recorder and the fee information for a certified license copy for you. You probably should keep your original marriage certificate in case you need it for something else."

The psychiatrist took a large manila envelope off his desk. "After you get the copy of your license, mail it with this paperwork. There's an addressed envelope inside. Be sure you fill in anything that's blank and sign it before you mail it." The receptionist walked into the office, glanced at Molly, who still sat on the floor coloring, handed the doctor a slip of paper, and left without looking at Trudy.

"It shouldn't take too long to process. I'm putting the address for the recorder and the fee information for the license copy in here, too." He added the slip of paper the receptionist had given him to the envelope and handed it to Trudy.

She took it and stood speechless. The psychiatrist would keep electrocuting Karl, torturing him, taking away his memories, and changing him into a stranger, and that even if it did make him "sane," it wouldn't last.

But you just gave me and my children a way to survive. What can I possibly say?

Her awkwardness hung in the air until Dr. Levinson broke the silence. "Trudy, I know you think EST is ineffective and cruel. But the therapy has been modified since it came into use. Patients are sedated and most have virtually no memory of their treatments." He looked down then raised his eyes to hers. "Maybe someday science will come up with something better. But Karl is here now, and this is what we have. It's his only chance."

"Dr. Levinson, I know you're doing what you believe is right. I can't help Karl. I'd like to think you can. I know you want to. I just can't stand the thought of him suffering and never understanding why. And if it don't last, is it really worth it?" Tears filled her eyes and she blinked them away. She straightened her shoulders. "Thank you for this." She lifted the hand that held the envelope he had given her. "I can't begin to tell you what it means to me and my children."

"You're welcome, Trudy. I'm sorry you've had to go through all this. We'll keep working with Karl. Don't give up hope. You'll be seeing us again."

"Mama, can we go home now?" Molly clutched her coloring book and stared up at her mother.

Chapter Twenty-five

Pennies from Heaven

A smile brightened Frieda's careworn face when Trudy told her about the disability payments. She pulled Trudy into her arms and held her for several moments. "You know you can stay here as long as you want to. We have the room. It's no bother. I'm just glad for your sake," she said as she released Trudy.

"I know. I appreciate all you've done. I had no one else to turn to." Trudy's in-laws had been the final straw she'd had to cling to, and she was more thankful than she could express that they'd been there. She hoped Frieda knew that. It was her turn to hug her sister-in-law.

"We'll always be here if you need us," Frieda said.

When Raymond returned from work, Trudy, Molly, and Martin left with him to reclaim their car. There was no point in staying in Big Spring longer. Dr. Levinson had sounded less than optimistic about Karl's recovering soon, if at all. When, or if, things changed, they would return.

I just want to be home. Wherever that is, it's not here.

When Trudy opened their door late that evening, with Martin asleep in her arms, she found a letter lying on the floor beneath the mail slot. She carried her son into the bedroom and placed him in bed, then returned to pick up the letter. It was from Mary, but the address was new. After Molly had been collected from the car and tucked into bed beside her brother, Trudy returned to the kitchen to read Mary's letter.

"Dear Sis," she read, "I hope things are still good for you and Karl and the kids. I am afraid I got bad news. Travis got arrested for burglary. Him and some guy he works with broke into somebody's house while the people was gone on vacation. I guess they left fingerprints, and that is how the police tracked Travis down. He got fingerprinted when he was arrested that other time when he was in high school.

"Anyhow, he is in jail now. I am staying with his parents, as you can see from the address on this letter. We are waiting for the trial. I am afraid this will go bad for him because he has a record. It may not count because he was a juvenile back then, but if it does, I am not sure what I'll do. Linda's not even two years old. Sorry to put all this on you. I know you have your own worries.

Love,
Your Sister Mary.

P.S. Betty and Tommy are fine. Mad at their daddy, naturally."
What next? What next? That little bastard.

She hoped she could find something encouraging to say when she wrote back. Exhausted, she returned to the bedroom and crawled into bed with her children.

***

The next day Trudy picked up her stroller from the Schumachers' and walked to the nearest Post Office. Martin rode sitting up now, a chunky little Buddha surveying his kingdom. Molly trotted alongside her mother, gripping Trudy's skirt and singing to herself.

At the Post Office, Trudy bought a money order, made it payable to the Monterey County Recorder, then placed it with the request for a copy of her marriage certificate into an envelope and mailed it off to the address she'd been given. She slipped her return letter to Mary into the same mail slot.

Back home, they dropped the stroller off at the Schumachers' and stayed for tea. Trudy related her experience at Big Spring State Hospital. "So," Mrs. Schumacher said, "will you be all right 'til the money comes through, Trudy? We'll be happy to help if we can."

Trudy looked at her, knowing how limited the couples' resources were. Evidence lay all around her in their old, though well-cared-for, furniture, and the tiny, cheap apartment, almost identical to hers. Their generosity and affection touched her heart. "No, I can manage." She smiled and fought back tears.

It took over a week to receive the copy of her marriage license. The day after, she stuck the copy along with the completed and signed disability paperwork into its self-addressed envelope. Adding an extra stamp to be sure she had sufficient postage, she thrust the envelope into the mail slot in the apartment door. Now all she could do was to wait and see, and hope that Dr. Levinson had been right.

While they were still waiting the rent came due again. Trudy had two choices: she could explain her situation to her landlord, and hope he would be sympathetic enough to give her more time for the paperwork to process, or she could find the money.

She barely considered the first option. She had a business relationship with the landlord, nothing more, and that was how she wanted to keep it. That left family, and the only family members she knew who had both resources and a responsibility to Karl's children were Frieda and Raymond.

They wired her the money, slightly more than she'd asked for, overnight. She picked it up at the neighborhood Western Union office.

When she called them from the drugstore payphone to let them know the money had arrived safely, Frieda told her she didn't need to pay them back. Trudy said she would. A week later, when the first government check arrived, the first thing she did after cashing it was buy another money order to repay the loan.

The relief of receiving Karl's first disability check and knowing that her and the children's material welfare was insured faded quickly. Worrying about their survival had kept Trudy's mind occupied. Now thoughts of Karl and what their future might be crept in. She thrust them away and fought despondency by concentrating on her children, watching their interactions.

Marty had begun to crawl, and as soon as she took him out of his playpen and placed him on the floor, he would make a beeline for the toy box he and Molly shared. Sitting beside it, he would reach into the toys and grab whatever came to hand. Seizing the toy in chubby fingers, he would fling it as far as he could, then grab another and repeat the process.

Molly would watch for a moment, then, frowning, crawl over to the toy box herself and begin retrieving the toys and placing them back inside. This appeared to delight Marty. He would continue more furiously than ever, chortling as he threw until he finally got bored and crawled away. The first time it had happened, Molly had looked at her mother.

"Mama, why is he throwing my toys?" Molly's expression was a cross between irritation and puzzlement.

"He's just a baby, Molly. He don't know how to play yet. He thinks he's playing." Trudy smiled, hoping the tenderness Molly read in her face would encourage her daughter to indulge her baby brother.

Thereafter, Molly tried to combat the chaos as best she could, sometimes sighing and frowning, but never showing the slightest trace of anger toward Marty. Trudy marveled at her little girl's patience.

***

When Trudy had written Mary right after returning from Big Spring, she'd kept her letter focused on Mary's plight and asked questions about how her children were doing and how they were dealing with the news about Travis. Mary replied that Betty had quickly forgiven her father, but Tommy moped around, refusing to discuss the situation. "It worries me a little, Trudy," she wrote. "But you know how men are. They hide their feelings."

Trudy had steered clear of her own situation so as not to lie outright, although she had said "Everything's fine here." She rationalized the statement by telling herself that everything was relative. It depended on what a person meant by 'fine'.

Nobody's died, anyway.

Mary told her in the next letter that they were still waiting for Travis's trial to begin. Trudy wrote back, filling the letter with the antics of her charming son and daughter and further condolences. Again, she avoided mentioning her own circumstances. She knew Mary had to wait for the outcome of the trial to make a decision, but wondered what options she was considering. "Are you thinking about moving back to Tahlequah to stay with Mama and Papa?" she wrote.

Then she received another letter. The trial was over. Travis had been luckier than he probably deserved. They'd tried him as a first time offender since his earlier break-in had been as a juvenile, and those records were sealed. He'd been sentenced to three years and was being transferred to the Texas State Penitentiary at Huntsville. Time off for good behavior was a possibility, as was parole. Trudy's mouth curved in an ironic smile as she read.

Yes. Time off for good behavior is pretty much a certainty, as is parole.

Trudy knew Travis could charm the hide off a rattlesnake. In prison, that would doubtlessly prove to be a critical talent. She read on. No, Mary was not thinking of returning home. She was thinking of moving herself and the kids to Amarillo, to be close to Trudy. Could Trudy help her find a place? Could they stay at Trudy's while they looked? She knew it would be crowded, but it should only be a few days. Mary had enough money to get into an apartment, and, with the baby and all, she was sure she could get public assistance to help pay the bills. She could also make some money taking in ironing or babysitting.

Trudy wrote back. Of course they could stay as long as they liked. Faced with Mary's imminent arrival, Trudy had no choice but to tell her about Karl. At least she could assure Mary that she and Karl's children were financially stable, thanks to her husband's witch doctors and the federal government.

***

The doorbell rang, and Trudy opened the door. It had been over fifteen long, hard years since she'd last seen her baby sister. She registered the fine lines surrounding Mary's eyes and knew she had many more herself. Bitterness flooded her, but was supplanted by a wave of pure joy.

They held each other, rocking side to side, then Trudy stepped back from her sister and noticed Mary's children for the first time. Betty and Tommy stood behind their mother, looking down at the landing. Betty balanced her baby sister on one narrow hip.

Trudy grinned, wiping her eyes. She stepped around Mary and wrapped her arms around the red-faced twelve-year-old boy with blue eyes and curly red hair then turned to his fourteen-year-old sister and hugged her and the baby together. "You both look exactly like your father!" Betty brushed her wavy red hair off her shoulder with her free hand then smiled at her aunt. Tommy's expression remained a bit sullen, as if that might not be a compliment. Mary smiled as she watched them. The baby, Linda, was beginning to twist in her sister's arms.

They all moved inside, brought the suitcases and closed the door. Betty set her baby sister on the floor. The assorted offspring regarded each other, and then Linda made for the toy box in the corner of the room. Molly looked at her mother.

Trudy grinned. "She's your cousin." Molly sighed.

I know, sweetheart, the things you have to put up with for family.

Leaving the children to get acquainted, Trudy and Mary carried the luggage into the single bedroom then returned to sit at the kitchen table. Trudy poured them cups of warmed-over coffee then reached across the table for her sister's hands. They squeezed each other's fingers. Mary sighed. "I didn't know who he was, Sis. What he was. I thought I did."

"I don't think we ever know another person. Not really. Hell, I'm not sure we even know ourselves. We just figure it out as we go." Trudy smiled as she raised the coffee cup to her lips.

Concern wrinkled Mary's brow. "Here I am feeling sorry for myself. At least Travis will get out one day, and I got my kids with me. What's happening with Karl and with your boys?"

"At least Karl's alive. That's the most I can say, and I'm not sure if that's a blessing or not. When I think about him getting those shock treatments ...."

"Shock treatments?" The look of horror on Mary's face grew as Trudy explained.

"They say it works, but he wasn't the man I married even after his first time in the hospital. I was getting used to that. But now? If they ever do let him out, it'll be like living with a time bomb, waiting for the seconds to tick down. I love him. He's my husband." Trudy heard her voice crack and struggled to maintain her control. She cleared her throat. "So I got to figure out a way to be there for him, but survive the explosion when it comes."

Wordless, Mary shook her head. "What about the boys? How are they doing?"

"They're growing up. I haven't seen them for almost two years now. I get letters." They sat in silence for a moment. Trudy felt tears rise in her eyes and saw them mirrored in Mary's. Suddenly she began to laugh.

"Shit, look at us. What a pair of sad sacks."

Mary joined her sister's laughter. "God, Sis, it's so good to see you!"

Chapter Twenty-six

Lullaby and Goodnight

Mary and Trudy shared the bed with Marty, and the three girls slept on pallets on the bedroom floor. As the sole boy, Tommy got the privilege of sleeping on the living room couch. It was better than the tent Mary had shared with Trudy and Joe years ago, but not much.

The day after she arrived, Mary visited the Amarillo Department of Public Welfare and learned she would receive eighteen dollars a month for Aid to Families with Dependent Children, another program subsidized by the federal government. She would also get commodities: canned vegetables, oats, rice, peanut butter, processed cheese, and powdered milk that were distributed as a result of federal agricultural subsidies. Trudy had a steady income from Karl's disability payment. Together, they could manage very well.

They decided to look for a bigger apartment and found one they could afford in a small complex across town in less than a week. There were three bedrooms complete with beds, one for Trudy and her children, one for Mary and her girls, and one not much bigger than a closet for Tommy. The mattresses smelled a little musty, so they bought mattress covers. The apartment was bigger than the home they'd grown up in, and, besides well-worn furniture, it had electricity, indoor plumbing, and even an old claw-footed bathtub.

The only difficult part of the move had been saying goodbye to the Schumachers. Trudy told herself they wouldn't be that far away. She promised to bring the children to see them at least once a week. Still she felt guilty as she hugged them goodbye. Now that Mary was here, her own loneliness was over, but she was abandoning them to theirs.

A greater source of guilt and sadness for Trudy lay in her separation from her older sons. Although she wrote to them at least once a week, return letters arrived less and less frequently. The day that she, Mary, and the kids moved into the apartment, Trudy wrote a brief note to her boys with her new address and dropped the envelope into the mailbox in the lobby of their complex. She hoped it would encourage them to respond.

A week later she sat on the worn Naugahyde couch, holding the first letter she had received from her sons in over a month. It was more like a school writing exercise than real communication. "Dear Ma, How are you? We are fine." A few wooden sentences gave her a bare minimum of information before they signed off with love.

She knew they were helping out at their father's truck yard, and he was actually paying them small salaries. Bobby hadn't gone back to school. He hadn't even finished eighth grade. It was as she'd feared: neither of her sons found much use for education.

She couldn't say why, but she got the feeling they might be having some troubles with their father. Maybe it was just that they always asked how Karl was doing as if they might be wondering when they could come home. Or maybe it was something else, like when she'd sensed that Bobby was hurt.

How long can I keep waiting, just floating like a damn leaf down a creek?

***

At first Marty's symptoms mirrored those of a cold. His nose was stuffy, and he fussed, chewing on his fingers. He was cutting more teeth, and that didn't help. That evening, he vomited. Trudy gave him a child's dose of Pepto-Bismol, and shortly after, he nursed to sleep.

The next day, he was more listless and fussy. Then, in late afternoon, he lay down on his back, raised his knees, pulling them toward his stomach, and cried. Thinking he might be constipated, Trudy stewed some prunes and, sitting beside him on the floor, managed to get him to eat a couple of bites. She lifted him onto her lap and held him to her breast, encouraging him to nurse. He turned away. Trudy began to worry. She decided to call the doctor first thing in the morning, then laid her son on the floor and unpinned his damp diaper. As she lowered it between his thighs, she glimpsed a flash of color. Pulling the diaper from beneath him, she saw a puddle of brownish red jelly.

"Oh, God! No!"

Mary had been preparing meatloaf for supper in the kitchen with Molly and Linda. She rushed in, a look of concern on her face. "What's wrong?" The girls trailed behind her.

"What's wrong, Mommy?"

"Marty's sick, Molly. I have to talk to Aunt Mary. Please take Linda back to the kitchen." Trudy fought for control until the children were gone.

"There's blood in his diaper, Mary!" Her voice trembled. She showed Mary the diaper. "I've got to take him to the hospital!"

Bending over, Mary laid her hands on her sister's shoulders. "I don't want you to drive. You stay here. I'll get a cab." She ran outside.

Trudy cleaned up her unresisting toddler, pinning a fresh diaper on him. She rolled up the old one, hiding the blood from view. Molly stuck her head around the kitchen door. "Momma, can we come out now?"

"Yes, baby," Trudy said. She lifted Marty and holding him close to her chest, rose from the floor. "I've got to take Marty to the doctor."

Molly ran up to her, with Linda close behind. "Can I go, Momma?"

Trudy shook her head. "I need you to stay with Aunt Mary. We'll be back soon."

Just then, Mary stepped back through the front door. "The taxi's on it's way, Sis. I borrowed the neighbor's phone. They said the closest hospital's St. Anthony's. Just tell the driver. It's on Wallace Boulevard. I'm sure he knows where. You need to go right now, but I'll get there soon as I can. I'll find Bobby and Shirley so's they can watch the little ones. Where's your car keys?"

"In my purse, on the dresser in our bedroom. Could you hand me that diaper? The doctor might want it. And get me my purse."

***

At the hospital Trudy waited. First, she waited for a doctor in the emergency room to examine Martin. He looked at the diaper, then took her indifferent son from his mother's arms and laid him on a small, padded table. He examined Marty briefly, pressing his fingers into his abdomen. The baby whimpered, but seemed to lack the energy to protest more strongly.

"Your son has symptoms of a condition known as an intussusception. His large intestine appears to have telescoped upon itself. It may require surgery. An X-ray will confirm that. I'm sending him down to radiology now, with a nurse. She'll show you where to wait."

"Can I go with him?"

"No, I'm afraid not. But it shouldn't take long."

The nurse wheeled the table where Marty lay down a hallway. Trudy followed. As they passed a doorway, the nurse motioned toward it. "You wait in there, Mom," she said, smiling. "We'll be back, quick as a wink."

It was a small, private room with a crib and two chairs. After fifteen minutes, the nurse brought Marty back and started to put him into the crib. Trudy touched her elbow. "I'll take him," she said, and the nurse relinquished her son to her.

Next, she waited for the surgeon to arrive to confirm the diagnosis. He did so. "We'll operate first thing in the morning. Your son's condition is serious, but not yet critical. You should put him in the crib and try to get some rest. A nurse can bring in a cot for you if you'd like." He patted Trudy's shoulder, and left.

After the surgeon was gone she waited for Mary, who arrived about fifteen minutes later. "I'm sorry to take so long, Sis. I couldn't find those darn kids. They went to one of their friend's houses, and I had to keep asking 'round 'til I found somebody who knew where it was. What did you find out?"

Trudy told her.

"Well, it sounds like they're gonna take care of it. Here, I brought you a sandwich. Eat it. You need to keep your strength up."

To reassure her sister, Trudy tried to eat, but finally put the meatloaf sandwich back in the bag, barely touched. Then she waited for morning. She held her peacefully sleeping son in her arms. She refused to put him in the crib. Mary dozed in the chair beside her.

Shortly before dawn, Trudy realized that Marty was gone. He'd never stirred. He'd never woken. He'd simply slipped away into eternity, cradled in his mother's arms. Frantic, unbelieving, she laid her ear against his chest. No breath. No heartbeat.

Mary awoke to Trudy's hysterical, sobbing cries and ran into the hallway to find a doctor.

No, no, no! My sweet baby. No! Anything else, dear Lord, please. Not this!

***

Trudy drifted like an abandoned ship through the next few months. Only Molly kept her anchored at all. She knew there were others who would grieve if she were gone, if she left to join her precious baby. But only Molly would be devastated, and Trudy could never trade her suffering for that of her little girl. So, somehow, she endured.

Molly tried in her way, based upon her mother's teachings and her own ritual nighttime prayer, to comfort her mother. Seeing Trudy sitting numbly on the couch, staring into space, she would climb up to sit beside her and pat her mother's hand, lying limply on her lap.

"Don't worry, Mommy. Marty's in Heaven. He's with Jesus and the angels. When we die, we'll see him again. He's happy there, Mommy." And Trudy would force herself to smile at her small daughter and squeeze her hand. Then Molly would hop down and run to find Linda.

Mary had handled everything associated with Martin's death: arranging the funeral, notifying relatives and the Schumachers, Trudy's only real friends. She did everything for Trudy except bathe and dress her, and sometimes she even helped with that.

After a time, although the pain was still there, the fog began to lift. Trudy began to think about the future. She couldn't live in limbo forever. She had to get what remained of her family back together. But whatever she did, Mary had to be part of her plan.

She found her sister in the kitchen, putting away the commodities she had picked up earlier that Saturday morning. Molly and Linda stood on chairs next to the table. They searched through the cardboard boxes filled with smaller boxes, bags, and cans, examining the contents. Each had a spoonful of peanut butter lodged in her mouth. The open jar sat near them on the table.

Molly pulled the spoon out so she could speak. "Look, Mommy!" She held up a box of powdered milk. "Aunt Mary's gonna cook with it. We can't drink it. It tastes nasty!" She giggled, looking at Linda. Linda giggled, too, then removed the spoon from her own mouth.

"Nasty," she agreed, pointing her gooey spoon at the box.

Trudy smiled at Linda and laid her hand on her daughter's head, ruffling her hair. The girls renewed their inspection of the commodities. "Mary, does Travis have any idea when he might be paroled?" She knew her sister had received a letter from her husband the day before.

Mary paused in her task, a can of green peas in her hand. "Yes, as a matter a fact, he does. I was gonna tell you. He says in three months he'll have served a quarter of his time. That makes him eligible. A course, it's up to the parole board. But he ain't worried. He's being good."

Or pretending to be anyway. Three months, then what?

"Do you know what he plans to do then?"

"Not yet. I don't think he's thought 'bout it much. Three months is a long time." She set the can of peas on the table, then stepped up to Trudy, putting her hands on her sister's waist. "Don't you worry 'bout it, Sis. You hear? Whatever we do, if we leave this place, you and Molly are coming with us. Far as I'm concerned, if he don't like it, he can get out." Her face softened. "But he won't mind at all. He's got his flaws, but meanness ain't one of 'em. Would you mind him being here?" She gazed into Trudy's eyes.

"No, as long as I've got you, I can put up with him." Trudy smiled and gave her sister a quick hug.

For a while anyway. Probably not forever.

Trudy stepped back at the sound of knocking. Before either she or Mary could respond, they heard Shirley yell from the living room where she'd been curled up on the couch reading a book. "I'll get it!" The door creaked on its hinges. "Daddy!"

Mary ran though the kitchen doorway. The girls scooted past, then stopped and stared. Trudy trailed, unbelieving. On the porch, just outside the door, his arms wrapped around his older daughter, stood a chunky, balding, red-haired man. Travis. His piercing blue eyes met hers, then darted away. Turning toward Mary, he grinned and moved Shirley aside, opening his arms wide as his wife ran into them.

Chapter Twenty-seven

Straighten Up and Fly Right

"I wanted to surprise you," Travis said. He sat on the couch next to Mary, his arm around her. Linda sat on his knee. Betty sat cross-legged on the floor in front of him. His daughter's eyes never left his face. "I got time off for good conduct. Ninety days. They counted it towards my parole." He glanced at Trudy. She sat across the room in their old rocker, holding Molly on her lap.

You wonder if I'm buying it. You fooled the authorities, but I know you're as phony as a three dollar bill.

She said nothing.

"They give me jobs, and I done 'em. I worked hard. You know I'm a hard worker, don'cha, honey?" He nudged Mary with his elbow, grinning at her.

She smiled up at him. "Sometimes, I guess. When you have to be."

"Well, who works hard if they don't have to? That'd just be stupid now, wouldn't it?" He bumped her shoulder with his own.

"You two have a lot to talk about. I'll finish putting away the food." Trudy slid Molly off her lap and rose. She went back to the kitchen, leading Molly by the hand. Her daughter tugged at her fingers, frowning.

Trudy tightened her grip, sweeping her little girl through the kitchen doorway. When they were inside and out of sight, she squatted until she was face to face with Molly. "Honey, they haven't seen each other for a long time. They need some private time. You can go back in a little while. But right now you can help me sort these canned vegetables."

Trudy knew it was the sort of task Molly loved, and, sure enough, she was immediately engrossed.

***

Travis inserted himself into the life Trudy and Mary had created like the serpent in the Garden of Eden. Betty and Linda moved into Tommy's room, and Tommy now slept on the couch as he had in the other apartment. He seemed less enthusiastic about his father's return than the rest of his family and found things to do away from home during the time he wasn't in school. Trudy sometimes caught him glaring at his father when Travis was unaware.

He ain't fooling you either, is he?

Trudy's dislike of the man sat like a boulder between her and her sister. But for the time being, things were up in the air. Mary could continue to receive welfare and commodities as long as Travis remained unemployed, but she couldn't support her family, including Travis, without Trudy's help. So Trudy couldn't even think about leaving until Travis found a job.

As she sat on the couch, hemming a dress that Molly had outgrown so that Linda could wear it, Trudy wondered how hard he would actually try while she and Mary were supporting him. She decided it was a standoff, smirked, and shook her head, her eyes fixed on her needlework. She could hear the occasional clunk of a cabinet door or clank of a pot as Mary put away the clean breakfast dishes.

They had the apartment to themselves for a change. Travis had gone to meet with his parole officer, borrowing Trudy's Chevy, as usual. Tommy and Betty were at school, and Molly and Linda were playing outside, making mud pies and possibly eating them.

Hearing the silence, Trudy glanced up. Mary stood before her, looking uncomfortable. "Sis, we need to talk." She turned and, seizing the arm of their rocker, dragged it closer to the couch and sat facing Trudy.

Trudy stuck the needle into the hem then set the dress aside, focusing on her sister's face. "What's up? Is something wrong?"

"No, I just need to see how you feel about something." Mary looked down. Trudy waited. "Travis wants to go back to Phoenix. He thinks it's a better place for us to live." Mary's eyes lifted to Trudy's. "Will you come with us? How would you feel about moving?" She rushed on, not pausing for an answer. "I know it's farther from Karl, but they don't let you see him anyways. If he gets well, you could come back, or maybe he could come out there. I know it's a long ways, but." She finally drifted to a halt.

A long ways from Karl, but closer to my boys.

Trudy took a deep breath. "But what about Travis's parole? Isn't he supposed to stay in Texas?" She watched conflicting emotions cross Mary's face.

Embarrassment appeared to win. Mary looked down at her hands. "You know him, Trudy. They didn't catch him the last time he run off, when he was a kid. He don't think they'll catch him this time neither."

They both heard a noise and turned toward the door. The knob was turning. Travis entered to find Trudy and Mary staring at him. "Uh, oh. Maybe I better leave." He turned, grinning, pretending to step back outside.

"I was just telling Trudy 'bout us maybe moving back to Arizona. Seeing how she feels."

"Well, how *do* you feel?" He walked across the room to stand next to Mary, resting his hand on her arm. His eyes locked on Trudy's. They were unreadable, but Trudy knew how he felt.

You don't want me along, but you need me. Unless maybe you plan to steal my car. I wouldn't put it past you.

"I'm still deciding. Are you sure about taking the risk? If they catch you, you'll go back to prison, maybe for longer." She studied his face.

"Don't worry me. Does it worry you?" He watched her, eyes narrowed, chin thrust forward.

"It's your life. No skin off my nose. But you might wanna think about Mary and the kids." She figured that was the least of his considerations, but she watched for a sign she might have struck a nerve.

He smiled, his face changing like a chameleon. "Don't worry, Trudy. They'll be fine. What I done was just a little chicken shit burglary. No guns, no harm to nobody. Hell, them people even got their stuff back. The cops ain't gonna bother with me. Outta sight, outta mind."

"I hope so. For Mary's sake."

"So, are you going with us?"

Mary grabbed his arm. "Honey, let's give her a little time to think about it. We can talk about it later."

"Sure, baby. How about I change clothes while you clean those girls up, and we take 'em to the park? It's nearly lunchtime. We could have a picnic." He went into their bedroom. Mary glanced at Trudy, then hurried outside to get Molly and Linda. Trudy picked up Molly's dress and continued hemming.

***

When Betty and Tommy arrived after school, Trudy told them where their parents were. Tommy said he was meeting a friend to do homework and took off. Betty left for the park almost immediately, only pausing to gulp a cold glass of Kool-Aid.

What fools we women are.

Trudy was almost paralyzed by the thought of moving to Arizona. What if her decision, whether yes or no, became something else to regret? She wandered around the apartment dusting, cleaning out drawers, straightening out cabinets, keeping her hands busy as her mind worked.

She'd learned that riding time's current was like finding her way through the woods without a lantern on a moonless night. She might end up safe at home, or trip over the edge of a cliff. She couldn't lie to herself that she had any control of the future. Her past had taught her that. She could only decide based on this single moment, and her decision might turn out to be wrong.

I guess this is why Papa put his life in God's hands. Does believing everything is God's will mean no guilt for wrong decisions?

Would she be abandoning Karl if she left? She'd only found him after years of trying to make the best of it. She would always love him. No one could ever replace him. A flood of memories of their brief happiness pierced her heart. But he was so far away from her now that he might as well be living on the moon. Would a few hundred miles make any real difference?

Mary was both her dearest friend and sweet sister. She and Molly were all that had kept Trudy hanging onto the edge of the cliff after she lost Marty. Trudy knew, even if Mary didn't, that Travis couldn't be relied upon. If he went back to prison, Mary would be stranded alone in Arizona if Trudy didn't go with her.

Arizona was closer to California. Bobby and Willie might be able to come home at last. She believed they needed her. She knew she needed them.

If this is a mistake, I'll deal with it in the future when I know what that is.

***

Mid-afternoon, when Travis, Mary, and the girls returned from the park, Travis went straight to the bedroom. Trudy heard the radio come on. The man reminded her of Joe in some ways, but for all his faults she knew Joe had more basic decency than Travis would ever have. Molly ran over to hug her mother, then raced after Linda to the kitchen. Mary followed. The girls came out carefully balancing glasses of purple Kool-Aid.

"Drink that outside, girls," Mary called, standing in the kitchen doorway. They pushed the back door open and stepped out. Betty got her own glass of Kool-Aid then followed them into the tiny backyard, closing the door behind her. Mary hesitated, regarding Trudy. "Well, I guess I better start supper." She turned halfway.

"No, Sis. I'll help you with that in a minute. We need to talk first."

Mary slowly approached and sat in the rocker. "I'm sorry that Travis tried to pressure you. He's sort of high-strung. We're not in that big a hurry."

Trudy shook her head, making a brushing motion with her hand. "I've decided. We'll go with you. I'm guessing Travis was planning on taking my car, if I decided to come along." Mary lowered her eyes, blushing. "That's fine. I'll pay for the gas, too. We'll keep track, and you all can pay me back half after he finds a job."

Mary rose and crossed the room to stand before her sister. She reached down to take Trudy's hands in hers. "Thank you, Sis. I couldn't bear to think of going without you." Tears filled her eyes.

Trudy rose and took her sister in her arms. "And I couldn't let you." Mary leaned back and smiled through her tears. They held each other for another moment then walked arm in arm to the kitchen to prepare supper.

***

Travis told them he wanted to leave as soon as possible. He and Mary went to Amarillo High School and Sam Houstin Junior High to withdraw Betty and Tommy. Mary told Trudy that Travis had done the talking. "He told 'em we was moving to Austin, and that the kids' new schools would be sending for their records. That way, when he don't meet with his parole officer, if the authorities start looking for him, maybe they'll concentrate on Austin for a while. I think they believed him."

Trudy's eyes searched her sister's face. "Does it ever bother you that he lies so easy?"

"Sure it does." Mary broke eye contact, then stepped over to the front window, gazing out. When she began to speak again, her voice was so soft Trudy could barely hear her. "But I can't change him. And he's my husband, Trudy."

Trudy walked up behind her, laying her hands on Mary's shoulders. "I know, but if you ever want to change that, I'll help you, Sis."

Mary remained motionless. "I still love him. God help me, but I do."

There was nothing more for Trudy to say. She pulled her sister around to face her. "Then we'll all just have to make the best of it."

Once again.

***

With everyone squeezed into the Chevy, there wouldn't be much room for anything else, but then, they didn't own much. The four children would fill the back seat, but Trudy and Mary managed to jam clothing, bed clothes, a large cardboard box of glasses and dishes wrapped in newspaper, and a smaller one of pots and pans, into the trunk.

Mary had left most of her personal items with her in-laws, to be collected after things settled down for her and Travis, sometime in the indefinite future. Trudy placed a small box of keepsakes, mostly photographs taken by her or Karl, on the far right side of the front seat. It would rest on her lap for safe-keeping. She still couldn't look at the snapshots of Marty without crying.

After they were packed, Trudy walked three blocks to a pay phone outside a drugstore. There, she placed three calls. First, she phoned Frieda to promise to call with her new address as soon as she had one. She was relieved to hear no censure in her sister-in-law's voice. On the contrary, Frieda sounded happy to hear that Trudy was moving forward.

Next, she called the Schumachers. Mrs. Schumacher sounded older and more tired than when she'd last seen her. Trudy felt a stab of guilt for her neighbors' loneliness, but she couldn't help it. She promised to write and keep them up to date on Molly's activities.

Finally, she phoned Dr. Levinson and apprised him of her plans, saying she would call to give him contact information as soon as possible. She thanked him for all he'd done for her. "I don't know how we'd have survived without Karl's disability check. If you hadn't helped me ...." There was an awkward pause. She heard the psychiatrist clear his throat.

"Trudy, I'm glad I could do something. And I'm glad you're getting on with your life." He hesitated. "I'm sorry to have to say this over the phone, but I think it's important for you to understand. I don't believe Karl will ever be completely well. He may have periods of lucidity, maybe even leave the hospital. But the improvement will in all likelihood be temporary. You need to let go, concentrate on your children. By the way, did you have a boy or a girl? I forgot to ask the last time you were here."

"A boy." Trudy realized she'd spoken too softly to be heard. Clearing her throat she repeated firmly. "A boy." She could say no more.

"Congratulations! One of each." Trudy could hear the sincere pleasure in his voice. She brushed the tears from her eyes and said her goodbye.

Chapter Twenty-eight

Sentimental Journey

Tommy huddled under Mary's old red and black striped Indian blanket on the living room floor, still asleep. When Trudy saw him there, images of Davy filled her mind. She hadn't seen her brother or heard his voice since the night she'd fled Mama's bitter accusations. She knew he'd made it through the war, but, according to Millie, it had changed him. "He's different now, Sis. Quieter. Grown up, but sadder, almost like a stranger, and he won't talk about it," Millie had written.

He is a stranger to me. It's been too long. Much too long. Papa's getting old. I can't bear not to see him again.

Trudy walked through the living room and out the front door. She stood in the front yard and looked back at the house. It was much larger than their Amarillo apartment. Ranch style, it was constructed of cement blocks newly painted a soft cream color with dark green trim. The large screened casement windows were flung open like welcoming arms. They kept out flies, but let the breeze from the window-mounted swamp cooler in the front room circulate.

Phoenix again. I'm like a cat finding its way back no matter where it's dropped.

Travis had filled out the paperwork for the rental, and Trudy suspected—*knew*, if she were honest with herself—that he'd lied about his employment. They'd paid the first month's rent and deposit with Trudy's money, but the agreement was in Travis' name. Trudy had mixed feelings, but Mary took it in stride.

"We don't want to hurt his pride, Sis. He's the man, after all."

Some man! How can you still trust him after all he's put you through?

The front door slammed, and Trudy turned to see Molly and Linda running toward her, giggling. "Mama, we want toast and jelly." Molly looked at the smaller girl standing beside her.

"Yeah, and Kool-aid." Linda looked at Molly.

"Yeah." They grinned at each other.

"Toast and jelly and milk," Trudy said, and walked back toward the house. The children ran ahead.

Maybe this could be home now, if we could just get rid of the rat in the woodpile—and get my boys back.

***

"Mama, we're done. Can we turn on the radio? It's time for "The Lone Ranger," Tommy said.

All of the children, including Molly, turned eager eyes toward Mary. She smiled. "Okay, so long as you remember you gotta do the dishes soon as it's over." Chairs scraped the linoleum floor as the cousins ran into the living room.

The sound of the announcer's voice burst forth. "And now, the further adventures of the Lone Ranger and his faithful companion, Tonto."

"Turn it down a little!" Mary smiled at her sister.

It had been a week since they'd moved in, and Travis, Trudy, and Mary sat at the dinner table nibbling the remains of canned green beans, fried Spam, and biscuits. As the sound of the radio dimmed, Travis made his announcement. "Well, ladies, I got me a job."

"What? You been home for hours and didn't tell me?" Joy and hurt puzzlement fought for Mary's expression.

"I wanted to surprise you. Besides, I didn't think it was fair to tell you first. It's important to Trudy, too." He glanced over at Trudy, smirking.

"That's great, Travis. 'Cause with you living here, and your name on the rent agreement, I don't think Mary could get public assistance." Trudy's words hung in the air.

"Well, she don't need it. She's got a man to provide for her." The contempt dripped from his voice. He stared at her, his upper lip curled.

We don't like each other much, do we?

Mary glanced at Trudy, anxiety in her eyes, then turned back to Travis. "What kind of job, honey?" Her voice was a pleading wheedle that pierced Trudy's heart. Staring at her plate, she cut a piece of leftover spam with the side of her fork, lifted it to her mouth, and chewed in silence.

"Mechanic, what else? I fudged a little on the employment dates, but Harry'll cover for me if they ever get 'round to calling him. But when they see what I can do, I doubt they'll bother."

No. They probably won't.

Trudy rose with her empty dishes and walked to the sink. Mary's gaze followed her for a moment, then returned to her husband's face. She scooted her chair closer to his and leaned over to kiss his jaw. When Trudy returned for the serving dishes, Mary waved her away. "Me and the kids'll take care of it, Sis. You go relax."

Trudy joined the children in the living room. The Lone Ranger was explaining his plan in a resonant voice to his loyal side-kick. She sank down on the couch between Betty and Molly, and Molly stuck her small fingers inside her mother's. Trudy blanked her mind and willed herself into the world of radio drama where justice was always served up.

***

"Sis, that's way too much!" Mary pushed Trudy's hand holding two twenty and two ten dollar bills away. "You done paid a whole month's rent, plus deposit last month. Maybe twenty, to help with the food, but that's it. Travis gets his pay today."

"Take it, Mary. If you don't need it, hide it someplace. You need some savings, just in case." A red blush seeped into Mary's cheeks, and she slowly took a ten and a twenty from her sister's hand.

"You keep the rest. You need to save some for yourself. To get the boys here, if Joe won't bring 'em." Mary stepped over to her sister and wrapped her arms around her. "Life is harder than we used to think when we was kids, innit? But we're together again. Thank the good Lord for that!" Trudy stepped back, hiding her skepticism from her sister in a soft smile.

God helps them who help themselves. Or maybe we just help ourselves.

Trudy was slicing potatoes into a frying pan puddled with sizzling lard while Mary chopped tomatoes when a car pulled into the driveway. She glanced through the kitchen window expecting to see Travis, home from work, climbing out of her Chevy. Mary looked up, too. "Lord, who can that be?"

The car was not Trudy's Chevy, but a dark blue Plymouth with one white fender. The door scraped open and Travis climbed out. Trudy saw him purse his lips and a shrill whistle pierced the air. Mary wiped her hands and ran for the front door. Trudy followed filled with trepidation. The two women stopped at the edge of the driveway. Trudy stood behind Mary as Travis grinned at his wife. "You like it?"

"Where'd it come from? Where's Trudy's car?" Trudy heard the concern in her sister's voice. She felt it, too.

What have you done, you jackass?

"Trudy's car's just fine. We'll go back to the garage so's she can get it. This here's our car!" Travis smiled at his wife, reminding Trudy of a toddler showing his mother a perfect mud pie.

"But, honey, we can't afford a car." Mary glanced over her shoulder at Trudy.

Travis glowered. "Sure we can. I got paid today, remember? Some guy brought this baby in, but didn't want to pay what it cost to fix it. I made him an offer, and he took it. I still got some money left." His smile returned.

"How much?" Mary glanced at Trudy again.

"Enough. Trudy's paying half the rent, ain't she? We still got groceries, don't we?"

"But ... Trudy paid all the rent last time, and already bought all the groceries we didn't bring with us, and her and Molly don't eat nearly as much as all of us do." Mary looked as if she were about to cry.

"It's okay, Sis. I can help out." Trudy grasped her sister's shoulders from behind and propped her head next to Mary's. She remembered when her sweet little sister had swallowed the nickel so long ago. Staring at Travis, she caught his eye and held it.

"Now Travis's got a car, so he won't need to buy anything else. He can start paying me back when he gets his next paycheck." Her voice was soft and soothing near Mary's ear, but her eyes on Travis's told a different story.

***

Travis came home from work at noon the next day. Mary and Trudy sat at the kitchen table sipping iced tea. He waved at them as he stepped inside then walked into the living room. Tommy and Betty sat on the old couch, legs curled under them, reading tattered Superman comics.

Molly and Linda sat on the floor dressing their baby dolls. They peered up at him, and he squatted down beside them. "Hey, kids. How's 'bout we go for a picnic?"

Betty set her comic aside and looked over at her father. She smiled. "Where?" Tommy continued to read.

"Don't know 'zactly. Somewhere along the canal. We can drive around, test out the old buggy, and find someplace we like. I might even give you a driving lesson. It's time you start learning. Don't want to be like your Mama." He glanced over his shoulder at Mary and winked.

"Maybe we could stop by Dairy Queen on the way back." He turned toward Tommy. "Get us cones with a curl on top. Mama took most of my money, but I still got a couple of bucks." Tommy put his comic aside but still didn't look at his father.

"Ice cream! We want ice cream!" Molly and Linda sang in unison, jumping up and down.

"Honey, could you make us some sandwiches?" Travis said.

Mary turned to Trudy. "What do you think? Sounds like fun, don't it?"

"Yeah, it does. But, sweetie, if you don't mind, I think I'll stay here. I didn't sleep very good last night. Can I beg off this time? Maybe relax in the quiet. Take a nap?"

Mary's eyes peered into her sister's then slid away. "Sure, if you'd rather not go."

Trudy grabbed her arm and pulled Mary into a brief hug. "Really, Sis, I'm just too tired for all the excitement. But I want you to have fun," she said. Mary smiled and turned toward the cupboard, reaching for the breadbox.

**

After they left, Trudy walked into her bedroom. She regarded herself in the mirror on the wall beside her bedroom window. The strong afternoon light highlighted the fine lines around the corners of her eyes and across her high forehead. A sprinkling of gray hairs dotted her temples.

She wasn't really tired, but she couldn't imagine an afternoon stuck in the car with Travis. He was like a branch scraping against the window in a rain storm. She could only stand so much of him. She tied a green scarf around her hair and tucked the gray hairs out of sight beneath it. Grabbing her sunglasses, she walked back through the house and out the front door.

Trudy walked north and passed a house where two small brown-skinned boys wearing baggy khaki shorts and nothing else played in the front yard of a frame house with peeling paint. A lanky brown and black mongrel lay beside them in the dried Bermuda grass. As Trudy passed, it leaped up and ran to the chicken wire fence, barking ferociously.

"*Cállate, Ladrón! Déjala en paz!*" The larger boy ran after the dog and swatted it on its rear. The dog stopped barking, but still growled under its breath. Trudy smiled at the boy, and he grinned back at her, showing missing front teeth.

A couple of blocks ahead, a truck filled with cement bags and concrete blocks stood on a lot along with the skeleton of a house. No one was in sight. On the same street, but across the road, stood a completed house with a sign in front bearing the name Lincoln Acres Construction Company. Farther west Trudy could see several similar houses. Each formed a chunky letter L. They varied in the direction the L's faced and the color, pale pink, blue, green, or gold. Some were slightly larger than others. A few had cars or pickup trucks in the driveways. Farther east from where she stood, Trudy saw a few vacant lots.

She crossed the street and peered at the sign in front of the empty house. Under the company name were the words "Build to Suit. Will Carry." Trudy took a quick breath and stood memorizing the phone number on the sign: BR-555-88. It couldn't hurt to call them and get information. She had a steady income from the government, and she knew she couldn't tolerate Travis much longer.

But I'd be close by when Mary needs me, which I know she will.

She started back, repeating the phone number to herself. When she passed the house where the dog had barked, neither dog nor boys were in sight.

If I buy one of them houses, if this becomes my home, I'll learn their names.

Chapter Twenty-nine

Look for the Silver Lining

"How much is the down payment?" Trudy stood outside Varela's Grocery the following Monday morning and spoke into a pay phone. She'd already discussed the price of a one bedroom house and what the payments would be with the Lincoln Acres partner on the other end of the conversation. The monthly payments would be less than her current share of Mary's rent.

"Depends. We carry, it's three percent. Bank carries, 'bout the same, unless it's a G.I. Loan. Did your husband serve during the war?"

"Yes, he did."

"Then he could probably get one. In that case, there's no down payment. The government guarantees it. If you're interested, come on down to our office and we'll see what we can work out."

"Where are you located?" Trudy took a pencil and scrap of paper out of her purse and carefully wrote down directions as he told her how to get there. After she hung up, she stood for a moment. She was benefiting from Karl's military service once again.

But none of this makes up for what that mule took away from me. Nothing ever will.

A bitter smile crossed her face. She clenched her jaw and pushed back against the overwhelming sadness that threatened to overpower her, turned, and walked back to the house to get the car.

***

Trudy called her sons long distance from the same pay phone that evening. The number Joe had given her two years before still worked, and the voice that answered was instantly recognizable, but deeper than she remembered. "Will?"

"Mama?" At the sound of surprise in her older son's voice, Trudy began to laugh and cry at the same time.

"Bobby, it's Mama!" Trudy heard her son relay the news to his brother. "What's going on, Ma? Is everything okay? How is it, being back in Arizona?" They caught up for a while, and Trudy was content just to hear his voice. But when she had to drop more coins into the phone she got to the point. She told him about the house. She'd contracted for an unfinished interior to save money, trusting that her sons could handle the parts left undone.

"I'll need your and Bobby's help to get it fixed up to live in after the construction company gets finished. Then, if you want to, you could stay here with me and your sister. I'd love that, but I know you're working for your daddy, so if you want to go back out there, I understand. But I'd love to have you here. I know you could find jobs." She hesitated. She didn't want to pressure him, but she couldn't help it. "I've missed you so much!"

"We missed you, too, Mama." Trudy's tears flowed anew. Willie must have turned away from the receiver because she could hear tones of a brief conversation with his brother, then he came back on the line. "Should we come now?"

Trudy hesitated. "Oh, I wish you could! But Mary's husband is sort of a jerk, and I'm not sure when the house will be finished. They're waiting to hear about the loan. It's approved. Just a matter of paperwork, but after that it could be a couple of months. It might be better to wait just a little while, so we don't have to stay with them that long."

"Okay." She heard the disappointment in his voice.

"No, the hell with him! I pay more of the rent than he does. How soon can you come? Will your father drive you?"

"Naw, we'll catch a Greyhound. He'll be too busy."

Is that sarcasm I hear?

"We could probably be there in two or three days, depending on the bus schedule. If you're sure that's all right? Can you call tomorrow? We'll find out and tell you when to pick us up." The eagerness in his voice resolved all Trudy's fears.

"Do you need me to wire you some money?"

"Naw, we're fine. He pays us. Bobby wants to talk to you."

"Hi, Ma. How's my bratty little sister?" Trudy was unprepared for the change in her younger son's voice. She hadn't spoken to him, except through written word, since he'd broken his arm. The teasing, high-spirited child's voice had been replaced by that of a young man. Her heart ached for the lost time, even as she rejoiced in the fact that she would see him soon.

But when she called the next day, the timeline had changed. One of Joe's customers needed some help on a construction project. The job would be full-time at a decent hourly rate for nearly three months.

"It'll give us a chance to save some money, Ma. It might take us a while to find jobs in Phoenix. We don't want to be a burden. We want to help you out, pay our share. We're not babies anymore," Willie said.

No, you're certainly not.

Trudy hated the further reminder of the time she'd lost with them, but felt proud of the independent young men they'd become.

***

Construction on Trudy's house began as soon as she, in Karl's name, was approved for the G.I. Loan. Loan officers had helped her with the necessary paperwork and Power of Attorney. Afterward, she and Molly strolled the few blocks from Mary's house several times a week to check on the progress of their new home. When it was time to pick the exterior colors the painter stopped by Mary's house with samples of those available.

"This one, Momma," Molly said. She touched a yellow paint chip with a chubby finger.

"I don't know, baby. That's a little bright. How 'bout this one?" Trudy tapped a pale cream chip.

"That's the same color as Linda's house."

"Yeah. But don't you like it?"

"I guess. But make the windows different." Molly chose a pale aqua for the shutters, and Trudy let it be. Her daughter had strong opinions about color. It wasn't that important to Trudy.

The house sat completed for nearly a week before Trudy got the keys. It didn't matter that much because the boys wouldn't be arriving for another week. The builder met her for a final walk-through. He pointed to the beams and walls of the living room. She could see electric wires strung through the bare framed interior walls and outlets mounted to the studs. Two bare pipes capped with faucets extended into the sparse kitchen area above an enamel sink resting in the framed-in center of a skeleton kitchen cabinet.

"Everything's in working order." Her guide reached out and flipped up a switch attached to the kitchen framing. A light bulb hanging by a cord suspended from a ceiling beam came on.

"Naturally, the water's off until you finish the plumbing. You'll need to put the electricity, gas, and water in your name before the first of the month."

Trudy stared up into what would be her attic after the gypsum board was hung then followed the man into the bedroom. The bathroom, between the bedroom and back of the house, contained two capped water pipes running up the interior studs next to the kitchen and another farther back above a large opening in the concrete floor.

"The toilet goes there. The drain is installed and comes out under the back of the house. You'll need to run a sewer pipe from there to the cesspool once you have one. Same for the sink drains. Water heater goes there in the corner." He pointed. "You can install a shower or bathtub over there." He pointed again. "But the house don't come with plumbing for that." He looked at Trudy and frowned. "You gonna be able to handle this? You got help?"

Trudy met his gaze. "Yes, we'll manage."

"Okay. Well I guess that's it. These are yours. The front and back locks are the same." He handed her two keys on a metal ring and left her standing in a house that looked more like a barn.

When she heard his car pull away, Trudy returned to the living room, plopped down cross-legged on the cold concrete floor and began laughing.

Home, sweet home!

***

Trudy stood, hands on hips, and watched the boys dig. Tommy raked dirt away from the deep hole. A few clods sprinkled down on top of Bobby's head. He took one hand off the shovel to brush away the dirt. "Hey, you little turd, watch what you're doing." He tilted his head and stared at Tommy.

"Bobby!" Trudy's tone held shock and admonition. Then everyone, including Tommy, began to laugh, and Tommy made a threatening motion with the rake.

Mary and Betty sat on a pair of blue kitchen chairs and leaned forward to reach the handle of a wooden ice cream maker. The mixture cranked with no effort, not nearly frozen yet. Molly and Linda sat beside a puddle of water filched from a pail of drinking water. The puddle was a mud pie factory. A spare slab of plywood held their treasures to dry.

Will and Bob had found and installed a cheap toilet and cook stove the day after they'd arrived. Now they were completing the cesspool. With drainage installed, they could turn on the cold water, have drinking water and a toilet to use while they worked, and start hanging the gypsum board.

The boys climbed up the ladder and out of the hole. Bobby picked up his shovel and grunted as he slammed it into the ground. "Tommy, make a stack of the longest, thickest boards, then go help your ma with that ice cream. We need something cold and sweet." They began to dig a trench between the hole and the back of the house.

It took the rest of the day, with time out to eat bologna sandwiches and ice cream, but by early evening they'd connected the kitchen and bathroom drains to the cesspool and covered the cesspool with a thick layer of wood and earth. Mary, Betty, Linda, and Molly had left for home soon after lunch. Trudy stayed until the boys finished, helping them when she could. When she couldn't, she sat at the kitchen table she'd bought second hand before the boys arrived.

She stroked the top. It was a deep, pretty blue, with sides that folded up or down as needed. They were down now, waiting. The four chairs were the same shade, but the tops of the backs were patterned in delicate pastel flowers of pale blue, yellow, pink, and green. It was used, but it was the prettiest table Trudy had ever owned.

She tapped a Lucky Strike out of the half empty package, lit it, inhaled deeply, and leaned back in her chair. She looked out the open back door and watched the three boys mingle horseplay and laughter with grueling physical labor.

How lucky I am.

Abruptly, the image of Karl, smiling at her as he examined the water faucet the day they'd moved into their Sunnyslope home, flashed into her mind. Taking a deep breath, she thrust the image away.

***

The next day Bobby and Willie rose early without needing an alarm. Getting a jump on the day's heat was a necessity for anyone who worked in construction. They were in the kitchen sipping coffee when Trudy entered. She yawned. Bob reached for a cup, and Will lifted the old percolator from the stove to fill it. Trudy looked at them as she accepted her coffee and reached for the Carnation.

"Ma, we're going to the house to see how much gypsum board it's gonna take. We'll close off the bathroom and bedroom first. We can work on the rest as soon as you got the money for materials. We'll take the car later and go see the guys I used to work for in Sunnyslope. I think they'll give us a good deal. If they remember me."

"They'll remember you." Trudy smiled around her coffee cup.

Will grinned back, then looked at Bob. Trudy saw something pass between them. Bob's eyes flickered from his brother to his mother. "Ma, we been thinking. We got water, power, the cook stove works, and now we got a toilet. Me and Will could stay over there while we do the rest of the work."

"Why?" Trudy looked back and forth between them. "There's no cooler there yet. How'll you sleep in this heat?"

The boys grinned at each other. "Ma, we'll be working there most of the day. We're used to the heat. Besides, we can get a fan for nighttime, and cover up with wet sheets if we have to," Bob said.

"We're both gonna start looking for work, too. I'll ask the Sunnyslope people 'bout that. If there's anything around, they'll know about it. We want to help you out, pay our share. We're not babies anymore." Trudy met her eldest son's eyes and smiled through her melancholy.

No, you're sure not. Only one baby left.

Trudy took a deep breath as Molly wandered into the kitchen, rubbing her eyes. She walked over to her mother and wrapped her arms around Trudy's thighs. "I guess you could stay there if you want, but I'm still not sure how it's better'n here. I know it's a little crowded, but you'd be sleeping on the floor there, too."

The boys looked at each other and Bob looked at the floor. "It *is* crowded here, Ma, and if you must know, we'd rather not spend too much time around Travis." Will glanced at his little sister and lowered his voice. "There's something about him. He was telling us stories about some of the things he done, you know?" He glanced at Molly again. "He seemed to be bragging, and he kept watching us, like he was trying to figure out how we felt about it. He makes us uncomfortable."

That damn bastard! Did he think they'd be impressed? Did he want to involve them in one of his schemes?

"All right." Trudy took a deep breath. "I know how you feel. I'd like to get away from the S.O.B., too. Soon as we can." Molly looked up at her mother, eyes full of curiosity.

"Want toast and jelly, baby? How 'bout you two?"

"Naw, thanks, Ma. We're taking some sandwiches. We'll be back for the car in a bit."

***

They burst through the front door an hour later. Trudy looked up in surprise from the pot of beans and cold water she was setting on the stove to soak. Travis had left for work and Tommy and Betty for school. Mary was out on the back porch with the girls washing clothes.

"What's wrong?" Wiping her hands on a dish towel, she hurried over to where they stood frowning. Her eyes darted from one to the other.

"Karl's at the house," Will said.

"What?" The dish towel dropped unnoticed to the floor.

"Somebody knocked on the door, and when Bob opened it, Karl was standing there." Will spoke, but both of her sons stared at Trudy, watching her reaction. "He asked where you was, but we didn't tell him. We said we needed to talk to you first. Did you know he was coming?"

Was that doubt she saw in Bob's eyes? "God, no! Of course not!" Trudy's mind raced back and forth like a rat in a maze. A memory of Karl's tales of traveling around during the depression, hitch hiking, riding the rails surfaced. If he knew where to go, he could get there. The boys stood in silence as their mother tried to make sense of what had happened.

Did they release him? Why didn't Dr. Levinson write me? Or Frieda, if she knew?

"How'd he seem?"

The boys looked at each other and shrugged. "He seemed, I don't know, like maybe he knew something we didn't? Like he had a secret. His eyes were … I don't know," Will's voice trailed off. "Maybe he's still mad at us from before. We didn't talk to him really."

"Is he gonna stay here?" Bob said, his eyes seizing hers. Trudy knew that was the key question for both her sons. Their younger faces as they climbed into the car with their father years before flashed into her mind. She couldn't lose them again.

"You're gonna stay," she said. "Whether he stays or not depends on how he is. If he's well, and can be good to you and a good father to Molly, maybe he'll stay. But I doubt it. I don't think he'll ever be well again, much as I wish that could be true." She heard the bleak despair in her own voice, but the resolve behind it was stronger. Some of the tension left the boys' faces.

"I guess I better go talk to him. Tell Mary what happened, but not in front of Molly and Linda." Trudy walked into her bedroom. She stood for a moment, staring into the mirror as she ran a comb through her hair. The face in the mirror was wan and sad, but determined. The set of her jaw reminded her of her mother.

The boys were waiting in the living room when she came out. "Do you want us to come with you, Ma?" Eddie said.

She smiled sadly and gave him a brief hug. "No, I need to do this by myself."

Chapter Thirty

You'll Never Know

Trudy opened the front door to find Karl standing in front of her kitchen sink, running a comb through thinning, wet hair. "There you are!" He smirked at her, and the secret knowing, the suspicion, was all there. An aching lump rose in Trudy's throat.

Did I really think it might be different?

"Hello, Karl. When did you get out of the hospital? How did you find us?" It was hard to speak as she looked into the eyes of the man she loved and saw only a stranger.

"Oh, so many questions! Aren't you happy to see me, Trudy? No, I suppose not." His expression changed from a smirk to a self-satisfied smile. "That's okay. Jesus can change that. You're still my wife, no matter what you've done, even that betrayal. I forgive you."

He thinks I betrayed him by leaving Texas?

"I didn't expect you'd be out so soon, or I would've waited. I was planning to come back when they released you. When did they let you out?" Looking at Karl's expression, Trudy couldn't imagine *why* they'd let him out. That was the bigger question, but of course he couldn't answer it.

"Let me out?" His voice mocked her. "*They* didn't let me out. The Lord got me out. He told me what to say that they'd want to hear. So I did, and after a while they let me walk around the grounds with a nurse, then on my own. Then, my angel told me it was time. Time to do my work. So we left, and now we're here. Getting you back on the Path of Righteousness comes first. How did you stray so far when your father is a man of God, like me?" Trudy sensed an odd gloating behind his false compassionate expression.

She tried to steer the conversation to information she needed. "How did you know where I was? Did Dr. Levinson tell you?"

The familiar smirk returned. "Jesus showed me the way, Trudy. He wants to bring you back to the fold. That's why he took your little bastard. I knew he wasn't mine the minute I saw him."

Time stopped. "Karl, please! Don't do this. I can't bear it. I loved you so much." Trudy's words tumbled out amid sobs and agonized whimpers. She felt his eyes and chilling smile upon her. Then an eerie calm descended. She took a deep, shaky breath and felt the last feeble hope flutter and die inside her. It was true. The man she had loved no longer existed. She did not love this stranger, although she pitied him.

She breathed again, deeper, and steadied herself. "Leave, Karl. This is my house. You are ill. You need help. Go back to the hospital. Never come here again."

Karl looked off to the right, over his shoulder. "Yes, yes, I know. Trudy is very stubborn. But she will come to understand her sins and beg the Lord's forgiveness. She will return to Jesus. 'I am the light and the way.' We'll bring her out of the darkness."

Trudy turned and walked through the front door, closing it quietly behind her. She could still hear him talking. Outside, as she faced the road, out of the corner of her eye, she saw the new mailbox. It stood atop a six by six raw wood post. The newly painted address brought a wave of realization. She'd written her family to give them her new address, but told them to continue to send their letters in care of Mary until she wrote that she'd moved in. But Frieda and Dr. Levinson didn't correspond so regularly, so she hadn't mentioned the delay when she'd written them. One of them had to be the source of Karl's information.

She lowered the mailbox door. Inside were a few advertising leaflets and two envelopes, both with airmail postage. One had the Big Spring hospital address imprinted at the top and her new address typed on the front. The other, handwritten, was from Frieda. She crumpled the advertisements in one hand and stuffed them into a pocket of her house dress. Gripping the unopened letters she glanced back at the house then walked quickly back to Mary's.

***

"Are you okay, Ma?" Bob said as she stepped inside the house. Will came up to her and caught her arms just above the elbows as he stared into her eyes. Mary hovered in the background, watching, frowning.

Trudy gave her son a brief hug, then walked past him into the kitchen. She pulled out a chair, dropped the letters onto the table, and sat. She stared at the table as she spoke. "No, but I'll live." She laughed, a harsh, bitter bark as hollow and lonely as a single raven's cry. "Karl's worse than ever. He'll never be okay. I think he escaped from the hospital. I'll know more after I read these letters." She looked up at her sons.

"I told him to leave and not come back, but I don't think I got through to him. Only angels can do that." She smiled ruefully. "I'm gonna call Dr. Levinson and see if I can get him committed again." Suddenly her face collapsed and a ragged sob escaped her. Mary rushed forward and wrapped her body around her sister's.

After a moment, Trudy patted her sister's hand and pulled back. She smiled up at Mary, tears on her eyelashes. "I'll be all right." She clenched her jaw and wiped her eyes with the heel of one hand. "I survived worse. My kids are here. That's all that matters."

All except one.

She turned to smile at her boys. They shifted from foot to foot watching her but didn't approach. She looked into their eyes. "Looks like we'll be here with Mary a while longer, but as long as I stay away from the house, Karl might leave on his own. If he don't ... I'll see what his psychiatrist says. I hope they'll put him back in the hospital. That's where he needs to be. So someone can take care of him." Her face threatened to crumple again, but she controlled it. "I can't. Not ever again," she said almost to herself. "I just can't. Now I have to read these letters."

"Can we take the car, Ma?" Will said in a subdued voice as she reached for Dr. Levinson's letter. "We wanna go see those guys in Sunnyslope. See if maybe they've got some work for us."

Just like your father. When in doubt, go to work. Work cures everything.

"Keys are in my purse on the bed." She rose from the chair and walked over to hug them. "Be careful. I couldn't stand to lose you."

"We're careful. We love you, Ma," Will said.

After they left and Mary went to check on the children, Trudy sat at the table, head resting on her crossed arms for a few moments. Then, straightening her back, she picked up Levinson's letter again and opened it.

***

The following day Trudy made the familiar trek to Varela's and called Big Spring State Hospital. The receptionist quickly transferred her to Dr. Levinson's private line. "Hello, Trudy," the familiar voice said. "You got my letter?"

She'd read the handwritten, personal letter inside the formal typed envelope several times, but still had questions. "Yes, Doctor, but I still don't really understand how this could happen. Wasn't he committed? How could he just walk away?"

"This isn't a prison, Trudy. Karl was not incarcerated. Unfortunately, after a patient seems to have plateaued, his treatment is delegated to less highly trained staff as it becomes more routine. Some patients can be extremely cunning. Karl is intelligent, though deluded. It appears he fooled his caretakers into believing that his mental state was enough improved to be allowed to walk around the grounds unattended."

"But wasn't he under your supervision?" Trudy couldn't help feeling this was somehow the psychiatrist's fault.

"Technically, yes. But in reality I have to focus my attention on those with a greater potential for improvement or those newly admitted and needing diagnosis. I received routine reports, but seldom saw him in person." He paused. "I'm sorry this has happened, Trudy. But it's likely that if he's still in this area, he'll draw attention to himself and be returned by the authorities. Without his medications and EST, he'll become more unstable and less able to hide his symptoms."

"But he's not there. He's here. In my house." Trudy could feel his shock through the phone line.

"How did he find you?"

"Do you remember his sister Frieda? She called you the day after he walked off?" Trudy leaned against the side of the booth, suddenly weak. She stared at a set of initials carved into the wood next to the phone.

"Yes. She said he was at her house looking for you. He told her he had been released, but she called me from a neighbor's house to be sure. We sent an ambulance to pick him up, but he'd left before she got back from the neighbor's. Did she give him your address? She said she hadn't."

"No, she didn't. But he got it. When she went back to her study after he was gone her desk was messed up, papers out of her drawers. Her address book was laying right on top. It was open to my name, and the address was right there."

"I'll be damned! Excuse me, Trudy. That was clever. He found his way to Arizona. I'm amazed he was able to do that."

Trudy explained how Karl had traveled around during the Depression. "Can you do anything? I have to get him out of my house. Will the police do anything? The Arizona State Hospital isn't far away."

She heard the doctor sigh. "Is he violent?"

"No. Not as far as I know."

"Is he threatening to kill himself? Is he depressed?"

Karl's gloating expression floated into Trudy's mind. "No. He don't seem depressed." Trudy wondered where these questions were headed, but they gave her a bad feeling.

"As long as he's not out in public posing a threat to himself or others, they have no cause to come to your house to get him. He's your husband. He has a right to be there. I can call the hospital, but unless he does something publicly ...." His voice sounded subdued. "Your sister-in-law told me about your son." Trudy remained silent. "I'm so sorry. I wish I could help you."

After a brief hesitation, Trudy spoke. "Karl believes my baby wasn't his child. He said that God took Marty to punish me. I can't even stand to look at him anymore. I know it's not his fault, Doctor, but I loved him so much, and now I can't even look at him."

"Get a lawyer, Trudy." The psychiatrist's voice was cold now. He sounded angry or perhaps just extremely tired. "Divorce Karl. You can't help him," he said. "Don't let this destroy you. Please don't do that."

***

Trudy thought about the doctor's words as she trudged back to the house. Mary sat on the couch, her fingers gripping her knees, and watched her enter. Anxiety sang in her voice as she rose. "What did the doctor say? Can he help you?"

"He told me to get a divorce." Trudy smiled, but the smile never touched her eyes. She summarized her conversation with Dr. Levinson. "He can't help me. He never really has, except with government paperwork. If he hadn't told me about Karl's disability payment, I don't know where I'd be now. But he's only human. He couldn't fix Karl, and he can't fix my life. I have to do that. If I can." She felt her lips curve in a bitter smile, and forced it away.

Self-pity doesn't help anybody. I can be stronger than that.

"Are you gonna get a divorce?" Her sister's anxiety hung in the air between them.

Trudy chuckled darkly. "Funny, huh, Sis? Back in tent city I used to worry about you jumping from the frying pan into the fire. Then I did it a second time myself." Trudy sank down on the couch next to her sister and reached for Mary's hand. Self-doubt welled up inside her. "Mary, do you think Marty dying was God punishing me, like Karl said? Maybe for divorcing Joe? I made a vow. 'Til death do us part. I could have lived with it."

Mary was shaking her head so hard her short, soft brown hair flipped across her face. "No. No. No! Remember what Papa taught us? God is love. He'd never punish you like that for divorcing a jerk like Joe," she said. Trudy was silent for several moments as her father's face and gentle smile filled her memory.

Yes, Papa, you taught us God is love. But you stood by and let Mama take me out of school, knowing how bad that hurt, and you were blind to all those times Mama threatened to kill herself. You never saw. All of us, even Mama, especially Mama, fended for ourselves, but we all still believed you were as close to God as a man can be.

She released Mary's hand and laid hers on Mary's check, smoothing the hair back out of her sister's face. "You're right, Sis. God would've never taken Marty to punish me. He just stood by and watched it happen. Yes, I'm gonna get a divorce from Karl."

***

That evening after supper Trudy found her sons sitting outside on the back porch smoking. A full moon grinned coldly down upon them, and their murmured conversation weaved among the chirps of crickets and emerged as soothing but meaningless sounds. Trudy made a point of clearing her throat as she approached them from behind. They looked up.

"Boys, I need you to do something for me." She lowered herself to sit beside Bob, tucking her house dress beneath her.

Bob moved slightly, making room. He laid his hand on the packet of cigarettes he had rolled up in the sleeve of his T-shirt. "Want a fag, Ma?" Trudy nodded, took the cigarette he offered, and leaned over so he could light it. She inhaled deeply, then leaned back on her arms holding the glowing cigarette between her first two fingers.

"What do you need us to do?" Bob said.

Trudy looked down as she tapped the cigarette against the side of the porch, then raised her eyes to her older son's. "I want to find out if Karl's still at the house."

"You want us to go over there?" A surprised look flitted across Will's face.

"Not exactly. I want you to drive by the house and see what you can see. But don't stop the car. If he's there, I don't want him to see or talk to you."

"Okay," Will said. "We can do that right now." He stubbed out his cigarette in the ashtray they'd brought from the house. "Let's go, Bob."

They returned a few minutes later. "Yeah, Ma. He's still there." Will said as they stepped through the front door.

Linda and Molly sat on the living room floor, rolling a ball back and forth between them through a line of toy animals. They looked up. Trudy twisted her upper body to face her sons and put a finger to her lips. As the girls went back to their game, Trudy rose from the couch, gripped Will's upper arm and guided him out through the back door. Bobby followed.

"How do you know?"

Will explained as Bob watched his mother's face. "When we drove by, there was a light in the living room window. You know there ain't no curtains, but we couldn't see nothing moving."

"Yeah," Bob said. "I told Will, he coulda turned it on, then left."

"So I decided to see if there's anything in the garbage can." Trudy frowned, but didn't speak.

"I told him you told us not to stop," Bob said.

Will frowned at his younger brother. "I knew you didn't want Karl to see us, Ma, but it was dark. I knew I could be sneaky enough so's he wouldn't see or hear me. Not any dogs close by to bark and maybe cause him to look outside."

"I was back to the car in less than five minutes. They shoulda picked up the garbage yesterday and probably did 'cause all the stuff we put in there is gone. But there's what looks like a Dinty Moore stew can, and a little can, looks like Vienna sausage, and a cracker box. Must've been put in after yesterday morning. So looks like he really is still there. Karl always was neat. Maybe he's not trashing up the place at least. Wonder where he got the money for the food? Pan handling?"

Trudy shook her head slowly, frowning. "I told you not to stop. You didn't listen."

"Ma, you said you didn't want him to see or talk to us. He didn't. You need to trust our judgment more." Her son regarded her solemnly.

"I guess I don't really have a choice, do I?" She looked from one to the other. Bob looked away, but Will continued to meet her eyes.

That night Trudy lay awake in bed long after Molly slept soundly beside her. Memories of Karl before his illness invaded her heart no matter how she fought to suppress them. She recalled when he had entered her life in Salinas. He'd been her refuge from Joe, and his humor had brightened her days. His passion and tenderness had at last freed her own, long after she'd given up hope of such feelings. And she remembered his joy when he'd learned she was pregnant with Molly.

At last Trudy eased out of bed, careful not to disturb her daughter. The house was quiet. She crept past her sons curled on pallets in the living room, opened the back door, and stepped outside. The night was bright with a million stars, but Trudy couldn't see them. She sat on the edge of the porch and, blinded by tears, said goodbye to the love of her life.

Chapter Thirty-one

I Get Along Without You Very Well

The next day Trudy called a divorce attorney she'd seen advertised on a billboard at 40th Street and Van Buren. She learned that there were precedents for divorcing mentally incompetent spouses. Karl's one hundred percent disability authorization, attested to by Dr. Levinson and accepted by the V.A., put his status beyond doubt.

If he wanted to contest the divorce, Karl would have to find a psychiatrist willing to swear that he was competent. That wouldn't happen. The attorney expressed confidence that the court would award Trudy the house and a small amount of child support which would be taken out of Karl's disability check before it was mailed. A court appointed guardian would administer the remainder of the disability payment as he or she saw fit on Karl's behalf. In the circumstances, it was unlikely Trudy would receive alimony. Was that a problem?

"I'll manage," Trudy said. The attorney didn't ask how. Trudy remembered when she had made the decision to leave Joe, her determination to survive on her own if her relationship with Karl hadn't worked out. Now that's what she would do.

The divorce would be routine, the attorney assured her. As soon as Trudy paid the attorney's retainer, it would only be a matter of waiting. She didn't hesitate, although the retainer would take all the money she had tucked away in the Folgers can. She made an appointment for the next day. That night at supper, after the children and teenagers left the table, Trudy told Mary and Travis about her conversation with the lawyer.

Mary regarded her with a worried expression. "Did he give you any idea what the child support'll be?"

"He guessed about twenty-five dollars a month." Trudy said.

"That's barely enough to make your house payment! How'll you buy food, clothes, pay water and electricity bills? If you could get Karl back in the hospital without divorcing him, you could keep his disability payment."

Trudy regarded her sister. "Don't you see, Mary? That wouldn't fix things. I want this to be over, once and for all. I can't help him. I can hardly stand to look at him. I'd feel guilty pretending to be his wife just to get his money. I'll get a job. It's time I stood on my own two feet."

Mary looked skeptical. "Maybe you could at least wait 'til Molly gets older."

"You and Linda can babysit her while I'm working. If she's with you, she'll barely notice I'm gone. The boys don't have regular jobs yet, but they will. They'll help me out for a while."

Travis had been quiet up until then, and Trudy fixed her eyes on his. "Until the divorce comes through, I'll keep getting Karl's checks. I need to save all I can. I wrote a list of the things I paid for before you got your job, Travis. Most of the furniture, all the gas for the trip out here, food, rent deposit. Stuff like that." She took a slip of paper out of her pocket and pushed it across the table to him. He stared at it, frowning.

"I know you planned to pay me back your half. You don't need to pay me in cash. You all can just let me and Molly stay here 'til this is over and take my share of food and rent out of what you owe me. The boys'll be happy to give you a little money to keep sleeping on your floor."

Travis's eyes shifted away. He looked at his wife for support. "Gee, Trudy. Of course I wanna pay you back. I just don't know if I can do it that fast. I don't make all that much money, but when I get a raise in a few months, I'll be happy to take over all the rent or give you the money I owe if you've moved out by then."

Trudy glanced over at Mary. She was looking at her husband, her mouth set in a firm line. She shook her head. "We can do it. If Karl hadn't showed up, we'd probably be doing it by now anyway. I'd never have let Trudy give us money if she wasn't living here. If she's gonna stand on her own, so are we. I'll take in laundry or something if I need to."

Travis looked back and forth between them. They both stared back, unblinking. Trudy fought to suppress a grin, delighting in Mary's strength.

He's probably seen our expressions on mules.

"You might have to." Travis gave a final jab as he rose from the table, but before he could escape, Trudy caught Mary's hand and spoke in a clear voice for Travis' benefit. "After I find work, I'll pay you for babysitting Molly, Sis." Mary squeezed her fingers.

***

Mary and Travis sat on the couch across from her. It had been over a week since Trudy had confronted her brother-in-law about the money he owed her, but he still avoided her eyes. Now he gazed into his lap, a faint grin on his face. His wife's fingers were intertwined with his and their hands rested on her thigh. She stared into space, smiling expectantly. Molly and Linda sat cross-legged on the floor their eyes fixed on the radio.

They were listening to *Amos and Andy*. Sapphire had just reminded

Kingfish about the time he'd said he could dance with her 'til the cows came home. Kingfish retorted, "Well, the way you danced tonight, I thought they was there."

The cousins' high pitched laughter joined the canned studio laughter. They squealed and rolled on the floor. Trudy smiled, more amused by their antics than the program itself.

You don't even know what that means; you just like an excuse to laugh.

A loud knock sounded on the front door. Looking over her shoulder at the radio, Mary rose and crossed the room to answer it. Curious, Trudy swiveled to face the door. A strange man in wrinkled gray trousers and a dingy white shirt looked at Mary.

"Missus Krause?" Mary turned toward Trudy and their eyes met.

"That's me," Trudy rose from the chair and stepped around it.

"Could I speak with you a moment? It's about your husband."

Trudy led him into the kitchen. There was no door in the entrance between the kitchen and living room. She took him to the far end of the table, out of sight of the couch. The radio would cover most of their conversation. "What about my husband?"

"I work for Holbrook and Son. I'm a process server," the man said.

"You work for my attorney." He nodded and handed her a card. She glanced at it without really registering what it said. "Is something wrong?"

"No. Just something you need to know. Mr. Holbrook asked me to stop by on my way home to give you some information. I went to the address you gave us for your husband, but no one was there. I tried the door to see if it was locked. It wasn't, but I didn't go in. We're not allowed to do that."

Yeah, I bet you didn't. I've seen three-year-olds better at telling lies.

"I called Mr. Holbrook to tell him the situation. He said he'd make some calls, and I should call him back in a couple of hours. When I called him back, he'd found Mr. Krause. He's in the State Hospital, up on 24th Street and Van Buren." He dropped his eyes, and his face reddened. "The cops picked him up downtown. We don't exactly know why, but they're holding him for observation. I can't serve him the papers 'til he can have visitors, but the office will check every day. In the meantime, Mr. Holbrook said you should move back into your house. That way, you have possession. That's legal jargon. It puts you in a better position. We'll serve him before he's released, if he is, so if you're in the house, you can keep him away legally." He looked at her, and his eyes shifted away again.

You feel sorry for me, don't you? Think I'm some pitiful woman. Well, you don't know me. I don't need or want your pity. I got myself into this. I'll get myself out.

"Thank you. I appreciate you coming by. It's late. I'm sure you'd rather be home." She rose, forcing herself to do so less abruptly than she wanted. She walked to the door and opened it. He followed and hesitated in the doorway as if he wanted to say something more. "Goodnight," Trudy said before he could speak.

He looked as if she'd slapped him. "Goodnight." He turned and walked across the yard without glancing back.

***

After Travis and the boys went to work the next morning, Trudy left Molly playing with her cousin and walked to the home she had not yet lived in. The door was still unlocked, but she saw no sign of intruders other than Karl. A wad of blankets lay in the living room floor, and a couple of well-worn shirts had been folded and stacked next to a wall. There was no trash. Even the lone pot that sat on the stove was clean.

You're still neat aren't you? I wonder if there are other things about you that haven't changed. I'll never know.

But near the stove, where her treasured blue table had stood, sprawled a monstrosity. The table and chairs had been painted white with a coarse brush. Near the tops of the chairs, the delicate flowers that had so enchanted her peered through the streaky white veil.

Trudy dropped into one of the chairs, propped her elbows on the table and her head in her hands, and cried. She found herself unable to stop. Her shoulders shook with the depth of her grief.

It's just a goddamned table, for Christ's sake. It's not that important.

Gradually she calmed and took a shuddering breath. She wiped her swollen eyes and looked at the table. It would never be what it once was, but she could make it better. She could buy blue paint, and let Molly help her paint it. They might not get the flowers back, but the memory of painting it with her little girl would be better than the table had been.

***

That evening, when Will and Bob got home, they went over to the house with a writing tablet, pencil, and measuring tape. They calculated the number of sheets of gypsum they would need to block off the bedroom and bathroom. The rooms were small. It wasn't much.

The following afternoon, the boys delivered it in a borrowed company truck and carried it inside for safe keeping. Their boss had given them a discount, and some of the material, scraps left over from a job, they got for free. She remembered the old farmer who had given Joe the wood for the tent floor and the outhouse. Her sons, like their father, were liked and respected as hard workers.

That evening after supper the boys packed up their clothing and bedding and loaded them in the car. Trudy said nothing, but followed them outside. After they put their things in the trunk, they walked back to where their mother stood. "We didn't want to walk to the house carrying that stuff, but we can bring the car back after we unload it, if you want us to," Will said.

"There's no point in that. You'll need it in the morning for work. But you should come by for breakfast."

Bob blushed. "Thanks, Ma. We was planning on that."

Will looked at his brother. "But just for tomorrow morning. We're gonna get a coffee pot and a few groceries. But we'll probably eat dinner here 'til the house is fixed and you get moved in. That way you can tell us if you're gonna need the car. We can always get somebody to pick us up like we did the day you went to see the lawyer."

Will stepped forward to hug her goodbye. Trudy grabbed his wrist and stared into his eyes. "I'm gonna call the lawyer every day to see if he's heard anything about Karl. They ought to be keeping him in the hospital for a while, but that didn't stop him before. Keep the doors locked. We can't let him back in the house. If he shows up, don't open the door. One of you sneak out the back, cut through that vacant lot, and come get me. We'll call the cops." She released Will's wrist, and he hugged her.

"Okay, Ma."

Bobby hugged her in turn, frowning. "Goodnight, Ma. See you in the morning."

***

Will and Bob worked construction nearly full-time for the next couple of weeks, although they had yet to be formally hired. Still, every evening, they put in a couple of hours hanging gypsum. They worked Saturday afternoons as well, and all day Sundays. Trudy moved into the house as soon as the boys finished installing the ceiling and covering the interior studs.

The inside walls remained unpainted, and the kitchen cabinets were only framed in. They were larger, but still they reminded Trudy of the wooden orange crates she'd used for the same purposes back in tent city. She planned to stitch up some curtains until her sons were able to find doors.

Trudy and her children settled into their new home, and she waited for the divorce to come through. She saved as much of Karl's disability checks as she could in the meantime. Staying longer with Mary would have allowed her to save more, but getting away from Travis more than made up for the difference. She began buying the Sunday Arizona Republic and searching the want-ads.

At first, Trudy waited on pins and needles for Karl to show up and pound on her door. It never happened. Then she received a letter from Frieda. Frieda had been working with Dr. Levinson who'd recommended to the court that she be named Karl's legal guardian. This gave her the authority to have Karl transported from the Arizona State Hospital back to the Big Spring facility, although she had to pay for his transportation. He was once again under Dr. Levinson's care. With luck, they'd keep a closer eye on him this time.

Trudy felt bad about transferring the responsibility for Karl to Frieda's shoulders. But she knew from experience that blood ties were more unbreakable than marriage vows. She also knew that Frieda had more resources and a less intimate relationship with her brother.

He's never been the center of your life. It'll be easier for you.

Chapter Thirty-two

This World Is Not My Home

For the first time in a long time, Trudy had the sense that she was moving forward. She rode in a creaky old wagon pulled by a half-blind dray horse over unknown territory, but at least she was moving, one step at a time, slow and steady.

She found a job. It was hot, grueling labor in a laundry and dry cleaners in the industrial heart of downtown Phoenix. She left the car to the boys, who had begun working full time. Every morning except Sunday, she dropped Molly off at Mary's and walked the half mile to 40th Street and Washington to catch the city bus into town at six-thirty a.m.

Saturday morning three weeks after she began, she got her first two-week paycheck. It was for forty dollars and fifty-three cents after taxes. After walking home from the bus stop at noon, Trudy went directly to Mary's to pick up Molly. She showed her check to Mary.

"That don't seem like much for two weeks." Mary looked at her doubtfully. "It's a whole lot less than Travis makes. Are you gonna be able to live on it?"

"It's over eighty dollars a month! The boys are giving me twenty dollars a month each. If the lawyer's right and I get child support, it'll add up to a lot more than I been living on." Trudy looked at her sister. "It's the first time I ever got a paycheck, Mary. We got paid in cash for picking cotton, you remember, and I made a little doing washing, but Joe took charge of that. He just gave me an allowance, like a child. But this is *mine.*"

She glanced over at Molly who sat on the living room floor next to Linda pretending to read aloud a Little Golden Book that she had memorized. "If Mama had let me stay in school like I wanted, it would be more. But we'll get by. And she," Trudy thrust her chin toward her daughter, "she'll start school next year, and she'll keep going. High school, even college if she loves school the way I did. She'll be able to do whatever she wants and never have to depend on anybody but herself."

***

The evening after Mama had ended Trudy's schooling, the family had gathered in the front room as they always did for Bible reading, prayer, and hymns. Imagining the shine of triumph she was certain would fill Mama's eyes if she glimpsed the pain she'd caused, Trudy sang as enthusiastically as she could, determined to hide her sorrow.

Mary was only eight, yet she had the best voice in the family. It rang high and clear above all the others. Evelyn was learning to play the guitar, and she kept up the rhythm. Papa played the fiddle. His old fiddle had been handed down in his family for generations, but still sounded as true as on the day it was made. Papa knew how to make it cry from the heart.

The music had actually helped Trudy feel better. They all sang "Amazing Grace" and "When the Roll Is Called Up Yonder." Then Mary jumped up and looked at Papa. "Please, Papa, play 'Turkey in the Straw'. We wanna dance!"

A harvest moon grin lit up Papa's face. Trudy could see he'd been waiting for the request. She clasped Mary's hands, and they pranced into the kitchen where there was more room. They danced, skipping and twirling in the lantern light. Everyone smiled. John and Mildred clapped along, and Evelyn fought to keep pace with her guitar. Even baby Davy began to clap.

When the song ended, Papa broke into Trudy's favorite, "Wildwood Flower," before they could sit. He tapped his foot in time with his bow. As the bouncy rhythm captured them and they danced, Trudy's mind filled with memories of the white and purple hyacinths that covered Tahlequah hills and fallow fields in springtime. No one planted them or watered them, yet they sprang up every year and bathed the hills in color.

***

Molly trailed her mother to Varela's, and, inside, Trudy reached into the icy water where the sodas were stored to push two small bottles of Coca Cola along between the rails to the release lever. Dropping two nickels into the coin slot, she pulled the drinks free, popped the caps, and handed one to her daughter.

They savored the fizzy sweetness as Trudy collected the weekly groceries. She presented her check at the cash register, and the cashier tucked it under the cash drawer, deducted the charge for her groceries, counted out her change, then handed her two cents for each of the now empty Coke bottles. They stopped by Mary's on the way home, and, over her sister's protests, Trudy gave her ten dollars for babysitting Molly. "Put it away, Sis. It's yours for when you need it." She knew Mary got her underlying message.

Don't give it to that little creep. You'll need it one day.

She was still receiving Karl's disability check, so she tucked the remaining money away in the Folgers can. It was a decent nest egg six months later when the divorce was finalized and Karl's disability payments stopped. A month later Trudy received her first twenty-five dollar child support payment.

***

The boys, now officially employed, continued to work five and a half days per week. When they got home at noon every Saturday, they stopped by the mail box before they came inside and left any mail they found on the kitchen table for Trudy. She always stopped by the house after walking the half mile from the bus stop to get a glass of ice tea and relax a few minutes before going to Mary's to pick up Molly.

As she opened the door one Saturday afternoon six months after the divorce was final, Bob rose from the couch and pointed to a letter on the table. "Hey, Ma. You got a letter from Aunt Evelyn. It's airmail. Must be important."

Trudy tore open the envelope and frowned as she read the letter inside. Papa was in the hospital. Evelyn and Davy, who still lived near Tahlequah, were waiting to hear what the doctors had to say. Evelyn had written Millie, John, and Mary as well. When they knew more, she would write again.

Oh, no! Papa!

"Your grandpa's in the hospital." Trudy's mind raced. She handed the letter to Eddie. "I need to talk to Mary, and I might need the car. Where's Will?"

Bob reached into his pocket and handed her the car keys as he read the letter. "I got the keys. Will and that girl that works in the office, you know, Sarah, they went to a movie downtown. She's gonna bring him home."

***

Mary hadn't checked her mail yet. She opened her own letter from Evelyn and read it as Trudy waited. When she finished, she looked at her sister. "What are we going to do, Sis?" Concern deepened the lines in her brow.

"I get a week's vacation this summer. I was hoping to go out to see them then. But this ...." Images of Papa flooded her mind, softly smiling, playing the fiddle and tapping his foot, praying, reaching his arms out to enfold her when she was crying.

"We have to talk to Evelyn. When we know more, we'll decide."

Dorelyn Kunkel

Trudy left Molly with her aunt, stopped at Varela's to get the number of the pay phone, drove to the Western Union office and sent her sister a telegram.

CALL ME TOMORROW STOP TEN AM STOP AL 535-68 STOP CALL COLLECT STOP

She left Molly at Mary's the next morning, walked to Varela's and waited beside the phone booth. When the phone rang, she picked up the receiver with a trembling hand. After accepting the charges and depositing quarters, she heard a faint "hello". It had been nearly nineteen years since she'd heard her sister's voice, but she would have recognized it anywhere. There was so much to say, but only one thing mattered now.

"Evvie, what's happened? Did he have a heart attack?"

"No, Sis, no. It ain't his heart. He's got cancer. Stomach cancer. They're doing what they can, but he won't last long."

Cancer.

Trudy struggled not to cry. "How long? Does he know what's happening? When did you find out?"

"We just found out yesterday morning. His stomach'd been hurting and he'd had diarrhea, but you know Papa. He took Pepto-Bismol and kept praying and reading his Bible. Then he started throwing up blood, and there was blood in his stool. Mama called an ambulance. He's not hurting now. They're giving him so much sedatives, he sleeps most of the time. But he's cheerful as usual when he's awake. Dying don't scare him none. Not like it would you or me."

"Did they tell you how much time he's got?"

"Probably a week or two at most."

"Jesus! We're coming out. I don't know who all yet. Can you find a place to put us up?"

"Of course we can."

When a request to deposit more coins came on, they said their goodbyes and hung up. Trudy didn't have money to spare. She'd have to pay for the trip, and she and her sister would have plenty of time to catch up when they saw each other at last.

Hold on, Papa. Hold on. I have to see you and say goodbye this time.

Trudy stumbled toward Mary's, blinded by tears.

***

The next few hours sped by in a blur. Mary met her sister on the front porch where she'd been waiting for the results of Trudy's phone call. Trudy told her, and they cried in each other's arms.

Trudy couldn't have said if she was talking to Mary or herself. "I never should have waited so long. But that's water under the bridge. I'm

208

going now, no matter what it costs. I think they'll give me time off, or I'll quit and find another job when we get back. The boys can take a few days off to help me drive. They'll never get to know their grandpa, but at least they'll get to meet him."

"Can you take me, Sis? I can bring some sandwiches, and help with the gas a little. I have the babysitting money." Mary looked at her doubtfully. Trudy smiled through her tears.

"Of course you'll come! When I said we I meant you, too. Bring some sandwiches, if you can. Me and the boys'll take care of the gas. What about Linda? You're gonna bring her, right? What about Betty and Tommy?"

"Yeah, I'll bring Linda. She can't stay home alone while Travis is working. I'd like for Betty and Tommy to meet Papa, but they're in school. They'll be fine here with their daddy."

The next morning, Trudy drove to work and explained her situation to her boss. He allowed her to take off two weeks without pay. Back home, the six of them packed into Trudy's Chevy, Mary and the girls took the back seat and Trudy sat up front with her sons. The boys would share the driving. They had more stamina and were less distracted.

***

It was late morning on the second day of the trip when Bob parked the car in front of the tall apartment building in Muskogee where Evelyn and Jim lived. The others waited on the sidewalk while Trudy entered through the lobby alone, climbed the stairs, and knocked on the apartment door. Trudy had been expecting Evelyn, but the haggard, middle-aged woman who opened the door was Mildred. A familiar, wide grin spread across her sister's face below the brown frames of her glasses.

Why, you look like an old school marm! What happened to my feisty big sister?

"You're here, Millie! Is Sam with you?" Trudy looked over her sister's shoulder but saw no one.

"Naw. He had to work. I took a bus and got here this morning." Mildred threw her arms around her sister. After a few moments she stepped back and held Trudy at arm's length. "Where'd you get them gray hairs?" she said, then added, "Looks kinda sexy, though." Her eyes twinkled behind her glasses.

Same eyes!

Someone Trudy hadn't been able to see stepped around from behind Millie: a short, wide woman with dark curly hair grayed at the temples. A shy smile lit her plain face.

Evvie! There you are! Still the same, just a little bit fatter.

Together they went downstairs to greet Mary and meet the rest of the family. They unloaded the car, then Millie left in Jim's truck to pick up Mama and take her to the hospital. Trudy and Mary prepared sandwiches for themselves and the children. Evelyn brewed tea. None of the sisters ate much, but the sweet dark iced tea tasted like home, bringing comfort as well as pushing back the exhaustion of the long trip. After lunch, Evie tore a sheet of paper from a lined writing tablet and drew a map of the route. Trudy and the others piled back into the car and drove to the hospital. Trudy, Mary, and their children joined Mama and Millie in a hallway outside Papa's room.

Trudy's heart broke at the sight of her father, but healed at his touch. The love they shared stood apart from time. He was still the same Papa she had turned to for comfort as a child, and he still had the ability to sooth her sorrow and guilt. Death held no power over him. He was on his way to meet Jesus. His certainty in that regard had never wavered, so why would he fear dying? Even if Trudy would never have his faith, the peace it brought him made the approaching loss easier to bear.

Davy joined them at the hospital that evening. He still looked like a young man, but his eyes had aged beyond his years, and although he greeted his sisters with hugs, a sense of distance loomed between them. Trudy had never been especially close to him because of the age difference and the fact that she had left home when he was still a child. But he was her brother, and she mourned the change the war had brought to him.

John flew in from California the day before Papa died. Trudy rejoiced in the reunion of her brothers and sisters as she accepted the loss of her father. The evening before Papa's funeral they all sat around the wood stove in the house where she'd been raised and talked about Papa and their lives.

Mama sat and smiled through the sadness in her eyes. Her children shared memories and experiences, and sometimes even laughed as they had so long ago. The whole family had survived the trials of their years apart. The ties that bound them were still strong. Will and Bob sat and listened to the family history while Molly, Linda, and their cousin Jimmy, Evelyn's youngest son, played on the worn rag rug.

Family is eternal, Papa. Time and distance can't change that.

***

The funeral skies were cloudy and the wind blew as they stood in the sparse graveyard on the hill outside the church that Papa had helped construct. Trudy couldn't help but remember the last time she'd been there, at the pie supper the night before she'd run away with Joe. She glanced at her mother who stood slightly apart from the others.

Are you remembering, too, Mama?

Her mother looked up briefly, and a shadow crossed her worn, pinched face. Trudy walked over and draped her arm around Mama's shoulders as the preacher began to speak. Her mother leaned into her.

So tiny. Do you need comfort, too? You always did, didn't you? But you pushed us away, and we never saw. Papa gave us comfort, but you made sure we had food and shelter and clothes on our backs. I've been so wrong, Mama. You might've been mean, but you loved us every bit as much as he did.

***

They left for home that evening after the funeral supper. Trudy hadn't seen many familiar faces at the event. It had been too long. But Evelyn and Davy seemed to know most of the mourners. There were many; nearly a hundred crowded the old church and spilled out into the cooling night. The rain had held off. A blessing, the congregation agreed.

Millie and the others tried to discourage them from driving at night, but the boys planned to work the day after next, so they needed to be home by that morning. Trudy would drive most of the second night so her sons could get some sleep. As Mary and the girls climbed into the back seat, Trudy promised Evelyn that she would come back the following summer. Mama stood a short distance away, staring toward the graveyard fence. Trudy walked over to hug her.

"Bye, Mama. I'll write. Evie can read you my letters. And I'll be back. I love you, Mama." She couldn't remember the last time she'd said that, but she knew she had. And it was true.

"I love you, too, Trudy. I hope you know that."

"I do, Mama." She bent to kiss her mother's forehead.

***

Everyone except Trudy slept as she steered the car along the highway outside Globe in the early morning hours of the second day of their trip home. Her mind returned to the last time she'd driven through these mountains with Molly asleep beside her and Karl in the backseat with his angel.

It seemed like a lifetime ago, and, in some ways, it was. It would be hard, but she would make peace with the past, with memories of Karl and Marty, with her guilt about leaving Papa, and with her resentment toward Mama. So much had happened she hardly thought about the hard times with Joe anymore. Time passed. She would put down new roots and make a real home for her children.

She pulled into Mary's driveway just as the sun topped a line of distant mountains and spilled orange and purple light across a thin layer of clouds. Mary, her head resting on Trudy's shoulder, jerked awake mid-snore as Trudy put on the brake. She looked around, dazed.

"It's morning! Time to rise and shine, Little Sis," Trudy said.

About the Author

Dorelyn Kunkel was born and raised in Phoenix, Arizona, and graduated from Arizona State University in 1967 with a B.A. in English. She has always had dreams of writing and won second prize for short story in an ASU competition, but after graduation, she returned to the university to earn her teaching credentials and a Master's in reading education. Aside from brief periods as a full-time mother after the births of her three sons and one daughter, she has devoted her working life to education. After retiring as director of a charter high school founded for English language learners, she returned to writing and completed Wildflower, her first novel. She is currently writing a second book of short stories based on characters introduced in Wildflower.

ALL THINGS THAT MATTER PRESS

FOR MORE INFORMATION ON TITLES AVAILABLE FROM
ALL THINGS THAT MATTER PRESS, GO TO
http://allthingsthatmatterpress.com
or contact us at
allthingsthatmatterpress@gmail.com